ABOUT THE AUTHOR

Maggie Anderson writes paranormal and contemporary
romance, urban fantasy, and supernatural crime thrillers.
She is currently working on the fifth book in her Dark
Legacy series followed by a new cozy mystery series.
Maggie resides in Brisbane, Queensland, Australia. You
can find out more about her books on her website:
www.m-anderson.com.au

BOOK THREE

WOLF LOVER

A MOON GROVE PARANORMAL ROMANCE THRILLER

MAGGIE ANDERSON

Bella Luna Books
Australia

First Edition
Bella Luna Books, Australia

Front and back cover photos from
canstockphoto.com and pixabay.com
Cover design by Amy Elizabeth Photography, Australia
and Maggie Anderson

ISBN-13-9780648483618

Published by Bella Luna Books
AUSTRALIA

ONE

Paige flicked off the overhead light and crossed the shadowed office to the glass door. Eli would arrive at any minute to pick her up. She had worked until after nine and wanted to go home, kick off her heels, and relax on the sofa in his arms for a while. Her business had picked up over the past few weeks and she had several new clients. Were they human? Not one. She realized her patients were more likely to be of the supernatural kind, her being a wolf now. As she reached to open the door a figure appeared in the alcove outside, startling her. Paige gasped, jerked her hand away and lunged backwards into the shadows. Her breathing quickened, along with her heart rate, and she took another tentative step further into the dark. Who could it be? And why now?

Life had been quiet for a short while and it had felt good not to have to be on her guard. But she knew it would be only a matter of time before a new threat ventured into their town, and their lives would be thrown into turmoil once again. Remus would make sure of it. The dark shape stepped closer to the glass and Paige dashed out of the way hoping she wouldn't be seen. She snatched her cell phone from her purse and pressed Eli's number as she sidled along the wall around the room to the door leading to the kitchen and back exit. Eli's voicemail kicked in. "Eli," she whispered, "someone's at the door of my office and I'm heading out the back. Please hurry."

Paige rushed along the short hallway and into the kitchen. When she reached the back door her cell vibrated in her hand, the sensation sending a shockwave through her body, and she jumped. Eli's name appeared on the screen and she pressed the green dot with her thumb. "Where are you?"

"Stay inside until I get there. I'll deal with whoever's outside."

"I thought I should get out the back door and meet you in the next street."

"Paige, please do what I ask."

"But…"

"No buts. I'm only a minute away."

A noise echoed along the hallway. "I think they're trying to break in."

"I'm almost there. Please stay inside. It's the safest place for you."

Paige didn't think so. "Eli, I need to get out of here."

"Paige…"

She rang off, dropped her phone into her purse, snapped open the locks on the back door, and whipped it open hoping to gain some distance between her and the unknown assailant.

The hooded figure stood right in front of her. "Hello, Paige."

Paige's anxious eyes widened and she sucked in a shocked gasp.

Eli screeched the four wheel drive to a stop at the curb at a skewed angle, threw open the door, and hurled his tall frame out of the vehicle. The perpetrator wasn't at the front door now... so where were they? He stalked along the sidewalk, turned the corner, raced down the alley to the small rear courtyard and thrust open the gate. The back door to the building was closed. Had Paige taken his advice and stayed inside?

He marched up to the red wood door and tried the handle. Locked. He balled his fist and pounded on the door. "Paige, it's me. Open up."

The door swung back and Paige greeted him with a smile. "Hey. Come in."

Eli frowned into her eyes. "Are you ok? Where'd the guy go?"

"It wasn't a guy, Eli, it's..."

"Me." Paige's mother stood up from the kitchen table.

Eli's racing heartbeat calmed. "Abbey. It's good to see you again."

She nodded. "And you."

Eli stepped into the small space. "I'm glad you finally made the decision to come and see your daughter."

"I had to be careful. You know that."

"Yeah, I do. Brent told us everything."

"I couldn't just waltz into Moon Grove and go knock on Paige's door. The council would've known the moment I set foot in this town."

"Remus and his cronies aren't here. They're in hiding. No one's seen them for weeks." Eli pulled out a chair and sat down, placing his Stetson on the table and running his long fingers through his wavy, dark brown hair.

Abbey's right eyebrow rose. "Oh? Why?"

"It's a long story, but I'll give you the brief version. Remus wanted to build an army of unstoppable vampires by using Paige's blood. One vampire, a mercenary Remus hired, drank from Paige after... well, after she'd been initiated and it turned him into a monster, a monster that wanted to kill anything in its path, including his own team."

"Oh, my God."

"Yeah. I lost most of my pack because of him. So you can understand why the members of the council disappeared." He wouldn't tell Abbey, Paige, or anyone else he knew their whereabouts. Not yet. He'd only inform them when the time came to rid Moon Grove of Remus's hold on the town.

"What happened to the vampire?" Abbey backed up to her chair and sat down, clasping her hands on the table top.

"We eliminated him."

"We? If he killed most of your team then who's *we*?"

Eli's gaze moved to Paige then back to Abbey. "The local editor is a vampire. He called in other vamps to help. And I still have one member of my pack alive, but he's pretty raw. A newbie."

"Vampires? Since when do vampires help werewolves?"

"Archer's a good guy, funnily enough. I trust him."

Abbey shifted on her seat and folded her arms. "You shouldn't. They always have hidden agendas. So what do you plan to do with the newbie?"

"Continue to train him. What else can I do? Brent asked if he could become a pack member." Eli's eyes met hers. "Are you ok with that?"

Abbey nodded. "Of course I am. You need him. He has abilities that can help you."

"Thanks. I wanted to check with you before saying yes."

"Brent makes his own decisions. No need to ask me. And I support him, no matter what."

"Ok, good to know. So now I'm asking you. Do you want to be part of my pack?"

Abbey's eyes moved to her daughter. Paige smiled and nodded. "Sure. Why not? We need to belong somewhere. We've been on the move for far too long now. And I've heard you take care of your wolves."

"Isn't that what any Alpha's supposed to do?" Eli leaned back on his chair and folded his arms.

"It is, yes. But some don't."

"There's a pack over near Bellehurst. They're primal. Live off the land. Have you seen any of them in your travels? Talked to them?"

"Matthias is their Alpha, but I haven't personally had any dealings with them. I saw him in Bellehurst once and he recognized me as a wolf. Acknowledged me with a cold look of awareness but left me alone."

Eli gave a heavy sigh. "I thought I'd go over there and talk to him. I need strong wolves on my team. I know I can't ask them to join me but I can ask for their help. Somehow we have to get rid of Remus and his vampires. They're destroying our town."

Abbey's frowning gaze met his. "I don't think they'll do it. Like I said, they stay to themselves and don't get involved in other peoples' problems. Besides, they're probably as afraid of the council as everyone else is."

"All I can do is ask."

Abbey shrugged. "No harm in trying, I guess."

Paige walked over and stood beside her man, placing a hand of support on his shoulder. "I think they'll listen to Eli. He has a way with people."

"Maybe." Abbey glanced at Paige before returning her gaze to the sheriff. "But before you do, there's something you need to know."

TWO

Eli stood behind Rosemarie sitting at her desk, hands on hips, watching the two *human* deputies walk through the office door. It would be strange not having his pack working with him, well, at least not all of them. He missed his wolf family... the men and woman he'd grown up with, had been initiated with. Lucky for him Cooper had decided to become a wolf or he'd be the sole survivor of Gregor's massacre and he wouldn't be able to accept that.

Cooper stood up but remained behind his desk. He wasn't feeling much like being social, nor did he feel like working with a new partner. Bobby had not only been his mentor he had been his friend, too, and he missed him, along with Rebecca, Ryan and Paul. They had been his family, one he hadn't had for a long time and his heart ached for them.

Eli watched his new deputies cross the room and stop in front of the receptionist desk and wondered how well they'd fair in Moon Grove, a town layered with deep, dark secrets that needed to remain hidden. Rick Jarvis and Taylor Brandis were fresh out of the academy. Could they do their jobs without getting themselves killed... or worse? He would have to keep a close eye on them for the first few months to make sure.

"Morning, Chief," Rick greeted with a smile before gazing around the old-fashioned police station, thinking he'd stepped back in time. "Where do we sit?"

Eli rounded the wooden partition and came through the swinging gate. "You're over there." He pointed to Bobby's old desk. "And, Taylor, you're over there." He'd had to set up a new workstation for her beside Cooper's desk.

"Thanks," the deputies said together, giving each other a smile and taking their seats.

"Later this morning, I'll give you a tour of our town. I'll also show you the places to stay away from and the ones to keep an eye on."

"That'd be great," Taylor said giving him a broad grin. "I'm ready to get started."

"Yeah, we need to get acquainted with Moon Grove and the townsfolk so they know who we are," Rick told him.

"I'm pretty sure they already do. Word travels fast in small towns, especially this one," Cooper offered, his gaze moving from one to the other. To him, it felt like an invasion of their work space, even though he knew they needed the manpower. He also realized the ongoing grief of losing his family had to be the reason for his resentment of the new deputies, and he'd have to pick up his game otherwise Eli would have him in his office telling him to play nice.

"Oh, yeah, I guess so." Rick's eyes moved to Cooper. For some reason the guy bothered him. He couldn't put his finger on it even though it oozed from him. He knew it would take a while to fit in, and he wanted to make a good impression on his new boss and teammate. There would be certain adjustments to make coming from the city to a rural country town, but he intended to make a go of it.

"Once you settle in I'll brief you on our procedures and we'll get out on the road. Ok?" Eli headed to his office and closed the door.

"Well I suppose I'd better introduce myself," Rosemarie said. "I'm Rosemarie. I've been with Sheriff Blackwood for a long time now. We're more like family than work colleagues. If you need help with anything don't hesitate to ask. All right?" She gave the pair a thin smile and tried to hide her sorrow. The station wasn't the same anymore. "Oh, and most people call me Rose or Rosy."

"Thanks, Rosy," Rick said. "It's good to meet you."

"You too," Rosemarie replied.

"Would you mind if I call you Rose?" Taylor asked. "It sounds nice."

"That's fine, hon. I don't mind either name." Tears burned the backs of Rosemarie's eyes and she blinked to prevent them from spilling down her chubby cheeks. "Oh, and he's Cooper." She pointed across the room. "Coop, say hi."

"Hi."

"You'll have to excuse him, he's still hurting. We all are."

"Yeah... we heard. Sorry for your loss." Rick and Taylor had been briefed on the incident that had taken the lives of the town's deputy, forensic guy, and a couple of civilians.

"Thank you. We appreciate that." She turned to look at Cooper. "Don't we?"

"Sure. Thanks."

Rick could feel the hostility radiating from Cooper. *What's his problem?* He and Taylor had come to a new town to assist with law enforcement so what made the guy so antsy? They were on the same team.

"So why don't you both get settled in while I go make some coffee." The receptionist rose from her chair and headed out to the kitchen.

Cooper popped up off his seat and followed her through the open doorway.

Taylor's eyes followed him. "Rick?"

"Yeah?"

"What do you think's wrong with Cooper? It seems like he doesn't want us here. Don't you get that vibe?"

"Yeah, I do. But like Rosemarie said he's still grieving. Maybe that's all it is."

"I hope so because I want this to workout. I don't want to have to go back to the city and tell the super I couldn't handle it because someone made my life difficult."

"I guess all we can do is give it some time. See how it goes."

Taylor nodded. "You're right, I guess."

Rosemarie came back through the door, followed by Cooper, carrying a tray with mugs of black coffee, a jug of milk, a sugar bowl and some homemade choc chip cookies. "Help yourselves. I'll just take this in to Eli." She picked up a mug of coffee and a small plate with cookies on it and walked over to his office. "Eli, I have coffee and cookies for you," she called through the glass panel of the wooden door.

The door opened and Eli took the mug and plate from her hands. "Thanks, Rosy. Come on in."

She turned around to look at the group standing by the

tray on her desk. Cooper gave her a dark stare and she smiled unsurely. "Won't be a tick. Why don't you three get acquainted?" She hoped Cooper would behave. She could tell he wasn't himself this morning.

The door closed behind her.

"Have a seat, Rosy."

"Thank you, Eli." She scooped her hands under her dress to smooth it out and sat down. "Everything all right?"

Eli sighed. "I think Cooper's having a hard time coming to terms with the new arrivals. I can smell the hostility from here."

"I know. He's still grieving."

"Aren't we all? We lost good people…"

"Yes, we did." She swiped an errant tear from the corner of her left eye. "Ones that can never be replaced."

Eli's right eyebrow arched. "What else could I do, Rosy? We needed the manpower."

"I understand that, Darlin', but it doesn't make it any easier." She picked up a cookie from off the plate. "You forgot to introduce us, you know."

"Damn! Sorry, Rosy." He reached across, picked up the mug and sipped his coffee.

"You're not yourself, either. I can see that."

"I miss my best friend. I miss my pack."

"I know you do. So do I, Eli, so do I." She took a bite of the cookie and dabbed another tear.

"These new deputies will do fine once they settle into a routine. Cooper just has to give them a chance. He can't be mad at them for what happened."

"I don't think it's that. I think he doesn't know how to handle the loss. He'd been without a family for so long and then he had us for the briefest time before that monster killed everyone. I think he has survivor guilt. But he'll work through it. I'll talk to him later and see if there's anything I can do to help."

Eli's frown rested on her. "I should be the one to do that, Rosy, not you."

"I don't mind."

He shook his head. "No, I'll do it. You need to take care of yourself."

"Don't be hard on him, Eli. He needs a gentle hand."

"Maybe he needs to talk it out with Paige."

"You mean as in patient/doctor?"

"Yeah."

"I think he needs you or me to talk to. If you send him to a shrink, pardon the description, Paige is wonderful, he'll think you feel he can't do his job."

"I'm not sure he can right now." Eli leaned back and folded his arms.

"You know he'll be able to hear us talking?"

"Yes, I know. Maybe you'd better tell him to come in." He watched Rosemarie cross the office. "And leave us to talk."

The receptionist nodded, opened the door and stepped outside.

THREE

Eli's gaze moved to the open doorway. He disliked having these kinds of conversations with his deputies. He hoped they would follow protocol and not need a pep talk. He remembered Craig. Craig always required a talking to. He hated being told what to do and could never adhere to the rules – pack or police – and look where it got him. Killed. Cooper stepped into the office.

"Close the door and take a seat." Eli gestured to the chair on the other side of his desk.

"What's up?" Cooper sat down and gave his boss a sheepish glance. He had a fair idea why his boss wanted to talk to him. He couldn't help overhear the conversation between Eli and Rosemarie.

"I'm not going to have to keep an eye on you, am I?"

"What do you mean?" He shifted uncomfortably in his chair.

"Cooper, the hostility is radiating off you. I'm sure our new deputies can feel it."

His deputy's frown deepened. "I'm not hostile with them. It's… the whole situation, you know?"

"We're all grieving. Losing the people we love hurts

like hell but we have to keep our role in this community professional." Eli leaned back in his chair and folded his arms. "Do you think you can do that?"

"Of course, Chief." Cooper's head bobbed.

"Good. Because I don't want to have this conversation with you again. Got it?"

"Yep." Cooper stood up.

"On the flip side, if you need to talk you know I'm here for you, right?

"Sure I do." Cooper gave him a brief smile.

"Ok. Good. Taylor's going to be your new partner. I'll have Rick with me until he gets used to our procedures and the layout of the town and then he can work alone."

"Can I go now?"

"Yes. But remember what I said. And do me a favor."

"What's that?"

"Don't give your partner any reason to suspect what you are. Ok?"

"Absolutely."

"Ask them to gear up and I'll give them the tour."

"Sure." Cooper crossed the office to the door but before opening it he turned around. "Thanks, Eli."

"No problem. Just remember Rosemarie and I care about you. You're not only a deputy or pack member, you're our family."

Cooper smiled and nodded. "Yeah, I know."

Five minutes later, Eli stepped into reception. Rather than brief them here he thought he'd do it on the drive. Might make more sense that way. "Ok. Here's what's happening." He tossed the four wheel drive keys to Rick. "You're driving and I'll sit passenger. Taylor, you're in back. Once we're on the road, I'll show you around town and introduce you to some of the polite residents."

"Polite residents?" Taylor gave an unsure smile.

"Yes. There are people in Moon Grove who don't welcome newcomers so we'll give them a wide berth for the time being." Eli headed to the door and opened it, motioning for the pair to step outside ahead of him. Once they were on the porch he turned around and looked at Cooper and Rosemarie. "Can you hold the fort?"

"We sure can," Rosemarie said, her eyes moving to Cooper then back to Eli. "Go. Show those young people around."

"If anything comes up radio me or call me on my cell."

"Will do."

Once the three were in the car Eli directed Rick where to go. "Do a U-turn and head back into town."

"Ok, boss."

"Call me Eli. I hate being called boss." He didn't actually hate it. Bobby and Rebecca used to call him boss and he couldn't bear to hear it.

"Oh, sure, ok... Eli." Rick flashed the indicator and turned the vehicle around. "Moon Grove is a... pretty town." He smiled as he drove down the tree-lined main street.

"Yeah, it is. But it has its undertones." Eli slid his sunglasses onto his nose and gazed out the passenger window.

"Undertones?" Rick chuckled. "What? A dog escaped the backyard and ran amok down town?"

"You have no idea." Eli turned to look at his new deputy.

"Is there something we need to know, Eli?" Taylor asked between the seats.

"Not at the moment, no. You'll be covering simple call outs for the first few weeks until you know where you're going and what you're doing."

"We've been trained to handle anything." Taylor frowned and folded her arms. She wanted to get into the cogs of what made Moon Grove tick.

"I get that. But there are certain things you don't know and until you do you'll follow my instructions. Ok?" Eli peered around the back of his seat at her. "Ok?"

Taylor's face flushed. "Yes, sir."

"Thank you." He pointed to the Tribune office. "Pull into the curb."

Eli stepped out of the vehicle. "I won't be long."

Rick's eyes met Taylor's in the rear view mirror. "What do you make of that?"

Taylor shrugged. "Beats me. Looks like we won't be told anything."

"I think the sheriff's looking out for us, being new to the town."

"Our job is to serve and protect. How can we if he won't let us?"

"Give it some time. It's only our first day."

Eli stepped into the Tribune office and Archer came up to him. "To what do I owe the pleasure, Sheriff?" He smiled.

"I wanted to let you know the two new *human* deputies arrived."

"Ok. Thanks for the heads up." He peered through the office window at the four wheel drive. "So you're showing them around?"

"Yeah. I want them to get a feel for the place without knowing what goes on here."

"And how long do you think it will last? They're bound to come across something supernatural at some point... and then what are you going to do?" Archer folded his arms.

Eli sighed. "I'll cross that bridge when I come to it."

Archer's left eyebrow rose. "Probably not the best philosophy."

"I know, but it's the best I can do for now."

"Tell them everything and turn them into wolves."

"Hamilton."

"I thought we were past the last name thing." He gave Eli a smirk.

"Yeah, yeah, we are. But I can't do that."

"Why not? You need wolves in the pack."

"Be serious." Eli frowned into the vampire's dark eyes.

"I *am* being serious."

"Where's your brother and his friends?"

"They had to go out of town for a few days. They'll be back."

"Good." He waited a beat. "I appreciate your and their help with Gregor."

"You already said that." Archer gave him a curious frown.

"I want you to know I'm grateful."

"Thanks. I know."

"Well, I'd better get going." He headed for the door. Archer opened it for him.

"Thanks. Tell your brother and his friends to keep a low profile once they're back."

"I will." The sheriff stepped out the door. "Eli?"

"Yeah?"

"Can we talk sometime soon? There's something I need

to tell you." He knew he couldn't keep drinking Paige's blood a secret for long. He had to tell Eli.

"Sure." He gave the editor a questioning frown. "Everything all right?"

"Of course."

"Ok. Can we do it later today?"

"Yeah, sounds like a plan."

Eli tipped the brim of his Stetson and headed back to the car.

Archer watched him climb into the Jeep and drive away before going back to his desk. If they were working together he had to be honest with Eli. He wondered how the sheriff would take his confession.

FOUR

Paige stepped out of her consultation room and headed to the kitchen to find Linda at the table having morning tea. The receptionist glanced up from the magazine she'd been reading and smiled. Eli and Paige had discussed the possibility of Linda being the mole but she didn't want to believe it. They didn't have proof, apart from the fact that she had worked for Ross Redmond. That in itself wasn't incriminating. And even though she worked for the unscrupulous mayor it didn't mean she had the inclination to follow in his footsteps. She'd given Eli information when he needed it so it had to be someone else. She hated to think it, but maybe it had been one of Eli's pack: Ryan or Paul or even Rebecca. She poured herself a mug of coffee and sat down.

"How'd it go?" Linda asked, sipping her drink.

"Good. I think we're finally making progress."

"Glad to hear it. Who'd ever have thought you'd be a paranormal shrink?" She chuckled.

"I guess it's a natural progression now that I'm a wolf."

"At least you've gained some trust with the townsfolk."

"It certainly seems that way."

"I hear Eli has two new deputies."

"He does."

"Human?"

"Yep. I doubt the academy knows anything of the town or its residents. Well, at least some of its residents."

"Do you think Eli will tell them what goes on here?"

"I doubt it. They're too new. He'll wait, and if they start asking questions then he might."

"I'm sure they will eventually. What happens in Moon Grove can't stay hidden forever."

"I know you're right, but let's hope they don't step into anything dangerous. From what he's told me, though, they seem young and impulsive so who knows what they could get themselves into." Paige's cell phone jingled on the table and she picked it up and checked the screen before answering. "Clarissa? Is everything ok?"

"Do you have some time to come and see me?"

"When?"

"Today."

Paige stood up and walked along the hallway to the reception desk to check her calendar on the computer. "I've got a couple of hours now."

"Good. I'll see you when you get here."

"Ok. See you soon." Paige frowned at her phone and pondered the call for a moment. She called along the hall to Linda. "I have to go out for a while but I'll be back for my 12:30 appointment." She whipped down the hallway, grabbed her purse, dropped her phone into it and headed for the door. "Might want to lock up for a while."

Linda came up behind her. "My thoughts exactly."

"See you later." Paige crossed the sidewalk and climbed into her car.

Paige pulled into Clarissa's driveway and turned off the engine. The old woman's call had been ominous, at best. What had been the reason for its urgency? She opened the car door and stepped out, gazing around the street, her eyes moving to the house she no longer occupied across the road. Perhaps she should rent it out. Something to consider. She sighed, pulled the keys from the ignition, and climbed the front steps. The door opened as she reached the welcome mat. "Hello, dear, come in," Clarissa offered with an affectionate hug. "How have you been?"

"Good. You?"

"I'm fine, dear."

"So why did you want to see me?" Paige stepped into the entry hall and Clarissa closed the door. She wasn't sure how she'd tell Paige what she'd discovered, or how it would affect her once she knew.

"Want some tea?" The old woman headed into the kitchen.

Paige followed. "Tea would be nice. Thank you." She sat down at the wooden kitchen table.

"How's my grandson?"

"He's good. He's training two new deputies."

"Yes, I'd heard we had some newcomers."

"Mm. I guess the townsfolk won't be pleased."

"They never are, dear." Clarissa brought the teapot and cups to the table then went to the refrigerator for the milk. "I have some brownies if you'd like one."

"I'd love one."

Clarissa picked up the plate from off the counter, set it down in the center of the table, and took her seat opposite Paige.

"I know you didn't call me for morning tea, Clary. What's going on?"

The old woman's face wrinkled even more. "I discovered something. Something you should know but…"

"If it's something I should know you need to tell me."

Clarissa poured the tea and passed a cup to Paige. "I will. But I want to explain something to you first."

"What's that?"

"I believe Archer Hamilton is a good… vampire. His heart is in the right place, if he had one that is. I think what he did is in the best interest of you and our town."

"Clary, what did he do?"

After dropping the deputies back at the station, Eli drove into Moon Grove to find out why Archer Hamilton wanted to talk to him. The editor had seemed pensive and to Eli that wasn't a good sign. Archer opened the front door when Eli reached the Tribune office and the pair stepped inside. He'd been outside waiting for the Sheriff to arrive. "What did you want to tell me, Archer?"

"Want to take a seat?" He motioned to the chair in front of his desk.

"No thanks. I'd prefer to stand." Eli removed his Stetson and rotated it between his hands.

"Would you please take a seat on the sofa?"

Eli sighed. "All right, if I must."

"Thank you." Archer remained on his feet. "I want you to know that what I've done is in the best interest of both Paige and Moon Grove. The governing body sent me here to help."

Eli frowned up at him. "Who?"

Archer paced. "There's a hierarchy more powerful than the council that governs all otherworldly creatures – vampires and werewolves alike, among others – they sent me."

"For what reason? And why don't I know anything of this so-called governing body?" Eli wasn't sure he liked where the conversation seemed to be heading.

"The governing body only makes itself known when there's a supernatural crisis to be dealt with. They'd received intel on Gregor and his team coming to Moon Grove and they wanted me to ascertain if Paige's blood had the capabilities they believed it did."

"Whether or not it would create a super vampire, you mean?"

"Yes."

"And?"

"While Paige and I were seeing each other I…"

"You what?" Eli stood up.

"I drank some of her blood to ascertain if it would affect me in the way the governing body hoped it would."

Eli could feel the moonstone ring's effect on him. His face flamed, his insides churned with anger and he wanted to rip the editor's head off his shoulders. "You did?" His voice deepened and became husky. He had to control his emotions or he would do something he'd regret.

"I did. And it's enhanced all of my abilities. Think of the possibilities, Eli. If we could create more vampires like me we'd be able to defeat any threat that arrived in Moon Grove."

"You have more of her blood?"

"A small amount that I think could be made into a serum that would do the same thing for other vampires. I meant what I said. I'm here to assist you in any way I can."

Eli's rage subsided. The town needed all the help it could get. The way Archer had initiated his task had been wrong, and once Paige knew what he'd done she would be furious with him. "Do you know someone who can make the serum?"

"I've sent it to a laboratory administrated by the governing body. It should be completed in a month."

"A month might be too far off."

"Well, at least you have me for the interim."

"I should…"

"What, Eli? You know I had no choice."

"You violated Paige's trust. How do you think she'll feel when she learns the truth?"

At that moment, the door opened and Paige stormed into the office. "You betrayed my trust, Archer. How could you do that to me?" She strutted up to him and folded her arms. "So you took me out for the sole purpose of drinking my blood, is that it?"

Archer swung around. "I did it for the good of the town, Paige. Please believe that. And, no, that wasn't the only reason." He gave Eli a sheepish glance. He'd had feelings for Paige. Still did.

"You mesmerized me and drank my blood without my consent."

"I know and if I could change that I would, but I had my orders."

"And you expect me to believe you?"

"I can get all the proof you need. There is something coming that is far worse than Gregor Petrov and we need to be ready for it."

Paige's eyes widened. "Something worse?"

"Yes. Much worse."

FIVE

Eli left his Jeep parked on the shoulder and trudged the sodden, leaf covered path into the woods. Matthias's pack lived in an old log cabin by the lake, somewhere that allowed them to track who came into their domain and offered an easy escape route if needed. The muscles in Eli's gut tightened as he got closer and he wondered what kind of reception he'd get when he arrived on the Alpha's doorstep uninvited. The sun had begun to slide into the distant horizon and the hazy shadow of night poured over the tree tops.

Trudging further into the woods, he remembered what Abbey told him. Matthias had once worked for Remus. Had he offered his abilities willingly or had he been forced into it with the threat of the council hurting someone he cared for? Eli would have that conversation with the Alpha once he knew for certain he had the packs' allegiance. He wanted to give Matthias the benefit of the doubt for now because he knew how Remus operated.

"Stop right there," a deep, powerful voice echoed from the surrounding legion of tall pines. "Don't take another step. Raise your hands where I can see 'em."

Eli stopped, raised his hands, and groaned inwardly. This would be more difficult than he'd envisioned. "Ok." His eyes roamed the shadows. "But I'd like to know who I'm talking to."

"Why are you here, Sheriff Blackwood? What could you possibly want with us?"

"I need to speak to Matthias."

"Why?"

Eli's eyes continued the search. "I'd prefer to discuss that with him."

A tall, muscular male stepped from behind a large tree trunk. He stood at least six feet, five inches, had shoulders broader than a Chicago Bears quarterback, and a solid frame with long legs. A true wolf. He wore jeans, T-shirt, an open black and white checked button through shirt, and leather hiking boots. "Ok. State your business."

"Matthias?"

"Yeah. What do you want here, Eli?"

"I need your help."

"With what?" Matthias folded his arms.

"I don't know if you heard, but I lost most of my pack in a situation caused by the council."

"I heard. So?"

Eli frowned at him. "So, I need more wolves to help me find Remus and his lapdogs and rid Moon Grove of the council once and for all."

"Why should I risk my pack to help you? The council has eyes and ears everywhere. If they find out I've offered assistance we'll be in danger like the rest of you."

"Something else is coming. Something that, without your help, will end us all."

31

Matthias's right eyebrow arched. "What kind of *something*?"

"We're not sure yet. But I can guarantee Remus is behind it. He wants the wolves gone from the town and surrounding areas… that includes you and your pack. I have one new wolf left and a couple of vampires…"

"Vampires?" Matthias shook his head and raised his left hand. "You can count me out."

"Will you at least hear me out before discounting what I have to say? They helped get rid of Gregor Petrov and they *will* help when the next threat arrives. If you don't want to trust them trust me as a fellow Alpha."

"Why should I? It's not like we've had anything to do with each other in the past."

Eli sighed. "If, between us, we can rid the town of the council our lives will be far better for it. People are scared of Remus and his adherents, and with good reason. I can't promise there won't be casualties, because there's bound to be, but what I can promise is peace once the council is gone."

Matthias's intense stare met Eli's and he searched the sheriff's eyes for any kind of deception, but couldn't find any. Should he help? Would it be the answer to their never-ending prayers? "And how do you plan to get rid of them? Kill them?"

"They won't leave willingly, so, yes, we would have to kill them."

"I'll talk to my guys and see what they want to do."

"Fair enough." Eli hoped Matthias would make the right decision. "I'll wait to hear from you."

"I'll be in touch when I have an answer." He turned on his heel and disappeared into the hazy trees.

Eli headed back along the path toward his car and when he emerged from between the trees someone hit him from behind. The last thing he saw was a swirling wall of black rush toward him as he hit the ground.

As night set in and the amber street lamps glowed to life, Paige stood outside her office waiting for Eli to swing by and pick her up. *He's late, which is unusual for him.* She frowned at the time on her watch and tugged her phone from the pocket of her jacket. Pressing speed dial for Eli she waited for him to answer. He didn't. Paige frowned at the screen and pushed her cell back into her pocket. *Where are you?*

Her anxious gaze roamed the street and connecting intersection. *He should be coming around that corner any minute,* she told herself, her heart beating that little bit faster. He had most likely been held up at the station, that's all. But he always called to let her know, so why hadn't he?

Archer stepped out of the Tribune office and spotted Paige across the street. He closed and locked the door then walked over to her. "Everything all right?"

"I'm not sure. Eli should've been here to pick me up ten minutes ago. It's not like him to be late or at least not to call."

"Have you tried the station?"

"Well, no, I wanted to give him a few more minutes in case he'd been delayed for some reason. He is dealing with new deputies." Her heart rate ticked up another notch. She could sense it now. "I think something's happened to him."

"What makes you say that?" Archer frowned into her eyes.

"I can't explain it. It's just a feeling I have." She snatched her phone from her pocket and pressed the button for the station. "Rosemarie, hi. Is Eli there?"

"No, hon, he's not. He didn't come back to the station. Shouldn't he be with you by now?"

"I've been waiting for over ten minutes and he hasn't shown up. Do you know where he might be?"

"He drove over to Bellehurst to talk to Matthias, but he would've been back ages ago." A slithering sensation curled its way through the receptionist's stomach, a sudden feeling of dread washing over her. "I'll see if I can get him on the radio. Can you hold the line?"

"Of course. Thanks, Rose."

"What's happening?" Archer asked, folding his arms.

"Rosemarie is trying him on the radio."

"Hon, you still there?" The receptionist queried.

"Yes, I'm here. Did you get on to him?"

"No, I didn't. He's not answering."

"Ok. Thanks, Rose."

"Is there anything I can do to help?" Tears stung the backs of Rosemarie's eyes, fear for Eli's safety rising inside her.

"Not at the moment. Let me see if I can find out what's going on and I'll get back to you. Are you heading home?"

"Cooper's on night watch so I might stay here with him for a little while longer."

"Ok. I'll call when I know something."

"Please do. I'm worried now."

"Don't worry. We'll find him."

"Who's with you?"

"Archer. We're heading over to Bellehurst. I'll be in touch." Paige rang off and looked into the editor's concerned gaze. "Let's get going. We have to find Eli."

The deserted streets sent a chill up Paige's spine as she and Archer drove through the town. Bellehurst seemed exactly like Moon Grove. Did it have a supernatural council of its own? Or did Remus rule the region? Once night set in, it seemed the residents knew to be indoors. Were there other localities that lived by the same conventions?

Her mother had given directions to get to Matthias's hideout. They would have to park the car at the edge of the woods and hike through the vegetation and trees down to the lake. Would Eli still be there? Paige's heart thumped against her ribs. She hoped so.

Archer pulled onto the dirt shoulder, turned off the headlights and looked at her. "Do you think we'll need weapons?"

Paige shook her head. "If we go in armed Matthias will think we're there to do them harm. We have to offer trust."

Archer frowned. "Ok. But I think we're setting ourselves up for a dangerous situation not having some form of protection."

She gave him a thin smile. "We're supernatural creatures. I think we can handle it."

The editor's left eyebrow arched. "We'll be outnumbered."

"We'll be fine."

The pair climbed out of the car. The night air had a chill to it and Paige shivered. She didn't think the cold had caused her reaction though. She gave a heavy sigh and her eyes roamed the hazy pined woods. "Ok, let's do this."

SIX

Both Paige and Archer could smell Eli's scent and knew they were on the right path. Could he still be in negotiations with the Alpha? A subtle glow shone through the trees and Paige pulled up short, the editor almost bumping into her back. She turned to glance over her shoulder at him with her finger to her lips. Archer nodded and the pair continued moving toward the light. When they reached the log cabin they remained hidden amongst the pines to survey the exterior and surrounding area.

No one appeared to be outside, at least not that either of them could see, which wasn't surprising. Paige's wolf hearing picked up male voices inside the house but she couldn't make out what they were saying. Could one of them be Eli? She frowned and strained her ears to listen. No, neither of the tones of voice sounded like his. She turned to Archer and whispered, "Can you hear what's being said?" Paige knew vampires had super sensitive hearing compared to wolves.

"Sounds like a general conversation."

"Ok. Perhaps we should go before anyone knows we're here."

A voice echoed out of the trees close behind them. "A bit late for that."

Paige gasped and swung around.

"Why are you here?" Matthias stepped out of the shadows.

"I – I'm Paige O'Connell… Eli's…"

"I know who you are. Why two visits in one day?" His eyes moved to Archer. "And why bring a blood drinker with you?"

Paige glanced over her shoulder. "Archer is a friend. He's no threat to you."

"Why don't you let me be the judge of that?" He took a step closer. "I told Sheriff Blackwood I'd get back to him. So I'll ask again, why are you here?"

"Eli didn't come back to Moon Grove. He's missing."

Matthias's severe stare met hers. He didn't like her unspoken insinuation. "He was fine when he left here."

"What time did he leave?"

"I don't know… around seven, seven thirty maybe. The sun had just gone down."

"Did he say where he might be going?" Paige dug her hands into the pockets of her jacket.

"No. Why would he?" The Alpha shrugged. "It's not like we're best buddies or anything."

"Something must've happened to him on the way back to town. Or even before."

The grim expression on Paige's face caused Matthias's heart to clench. He felt bad for her. "Look, I'll send my guys out to sniff around and see if they can pick up anything, but that's all I'm prepared to do."

"Did Eli tell you what happened and what we believe is coming?"

"Yeah."

"And you don't feel a sense of responsibility to your own kind to protect them from it?"

"We live a quiet life out here. Stay out of other peoples' business. It's worked well so far so why change it? We like remaining off the council's grid. Off anyone's grid, for that matter."

Paige thought him a coward but didn't vocalize it. She held back and bit her tongue. He'd offered to help find out what had happened to Eli and she had to be grateful for that. "I appreciate your help in trying to locate Eli. Thank you."

Matthias tugged his cell from the pocket of his jeans. "Give me your contact." He thrust the phone at her. "If I find out anything I'll be in touch."

Paige keyed in her number, handed him the phone, and thanked him again before following Archer back to the car. Stopping at the passenger door, she turned around. "I can't believe he doesn't want to get involved. I think he's a coward. I wanted to tell him, but thought better of it. If his pack can find out what happened to Eli…"

Archer gripped her shoulders. "We don't know what kind of dealings he's had with the council before. Maybe that's why he wants to keep a low profile. If that's the case then I understand. Who wouldn't?"

Paige let out a frustrated breath. "We're going to need all the help we can get. Alone, we're not strong enough to fight what you think is coming." Archer opened the door for her and she climbed in. "I wish there were more wolf packs in the area that we could call on." The editor closed the door, rounded the hood and climbed in beside her. Paige's eyes met his. "Do you know exactly what we're up against?"

"I'm waiting on the intel. Once I know you'll know." He gave her hand a gentle, reassuring squeeze. "We're in this together."

"I'm glad you're here." Paige eased her hand out of his, clipped in her seatbelt and gazed through the windshield. As Archer started the engine she cried out, "Stop!" She'd spotted a glimmer of bright white light in the distance.

"What is it?"

She threw off the seatbelt, thrust open the door and jumped out of the vehicle.

Archer followed. "What did you see?"

Paige pointed along the road and the pair trudged the graveled shoulder for a hundred feet. She gasped. "It's Eli's Jeep." The four wheel drive had gone off the road into the scrub. Her stomach did a sickening flip flop. *Is he injured? Or...?* She shook the thought from her mind. No, he couldn't be, she would sense it... wouldn't she?

Archer scrambled down the embankment to the driver's door. "There's no one inside." He circled the car and listened for any sounds – a heartbeat, moaning. Nothing. "Eli's not here." He made his way back up the embankment to her.

"Then where is he?" Her voice shook, her anxious eyes roaming the surrounding vegetation.

The editor's serious gaze searched the trees. "Do you think Matthias told us the truth?"

"He doesn't seem like a dishonest man."

"Then that means someone followed Eli out here and took him."

Paige's tear-filled eyes met Archer's. "Who would do that?"

"My guess would be one of Remus's henchmen. I got a whiff of vampire scent around Eli's truck. They want the ring and this is the only way they can get their hands on it."

"But..."

Matthias came up behind them. "My guys did a sweep of the woods and picked up vampire scent. It looks like the sheriff's been taken by bloodsuckers." He stood with hands on hips, his stern gaze meeting the editor's.

Archer raised defensive hands. "Well don't look at me. I've been with Paige... and I'm Eli's friend."

Matthias frowned. "Then it has to be the council's work."

"We came to that conclusion too. Remus and his cohorts have gone into hiding and no one knows where they are." Archer folded his arms.

"Someone needs to find out. And fast." Matthias turned on his heel and headed back along the road.

"Matthias, wait." Paige hurried up to him. "We need your help whether you want to give it or not. If anything happens to Eli I'll come back and I won't be alone."

The Alpha's right eyebrow arched and he stared into her eyes. "Is that a threat?"

"You bet it is. You have the power to offer your support. Without your pack we're doomed. Do you think the council will stop at us? If you do you're a fool. Once they eliminate our pack they'll come after yours. Is that what you want?"

Matthias didn't like hearing the truth. "You're a tough Alpha, Paige O'Connell."

41

"I've had to be. Now are you going to help us or not?"

Eli came to in a windowless underground room. The dank, rocky walls were covered in slimy green moss, the ground beneath him damp but firm. He realized his wrists were shackled, along with his ankles, and his boots had been removed. His wolf gaze roamed the unfamiliar, unlit space. *Where am I? Who brought me here?*

He flexed his biceps in an attempt to fracture his restraints. No amount of strength would weaken the metal. The cuffs and chains had been forged to hold a werewolf. Could this be part of the new threat Archer had told them would come to Moon Grove? Had he been taken by some formidable foe that wanted him out of the picture so they could decimate his town?

Eli knew Paige would figure out what had happened to him. And, if so, she'd be looking for him right now. *Could Matthias have something to do with this?* The Alpha seemed like an honorable man, despite his apathy. So who? Remus? His gut twisted into a tight knot of nerves at the thought. If the vampire head of the town's governing body had anything to do with it, Eli's life hung in the balance because Remus had been warned of his intention to rid Moon Grove of the council. The mole had given him the information. Could it be Linda, as he and Paige suspected? He didn't want to believe it. They had been friends a long time. But who else could it be?

Another thought crossed his mind and he checked for the moonstone ring… and his finger. Still there, at least for now. He'd had an aversion to silver until he placed the ring on his finger. Clary had told him the stone prevented him from having a reaction to it. His mind returned to his current situation. *How long have I been down here? What time of day is it?* Being in the dark and unable to see outside made it difficult to distinguish.

Eli raised his head and inhaled a deep breath through his nostrils. He couldn't smell vampire or any other creature in the air which meant it could be Remus's doing. Some wolves could pick up vampire scent, but he'd never been able to. He pumped his biceps once again, using all the wolf strength he had, and tried to break his restraints. Futile. Whoever had taken him made sure he couldn't get free.

The question on his mind… what did they plan to do with him?

SEVEN

Paige messaged the remaining pack members on her way back to Moon Grove, asking them to meet her and Archer for an emergency meeting in the church at nine. "We have to come up with a way to find Eli before anything happens to him, if it hasn't already." She gave a heavy sigh. "I believe you and Matthias are right. It has to be the council. Eli told me Alistair visited him a couple of times asking him to relinquish the ring and wasn't happy when he saw Eli wearing it."

"It's the only explanation. Remus has to be behind Eli's abduction. He wants the moonstone ring and will stop at nothing to get his hands on it." He flipped on the indicator and turned left. "At least Matthias has changed his mind and is willing to help us now."

"Yes, I didn't think I could persuade him to do it, but I'm glad he's going to join us in the fight to rid Moon Grove of the council and whatever's coming. We couldn't do it alone."

Archer smiled at her.

"What?" She frowned.

"You've grown so much in such a short period of time. You are a true female Alpha, Paige O'Connell."

She waved the comment off. "I'm only doing what I know Eli would do in this situation. It's all him, not me."

"Don't underestimate yourself. You have more strength inside you than you know." Archer accelerated up the hill to the white church and stopped outside the front doors. "You go in and I'll park."

Paige unclipped her seatbelt, opened the door and climbed out. "Don't be long, I want to get started."

"I'll only be a couple of minutes." He backed up and headed for the parking lot out back.

When Paige reached the front steps, Matthias and his pack members appeared out of the trees. "Glad you could make it," she said. "Come on in."

Matthias waited for her to step through the door then he and his men followed her inside.

Paige wandered down the nave to the front of the pews. Rosemarie, Cooper, Linda, and Brent and their mother were sitting along the front row. Matthias and his pack sidled into the row behind them and sat down.

"Thank you all for being here on such short notice. We have a situation."

Rosemarie wrung her hands together and her teary eyes met Paige's. "No word?"

Paige shook her head.

"What's going on?" Linda asked.

Archer walked through the door, locking it behind him, came down the nave and sat next to Paige's brother.

"Eli is missing. We believe the council had him abducted."

"What?!" Linda popped up off the seat, appearing shocked by the news.

"Right now, we have absolutely nothing to go on but we need to work together to come up with a plan to find him and get him back safely." She moved her gaze to Linda. "Would you have any idea where Remus would hide Eli? Maybe a property the council owns besides the mansion?"

"What makes you think I'd know anything regarding the council's investments?"

Paige walked along to her. "You worked for the mayor. You may have seen something cross Redmond's desk that would give us some kind of indication of where they might be… and where they've taken Eli."

"I don't. But I can find out." She rummaged through her purse and pulled out a small set of keys. "I still have these. I thought they might come in handy one day and Ross never asked me for them back, so we can get into city hall and look for ourselves." She gave Paige a satisfied smile.

"That's great. We'll head over there after the meeting." Paige moved back to center. "I want to introduce Matthias and his pack – Justin, Samuel, Peter, Heath, Nathan, Chad, and Ben. He has graciously offered to assist us with finding Eli and ridding Moon Grove of the council."

Everyone in the front row turned around and welcomed the pack. Matthias's gaze moved to Paige and she could see by the look on his face he wasn't happy. He preferred to keep life low key, but stood and thanked them anyway.

Would he challenge her decisions, being the Alpha of his own pack? Or would he abide by her pack rules and do what she asked of him? Only time would tell. She realized she could use his expertise, being an Alpha longer than she, and Paige would take advantage of his knowledge.

A thump on the doors echoed down the nave and everyone in the church jumped and swung around. Archer jumped to his feet, headed up the aisle to the double doors with Paige and Matthias close behind. A small, staved window with a latch sat at eye level in the wooden door and Archer opened it. He wouldn't risk everyone's safety.

A face appeared in front of the tiny square. "I'm here to help. Let us in."

Paige moved to the window. "Who are you?"

"I'm Daniel." He stepped aside. "And these guys are my pack."

"There are no other packs in the area." Paige wondered if they had been sent by Remus.

"I know. We've come from Lakeview."

"Lakeview? That's…"

"Yeah, a couple hundred miles from here."

"How did you find out we needed help?"

"Brent called me."

Paige glanced over her shoulder. Her brother had contacted more wolves to come and help them. Brent came up to the door. "They're good guys, Paige. You can let 'em in."

Archer unlocked the doors and swung one back.

Daniel and his pack strutted inside. "Brent told us what's been happening here. It's time we worked together to get this town back on its supernatural feet." He turned around and pointed to each of his pack. "This is Ethan, Thomas, Braydon, Leo, Patrick, Stephen, and Joshua."

"It's good to have you here. We could use the help." Paige couldn't believe they had more on their team. Her heart felt elated, but only for a moment. Eli's abduction had to be her main priority right now, not the impending battle.

The only door to the dank underground room opened and a figure stood in the doorway. "I tried to warn you, Eli. I knew it would come to this."

"Alistair. I should've known."

The vampire entered the dark space. "Don't blame me for this. You had the option of handing over the ring and you chose to wear it."

"It belongs to my pack." Eli's voice tightened.

"That may be, but when Remus sets his mind on something he does not let it go."

"So why hasn't he taken it?"

Alistair moved closer. "Because he cannot. Well, that is not entirely true. He could kill you for it but for some reason he does not want to do that. What he wants is for you to offer it to him."

"Does he know I can't get it off my finger?"

"Yes, he is aware of the eccentricities of the moonstone ring."

"How does he expect me to *offer* it to him when it won't come off? And what does he plan to do with me once he has it?"

"I do not know."

Eli sighed. "Why are you here, Alistair? Guilty conscience?"

"Not at all. I did my best to persuade you to hand the ring over to Remus but you decided to put it on your finger instead."

"Then you have no reason to be here. So why don't you leave me alone."

The vampire's left eyebrow arched. "I thought I could talk some sense into you. Make you see reason."

"There's nothing more to say, Alistair. Remus will kill me once he has the ring, we both know that. The power it contains will turn him into an even bigger maniac."

"I am sorry it has come to this, Eli."

"Don't lay your pity on me. Go away."

Without another word, Alistair turned on his heel and closed the door behind him, leaving Eli in the dark once more.

EIGHT

Paige, Archer and Linda crossed the road and scanned the street before entering the building. Being supernatural creatures, none of them needed any light to see by so it would be easy for them to search the mayor's files without anyone who happened to be passing by noticing a light on in his office at such a late hour. The new mayor wasn't under the control of the council, since they had gone into hiding and hadn't been seen in weeks, so he had no knowledge of the reason for his quick succession into his mayoral role. Ross Redmond had been murdered because of his association with Eli's father, and Remus and the council.

The trio made their way along the shadowed hall to the solid wood door at the far end, with *Mayor's Office* etched into a black and brass plaque set at eye level, and Linda unlocked it. The files were in a closet to their right.

Linda searched the keys until she found the right one and pushed it into the lock with a click. "Ok. Anything to do with the council will be on the left."

Each of them picked a filing cabinet and started sifting through the files.

"They seem to have a large portfolio of properties," Paige said, fingering through the manila folders in the drawer. "How are we going to cover all of these?"

Archer turned to look at her. "We divide them up and hand them around."

"We have enough people on board to help us check out all these properties," Linda told them. "Thanks to you, Paige. I don't know how you talked Matthias into helping but I'm glad you did."

"And don't forget Brent calling in another pack to give us a hand." Paige couldn't believe her brother knew Daniel and his team, but felt a sense of gratitude for the increased numbers.

Archer moved closer to her. "Here, give me some of those so we can get out of here."

"We're taking them with us?"

"Of course." He shrugged. "We can't stand here all night snapping photos of every page."

"You're right."

Linda's face paled. "But they'll be missed."

"So what?" Archer glanced at her over his shoulder. "It's not as though they're going to know who took them. It could be anyone who has access to these cabinets."

Linda nodded. "You're right, again." She stepped up beside Paige and eased a large bundle out of her hands.

"I'll need to call another meeting so these addresses can be distributed and checked out."

"Later this morning?" Archer asked.

"Yes. The sooner we get started the better."

The trio left the mayor's office the way they'd found it, except for the files, and headed down the stairs. A flashlight shone into the entry hall from outside through the frosted glass front door and Linda gasped. "Quick, this way." She led them through the building and out the back exit before the security guard could spot them making their getaway when he entered. They circled city hall and came out of the alley beside it, crossed the street and piled the folders into the trunk before climbing into the car and driving away. People got up early in Moon Grove to start their day and they couldn't risk being seen by someone out walking their dog or taking a morning jog.

By the time they reached the church the sun had risen completely above the surrounding trees. It looked like it would be a beautiful day. Paige unlocked the doors and the three carried the folders inside, laying them on the altar at the front of the hall.

"I've sent out a text to everyone so they should be here within the hour, depending on where they're coming from."

Rosemarie and Cooper appeared in the doorway. "Mornin' all," the receptionist's voice echoed along the nave. She and the deputy made their way down to the chancel. "Is there any news on Eli?"

"Morning, Rose." Paige shook her head. "No, nothing unfortunately. But we have a list of properties owned by the council and I'm assigning areas to be checked out. He has to be at one of them."

"I'm in," Cooper said. "We need to find him ASAP."

"Thanks, Coop. I knew I could count on you." Paige smiled.

"Always." He took a seat on the front pew next to Rosemarie.

Within minutes, Brent and his mother arrived and joined the seated pair. "No word?" Brent asked.

"Afraid not."

"So what are we doing here?" her brother wanted to know. "We need to be out there."

"We've discovered properties owned by the council and we're dividing up the list so these areas can be checked out."

"Ok. Let's do it." Brent bounced to his feet.

Paige motioned for him to sit back down. "We're waiting on the others to arrive before we get started."

"The longer we wait the more time will elapse." He wanted to get out there and search for Eli.

"I know that, Brent, but we have to do this in a systematic way or we'll be running amok. So, please, take a seat until they get here."

Brent huffed out a frustrated breath, shoved his hands into the pockets of his hoodie, and backed into his spot on the pew beside their mother.

At that moment, Matthias and his pack stalked down the nave and sat on the left-hand side front pew.

"Good morning. Thanks for coming," Paige greeted.

"No problem." Matthias gave her an intense stare as he took his seat.

Paige figured he always looked that way. She hadn't once seen him smile.

Daniel and his guys arrived shortly after and sidled into the pew behind Rosemarie and the others.

Archer and Linda sat down next to Abbey and Brent.

"Ok. Now that we're all here let's begin."

A voice echoed around the huge hall. "Wait a second. Can we get in on this too?"

Max, Archer's brother, and his friends Blake and Christopher stood at the door.

"You certainly can. Come on in. The more people we have the better our chance of finding Eli quickly." Paige knew it would make the search that much easier. She wished she could include the new deputies, but they were unaware of the town's eccentricities and she couldn't risk their lives. That may change in the future, but until it did the responsibility for their safety rested on her.

She looked at Rosemarie. "Rosy?"

"Yes, Paige?"

"Would you do me a huge favor?"

"You know I will."

"I need you to take command of the station while Eli is out of action. Someone has to be there for the new deputies. We can't have them asking questions."

"So, if they ask where Eli is what should I say?"

Paige gave the question some thought. "Tell them he had to go out of town unexpectedly for a few days. If they ask anything else say you don't know." She shrugged. "That's the best I can offer for the moment." She had more important issues right now, like finding Eli alive.

The receptionist gave her an uncertain frown. "Ok. I hope it'll be enough to satisfy their curiosity."

"Me too, Rosy, me too."

Eli started awake, his eyelids snapping open to a black wall of darkness. How long had he been asleep? His skewed internal body clock no longer offered any concept of time. He struggled to his feet, his restraints pulling against his tall frame. He jerked at the chains attached to the cuffs on his wrists with all of his strength but they wouldn't budge. He let out a frustrated growl. It seemed hopeless. He sat down again.

His wolf vision widened, allowing him to see a little more clearly in the gloom. He spotted something on the floor not far out of his reach. What could it be? Eli's pupils dilated further. A key? Had Alistair dropped it on the floor for him to find? But why would the vampire help him? Out of past friendship or guilt perhaps?

Eli struggled to stretch out his left leg, pointing his toes in an attempt to connect with the metal object just out of his reach. He let out an agitated grunt. "Dammit!" He shuffled closer along the floor on his behind but the shackles pulled tighter. Maybe if he stood up. He climbed to his feet and stepped sideways. Still no luck. His heartrate kicked up a few notches as his wolf tried to emerge and he noticed a dull glimmer from the ring on his finger. Maybe Archer had been right. Maybe he needed to turn to activate it. Eli took a deep breath, closed his eyes, and permitted his body to shift. The change ripped the restraints clean out of the rocky wall. *I'm free.*

Turning back to human form, Eli snatched the key off the floor, dashed over to the heavy metal door and rammed it into the lock. It snapped open. He eased the door back and peered outside. More darkness. Stepping into the passageway, he remembered his clothes had been shredded when he'd shifted. Where could he find something to cover himself? He continued forward to another door and hesitated before reaching for the handle. He pressed his ear to the metal. No sound on the other side. Knowing it could be a trap he gripped the handle and pushed the door open. The lit corridor gave him his location. He'd been here before.

NINE

Rosemarie unlocked the station door and stepped inside, flicking on the overhead light as she shrugged out of her jacket and hung it on the coat rack. Crossing the office, she gave a heavy sigh, pushed open the swinging door, and dropped her purse onto her desk. The place wasn't the same anymore without Bobby and the others. And now she had to lie to the new deputies because they knew nothing of the town's secrets.

Lucky for her she'd arrived before Taylor and Rick showed up for their shift otherwise they'd have been bound to ask questions. They would anyhow, with Cooper and Eli missing from the office. Rosemarie hated lying, and she wasn't good at it. She never could maintain a poker face. She wandered through to the kitchen to brew a pot of coffee and heard the front door open.

Turning on her heel, she headed back into the office.

Rick and Taylor were hanging up their jackets and Stetsons.

"Morning, you two. Ready to start the day?" She gave the pair a pleasant smile despite her feeling of apprehension over Eli and tried to pretend *business as usual*.

"We sure are." Rick's gaze moved around the station and through the glass window into Eli's office. "Where's Cooper and Eli?"

Rosemarie wrung her hands together, her heart rate ticking up a notch. "Oh... well... Cooper's doing his rounds and Eli... Eli had to go out of town for a couple days." Her voice had a nervous tremor to it and she knew she wasn't as convincing as she should be.

Rick's eyes stopped on her. "Cooper went out without Taylor?"

"Uh, yes, he wanted to get an early start. Besides, he's still a bit... you know. Perhaps you and Taylor could ride together today." Rosemarie knew it could be dangerous allowing the new deputies to go out on their own, but she didn't have a choice. Cooper and the others had been assigned to search for Eli and that took priority right now.

"But Eli said we couldn't ride together right away," Taylor said, giving the receptionist a curious stare. Something felt wrong.

Rosemarie mustered up the fortitude to be assertive. Something else she wasn't good at. "Well, I'm in charge while Eli's away so you'll do as I say. All right?"

"You're not a police officer. How can you be in charge?" Rick folded his arms and gave Taylor a sideward glance before returning his questioning gaze back to the receptionist.

"I'm an honorary police officer. Eli made me one." She whipped her badge wallet out of her purse, opened it and thrust it at the pair. "So you'll do what you're told without questioning my decisions. Understood?" Rosemarie's heart pumped so hard she could feel it in her throat. She hated being mean to anyone but, again, she didn't have a choice. Paige counted on her and she wouldn't let her down.

Rick raised defensive hands. "Ok, ok. Just asking."

"Well, now you know." The heat in her cheeks subsided. "Do you want some coffee before you head out? I'm going to make a pot." Rosemarie walked over to the hall doorway.

"Uh, no thanks. I think we'll get going." Rick plucked the patrol keys from the key cabinet behind the reception desk then headed over to the door, grabbing his jacket and hat off the coat rack.

"All right, well, stick to the areas Eli showed you, and don't deviate. Ok?"

"Yeah, we will." Rick pulled the door open.

Taylor stood watching Rosemarie, her stomach wound tight. She knew she had to trust her gut... something wasn't right.

"Are you coming?" Rick asked, holding the door for her.

The deputy swung around. "Oh. Yeah. Sure." She grabbed her jacket and hat and followed Rick out, glancing over her shoulder through the glass before heading along the porch behind him.

Rosemarie let out the breath she'd been holding in one long whoosh. She didn't know how long she could keep this up.

The police patrol cruised the quiet main road and turned onto the side street that led to the church on the hill. Both deputies gave each other a sideward glance before Rick drove the black and white up the incline. He'd noticed the tall, white spire in the distance the day Eli had taken them out on a tour of Moon Grove and he wanted to take a closer look.

"Did you get an odd vibe from Rosemarie this morning?" Taylor asked.

Rick pulled up at the front doors and turned off the engine. "What do you mean?"

"Couldn't you feel it?" She unclipped her seatbelt and stepped out of the wagon.

"No. Not except for her attitude. Why? What do you think's wrong?" Rick closed the patrol door and came around the vehicle to her.

"I'm not sure. But don't you think it's strange that Cooper went out without me, especially after Eli saying I had to ride with him? And don't you think Eli going out of town is a bit sudden?"

Rick shrugged. "Could've had a family emergency or something."

"Maybe." Taylor frowned at him. "Rosemarie seemed edgy. Didn't you think so?"

"I wasn't paying attention."

"You're a cop. How can you say that?" She folded her arms. "We're meant to notice everything."

"I noticed her grilling me."

"See. That's what I mean. It's not like her, is it?"

"How do we know? We haven't been here long enough. Maybe it is like her." He walked over to the double, wood doors and tried the handle. Locked. "Now that's strange."

"What is?" Taylor followed him.

"Church doors are usually open for people to come and pray. At least the churches where we live are." Rick tugged the other handle and frowned. "Don't you think that's odd?" He walked past Taylor and peered around the corner of the white, wood structure, then wandered along to a side door. Also locked. He turned and looked at his partner. "I wonder why it's locked up."

"Maybe because it's up here away from town." She stood with her hands on her hips and did a 360 degree turn. "Maybe they're worried vandals might go in and smash up the place."

Rick's suspicious gaze remained on Taylor. "Maybe. But a place of worship is meant to be accessible, not closed."

She shrugged. "What else could it be?"

"Good question." He headed back to the car, Taylor in tow.

"The streets are extra quiet today. I wonder why." She opened the door and climbed into the vehicle, clipping in her seatbelt.

Rick got into the driver's seat. "Yeah, I wondered that myself. When we went out with Eli it didn't seem so deserted."

"I know, right? The town is as pretty as a picture but it doesn't feel right, at least not to me."

"It's not only you, Tay, I've noticed it too."

Taylor turned in her seat. "I'm telling you there's something wrong. At least as far as Eli and Cooper are concerned."

Rick glanced at his watch. "We'd better get moving or we'll have to explain why we're late getting back."

By the time Rick and Taylor arrived at the station Cooper had returned, along with a couple of people the deputies hadn't met before.

"Everything all right on your rounds?" Rosemarie asked.

"Yeah. Sure. All good," Rick told her.

"Good. There's fresh coffee and donuts in the kitchen, if you're hungry."

"Thanks."

The pair hung up their jackets and hats and headed out back to the kitchen.

Rosemarie turned to Paige, Cooper and Archer. "They're starting to ask questions. What am I supposed to keep telling them?"

"Don't panic, Rose. Just keep doing what you're doing. Eli would want us to hold the fort while he's not here, so let's do that... for him." Paige's eyes moved to the door the pair had stepped out of.

"I'm not a good liar, Paige. I'm sure they're going to suspect something's wrong soon enough."

Paige placed her hands on Rosemarie's shoulders. "I have total faith in you. You can do this."

The receptionist nodded and gave a flustered sigh. "I can do this." She glanced at Cooper then Archer. "How's the search going?"

"Nothing so far," Cooper told her.

"The places I checked out were empty. I don't understand why the council has so many properties they don't utilize." Archer folded his arms.

"Power." Paige's eyes moved to him. "They want to

control everyone and everything in our town and beyond its borders."

She turned to Rosemarie. "We have to go. Will you be ok?"

"I'll be fine." She looked at Cooper. "Can you make an appearance once in a while today so the newbies don't get more suspicious?"

"I'll do my best, Rosy."

"That's all I can ask for. Now go find Eli."

The three left the station.

Rosemarie glanced over her shoulder and sighed. She had to be convincing so Taylor and Rick wouldn't become suspicious. Could she do it? She didn't have a choice.

TEN

Eli continued along the passage until he came to another door. A small, square panel slid open and Remus appeared on the other side. "So, you thought you could escape us, Eli Blackwood. I am sorry to disappoint you, but there is no escape for you." A satisfied smirk crossed his chiseled, pale face. "You see, I want the others to come looking for you. And when they do we will be waiting."

"I thought you were out of state." Eli couldn't believe Remus and his cronies were back in Moon Grove, and in their mansion.

"Yes, well, appearances can be deceiving, Sheriff. Technology is a fascinating tool."

"So I'm your bait?"

"You are." He turned on his heel and marched along the short hallway.

Eli gripped the bars in the panel. "Remus."

Alistair appeared at the opening. "I am sorry, Eli." The panel snapped shut, the acute sound echoing along the concrete walls behind him.

He'd been set up. He should've known better than to place any trust in a council member. They always had their own agenda.

Despair turned to rage. He would not let Remus win this battle. If he gave up now the town would be at the council's mercy and he couldn't let that happen. Something was on its way to destroy Moon Grove and he *would* be there to stop it. The moonstone ring glowed, its aura increasing in strength as his fury grew. Eli could feel the power of the ring surging through his tall frame. His muscles clenched, claws pushed through his fingertips, and with one almighty growl he shifted into wolf form, leaping at the door with all his Lycan strength and knocking it to the ground.

Bounding along the passage, he came to a set of stairs and stopped. Using his Lycan hearing, he listened for voices above. Nothing. Were Remus and the others staying at the mansion or were they using it only as a place to hold him? He shifted back to human form and climbed the treads one at a time with caution. Once on the landing, he pressed his ear to the door, his heightened Lupine senses searching for any voices or movement on the other side. Nothing.

The vampire leader had underestimated him once again. Eli jiggled the brass knob. It twisted in his hand and the door popped open. Easing it back, he peered around the staircase. No one in the entry hall. He stepped out and gazed up the stairs. The mansion appeared deserted. A coat rack nearby yielded a knee length, black jacket. He whipped across the foyer, yanked it off the hook and shrugged into it. A tight fit, but better than nothing. Where had Remus and his adherents disappeared to? Not knowing where they were posed too many issues for his town.

He heard a sound outside the double front doors and darted into the curtained hallway. Had they returned?

One door squeaked open and Alistair stepped inside.

When Eli saw him he came out of his hiding place. "What are you still doing here?"

The vampire's eyes widened. "How did you get out of...?"

"My wolf."

"I came back to set you free, Eli."

"How can I believe anything you say?" He folded his arms.

"Because it is the truth. I hadn't planned on Remus wanting to check on you. He never bothers with such menial things, but because *you* were his captive he made an exception."

"What will happen to you if he finds out what you've done?" Eli's frowning gaze remained on Alistair.

"He won't. He trusts me implicitly."

"Don't be too sure of that."

"Do not concern yourself with me, Eli. You have more important matters to deal with."

"What do you mean?" His gut shrank into a tight knot of nerves.

"There is a coven of thirteen witches coming, the Circle of the Full Moon. These witches are not your ordinary kind of spell casters. They have powers beyond your wildest imaginings and they will destroy the supernatural residents of Moon Grove, and anyone else who stands in their wake. They wield their powers like weapons. That's why Remus chose them."

"Why are you telling me this?"

"Because I cannot stand by and watch our town crumble. Remus has gone too far this time. His quest for power has overshadowed his judgement."

"How long before they get here?"

"Two, maybe three days. You need to be prepared, Eli, otherwise you'll fall alongside everyone else in this town."

Eli pushed past him. "I won't let that happen."

"Wait. Did Mayor Redmond give you the key to the safety deposit box?"

"What did he tell you about it, Alistair?"

"It offers a way to destroy Remus. Once he is gone the others will listen to me."

"Again, why should I trust you? How do I know this isn't a ploy to get your hands on whatever's inside that box?"

"I want to lead the council in the right way, Eli. Work with you to build trust in this town, not lord it over the residents to elicit fear. I have only tried to help you, and I am still offering my help."

Eli's frowning gaze remained on the vampire while he attempted to ascertain whether or not he could believe him. With no time left to refuse help, he said, "All right, I believe you. What's in the box?"

"What if the council has taken Eli to wherever they're holed up? How are we supposed to find him if he's not in Moon Grove?" Matthias stood in the nave, hands on hips. To his mind the search would be pointless with nothing to go on. They'd been summoned to another meeting at the church to advise Paige of their progress, which, so far, had been zero.

Paige walked over to him. "We don't know that so…"

"That's my point. We don't know anything." Matthias stood his ground.

"So we keep looking until we find something," Archer stepped up beside Paige.

"And how long do you think we should continue this charade? Indefinitely? What if he's already dead?"

Paige's right hand connected with the Alpha's cheek in a sharp slap that echoed around the hall. She hadn't meant to hit him, but frustration, worry, and his attitude had caused an automatic reaction. She gasped, raised her hand to her mouth, and stepped backwards. "I – I'm sorry, Matthias. I didn't mean to do that."

The Alpha's dark stare met hers and he inhaled a deep breath through his nostrils, contemplating whether to leave or stay. She had insulted him, and as Alpha of his pack he had every right to withdraw their help. But he knew how much pressure Paige was under, so he'd give her some leeway… this time. "Apology accepted." He leaned in, his mouth close to her ear. "Don't let it happen again."

Paige nodded and gave him an uncertain smile. "Thank you." She knew he could leave at any moment and without him and his pack they were in serious danger. She would need to keep her emotions in check from now on otherwise she would lose an alliance they so desperately needed.

At that moment, one of the double front doors opened and Eli stepped into the church hall.

Paige's gaze moved from Matthias to the doorway. When she saw Eli she raced up the nave and threw her arms around him. "Oh, my God, you're here. Where have you been? What happened?"

Alistair came up behind him and stepped across the threshold into the church.

Everyone in the pews stood up and turned to look at him.

"It's all right. He helped me escape. And he's here to offer his assistance."

"How can we trust a council member?" Matthias asked, his intense gaze resting on the vampire. He'd had dealings with Alistair before.

"Like I told you out at your place, you can trust *me*." Eli walked down the nave, Paige still hugging him close to her side. "I know what's coming and we don't have much time."

ELEVEN

The next morning, as Clarissa made a cup of tea she felt an unnerving shiver crawl up her spine and spilt the hot water onto the kitchen counter. She had always been able to sense other witches close by and she could feel it now. She could also sense the blackness of the magic the coven possessed. The most dangerous kind. Grabbing the nearby dish cloth, she set the electric kettle on its base, mopped up the spill then walked over to the telephone on the wall, picked up the receiver and dialed the station. "Hello, Rosemarie, is Eli there by any chance?"

"Sorry, Clarissa, he's out at the moment. I can try him on the radio, if you like?"

"No, don't trouble him while he's working. Would you please ask him to call me when he's back?"

"I certainly will." Rosemarie picked up the yellow Post-it note pad from off her desk and jotted down the message. "You have a nice day now." She dropped the digital phone onto its base, walked over to the glass paneled door to Eli's office and stuck it slap bang in the center of the window at eye level… his eye level.

"You too." Clarissa said to the empty, buzzing line. She turned around and bit her bottom lip. Even though she didn't want to disturb Eli while he was working, she needed to call him on his cell right away. The continuous ring on the other end of the line unnerved her. Why wasn't her grandson picking up? She tried Paige's number. No answer there, either. "What's going on?" She thought for a moment, then decided to call Archer Hamilton.

"Welcome to the Moon Grove Tribune, Archer speaking."

"Mr. Hamilton, it's Clarissa Baker. Do you have any idea where Eli and Paige are? I've been trying to call them and no one's answering."

The editor knew he couldn't tell Eli's grandmother what had happened to him. Eli would bite his head off if he did. Literally. "Sorry, Clarissa, I don't." Eli and Paige had gone to Chicago to retrieve the safety deposit box the mayor had bequeathed to the sheriff. Archer wondered why Eli hadn't mentioned it to his grandmother. "Let me see what I can find out and I'll call you back."

"Thank you, Mr. Hamilton, I appreciate your help."

"It's no problem at all. And, please, call me Archer."

"Thank you, Archer. I'll wait to hear from you." She set the receiver back in its cradle.

The editor pressed speed dial for Eli. No answer. He tried Paige's cell. No answer there, either. Maybe they were at the bank in the vault and had no reception. That's all he could think of right now. He'd give it another try later.

As he sat down at his desk the phone rang. Thinking it might be Eli or Paige returning his call, he pressed it to his ear. "Hello."

"Archer, it's Carmichael. I have excellent news. The serum is ready ahead of schedule."

"That is good news, my Lord. We need it here ASAP. We have intel on what is heading to Moon Grove and we'll need to use the serum to help us win the fight."

"Give me the details."

"Have you heard of the Coven of the Full Moon?"

Silence.

"Carmichael?"

"I am here. Yes, we have heard of this particular coven. They are an extremely dangerous group of black witches that use their powers to destroy anything in their path. They have annihilated whole towns across the globe and yours will be no exception. I'll expedite the serum to you post haste and also send others who have already trialed it. You will need more assistance than you have already."

"Thank you, my Lord. Is there anything on this coven you can email me, to prepare us for the battle?"

"I will have it to you by the end of today. Do you know when they're arriving?"

"Two days."

"You will have the information within the hour and I will arrange for the other vampires to get to you as soon as possible."

"I will await your email." Archer rang off, dropped the phone onto his desk, and ran his hand through his dark hair. This would be some war.

Eli and Paige stepped out of the bank and headed along South LaSalle Street, the sheriff carrying a bag with a journal, a sealed wooden container, and documents they had collected from the safety deposit box. Once back at their hotel, the pair would go over the information they had been bestowed by Ross Redmond and find the only way to end Remus's rule on Moon Grove.

As they walked the few blocks back to the Marriott, Eli's cell chimed. He plucked it from the pocket of his jacket and looked at the screen. It was Archer. "What's up?"

"Your grandmother called me. She's been trying to get onto you and Paige and is concerned that you're not picking up. She wants you to give her a call."

"Ok, thanks, I will."

"I have other news."

"Yeah? What?"

"The serum is ready. It's being shipped to me as we speak, along with some hybrid reinforcements who were part of the trial."

"That's great. I hope they'll be enough to defeat the coven."

"I'm also being sent intel on the coven. I should have it within the hour. There could be vital information we can use against them."

"We're on our way back to the hotel to go over what we've found then we're heading home. We should be back in Moon Grove by sundown."

"Ok. I'll see you when you get here. Don't forget to call your grandmother."

"I won't. See you later."

"Any news?" Paige gave Eli an inquisitive frown.

"Archer said intel's on its way. He also said Clary's been trying to reach us." Checking his cell, he found he had several missed calls on it from his grandmother.

"Oh?" Paige checked her phone. "The thick concrete walls of the vault must've prevented the signal."

"Yeah, most likely."

The pair picked up their pace. They needed to find out what Ross Redmond knew and get back to Moon Grove quickly.

The weight of worry lifted from Clarissa's shoulders when she heard her grandson's voice on the other end of the line. She had been concerned that the discomfort she'd experienced might have been the reason for his and Paige's silence. "Eli, I've felt something."

The sheriff knew he couldn't discount anything his grandmother sensed. "Like what?"

"There are other witches here. They practice the darkest form of magic."

Eli's gut shrank. He'd thought they'd have more time. "Do you know how many?"

"A black magic coven usually has thirteen witches. And they're nearby. Perhaps not in Moon Grove, but somewhere close to town. I wouldn't be able to sense them otherwise."

"Thanks for letting me know, Clary. We'll stop by in a bit. I've got something I need to do first."

"All right. I'll have the kettle on."

Eli pressed the Bluetooth phone button on the dash to end the call and glanced at Paige. "The witches are already somewhere near town. Clary has sensed them."

Paige's gaze moved through the windshield and along

the road ahead of them. "Then we need to get back home *now*."

TWELVE

Scarlet stepped from the silver, Chevrolet Express van, her emerald eyes roaming the luxury wood cabin set among the towering pines: wrap around porch with striped deck chairs, fire pit, and a Jacuzzi set into the corner. Perfect. The property, owned by the council, had been purchased in secret, and the coven members were permitted to reside here until they completed their task, however long it might take. As High Priestess of the Coven of the Full Moon, she would enter the house first and offer an incantation to their dark lord before her sisters stepped across the threshold.

Their coven consisted of thirteen witches, including her, with varying attributes: Minerva, Tamsin, Ursula, Morgan, Celeste, Jasmine, Molly, Opal, Nora, Raven, Salina, and Poppy were the most powerful dark magic practitioners in the world. Their powers were a gift from Satan and their reputations preceded them wherever they traversed. Witches across the globe feared them... and with good reason.

Scarlet climbed the front steps, opened the door, stepped into the living room and ran her gaze around the comfortable surroundings. They would enjoy their time in this elegant space. Stepping back out onto the porch, she asked her sisters to wait while she performed the blessing, then joined them at the van to retrieve her luggage.

"This place is great!" Morgan said, wriggling her finger and watching her suitcase float up the front steps onto the porch. "I'm going to love that Jacuzzi."

"How many bedrooms does it have?" Salina asked, hoping to have one to herself. She hated having to share.

"There are seven bedrooms, so you will have to pair up I'm afraid," Scarlet told them. She always had a private room.

Salina groaned and gave a heavy sigh. "I had hoped for a little space."

"Sorry, sweetie, there's nothing I can do." Scarlet zapped her bag and it disappeared. It would be waiting for her in her room – the master suite with its own bathroom.

"Why can't we use our magic to create an extension while we're here? Then everyone can have a room to themselves," Tamsin offered.

"Because we don't want to draw attention to ourselves. People hike through these woods. There are most likely forest rangers in the area who keep an eye on properties out here too. What do you think would happen if they saw that the cabin had been extended virtually overnight?"

Tamsin grimaced. "I only thought it might make everyone a bit more comfortable."

"Your heart's in the right place, but we can't."

"Sorry." Tamsin climbed the front steps and disappeared into the cabin.

Molly tugged her suitcase from the back of the van, set it down beside her, raised her hand and sent it up the steps.

Raven spotted it, pointed at the case, did a twirl with her index finger, and the lock popped open spilling Molly's clothes and other items all over the staircase.

Scarlet noticed. "Raven, clean that up right *now*."

Raven glared at Scarlet and raised her defiant chin in the air. "Why should I?"

"Because we don't treat our sisters with disrespect." Scarlet stood with arms folded. "Now, please do as I ask."

"No." Raven flew up to the porch, landed on the deck, and marched into the cabin.

Scarlet shook her head and sighed. Raven had become even more difficult to handle lately and her unruly behavior affected them all. If she couldn't take direction now what would she do when the battle began? She ran her index finger back and forth, the clothing and other items refolding themselves and returning to Molly's suitcase. "I'm sorry for Raven's behavior, Moll. She knows better."

"It's ok. I'm used to it." Molly climbed the front steps, picked up her bag and took it into the house. She would work on a spell later to get back at Raven. Something ambiguous that wouldn't be linked to her.

"Raven has some attitude. Maybe you should discipline her," Poppy said.

"When I do she defies me even more. I'm not sure what will work with her anymore."

"Mm. I hope you figure it out before she does something impulsive and lands us all in trouble. Hey, don't you think Tamsin's idea is pretty cool?"

"Yes, I do. It's unfortunate we can't do it."

"What if we used a cloaking spell?" Nora suggested.

Scarlet allowed the idea she should have thought of herself to circle her mind for a moment. That could work. "Tamsin," she called. "Can you come out here, please?"

Tamsin stepped out the front door and leaned against the railing. "What is it?"

"We're going to give your idea a try and use a cloaking spell."

"Yay!" Tamsin clapped her hands together and did a little happy jump.

"Want to join us?"

"Of course." She raced down the stairs and stood with her sisters. Glancing around her, she asked, "Where's Raven?"

"Sulking."

"Oh." Everyone knew to stay out of her way while Raven brooded.

After securing what they brought back with them from Chicago inside Eli's secret floor safe, the pair climbed into the Jeep and headed to Clary's. Archer had called Eli to let him know he'd received the email and also news of the impending arrival of the other vampires. Once Eli and Paige spent time with his grandmother, they would head over to the Tribune office to tell the editor what they'd discovered. They needed to prepare for the upcoming battle and anything that would help them defeat the coven would bring them one step closer to victory. There had to be a way to win the fight because Eli wouldn't allow a group of witches to destroy his town.

Clarissa met the pair on her front porch and ushered them inside, roaming the street with her eyes before closing the door and following them into the kitchen. Eli and Paige sat down at the table while his grandmother poured water into the teapot. Setting the pot on the round, cork heat mat in the center of the table, she took her seat. "The dark magic the coven possesses is incredibly powerful, Eli. It comes from Lucifer himself."

"How powerful?" Eli picked up his mug of tea and took a cautious sip.

"The kind of magic they command can kill with a look."

Paige's face paled. "So one of them could look at me and I'd be dead?"

The old woman gave a nod and a thin smile. "Puts a whole new spin on if looks could kill, doesn't it? And, who knows, perhaps that's where the saying stemmed from."

A shiver ran the length of Paige's small frame. "Yes, it does. So how are we meant to stop them?"

"That's the tricky part." Clarissa passed a cup of tea to Paige. "There has to be some kind of talisman that provides them with protection. If we can find it, it would reduce their powers. You would still have a fight on your hands though, because their combined dark energy would still be strong."

"But they wouldn't be able to kill us with a look, right?" Paige's heart rate ticked up a couple of notches at the thought.

"It depends. The High Priestess of the coven maintains a certain amount of satanic power regardless of where the talisman is."

Eli felt out of his depth. The town had never encountered witches with these kinds of abilities before. He couldn't send his team out to be killed. "If we can't find the talisman what else can we do?"

"I'm working on that. When I find what I'm looking for I'll let you know. And I won't stop searching until I do."

"Thanks for the information." Eli checked his watch and stood up. "Sorry, Clary, but we have to see Archer. He could have some news that will help us."

"That's all right. You go on, dear. And keep safe."

"We will." Paige walked around the table and gave the old woman a hug. "You too."

"Don't worry. I'll be fine." She remained seated at the table. If the coven learned of her attempts to thwart their plans they would end her life. *What can I do to help Eli and Paige?*

When the front door closed Clarissa got up from the table and headed for the living room. She'd consult the cards. There had to be an answer to their current dilemma.

THIRTEEN

When Eli and Paige stepped into the Tribune office Archer left his desk and walked up to the pair. "Hi, come with me." He led them through the back to a small, private office where they could talk uninterrupted and unheard. He had received the intel he'd been expecting and wanted to discuss what he had learned with them.

The trio stepped into the claustrophobic space and Archer closed the door, rounded the desk that took up most of the office and sat down. "Take a seat."

Paige and Eli did as he requested, giving each other a sideward glance. "Did you find out how we can defeat the coven?" Eli needed to protect his pack and the other packs offering their assistance from the serious threat they would face.

Archer rested his elbows on the chair arms and clasped his hands in front of him. "From what I can see, they have been unstoppable for centuries. Those who have tried," he said, giving them both a grave stare, "have died."

Paige's stomach did queasy flip flops underneath her jeans. "There has to be a way."

"There may be… but not only is it a risk, it may not work."

Eli moved forward on his chair. "What is it?"

"We need a witch to do a binding spell."

"You mean to stave off their ability to kill?" Eli knew what the editor had in mind and didn't like it.

"Yes." Archer straightened in his seat and leaned on the desk. "Would Clarissa be willing to help us?"

"She's an old woman…" Paige attempted to protest.

Archer raised his hand to stop her. "But she's an established witch. One who has possessed her powers her whole life. She has the capacity to cast this spell. Do you know of any other witch in the area that would be willing to risk her life to help us?"

Paige and Eli sighed together.

"No, we don't," Eli replied.

"Then there's no point in debating this. We need her assistance." Archer stood his ground.

At that moment, Clarissa knocked on the door. Eli jerked from his chair and opened it for her. "What are you doing here?"

"I know what needs to be done." She stepped into the small space. "I consulted the cards and they told me we must try a binding spell to prevent the coven from using their most dangerous powers. It's risky and it might not take effect, but we have to try. The first task we need to undertake is finding them and their talisman."

Archer wondered why he hadn't spoken to Clarissa in the first place. She seemed quite astute when it came to these kinds of matters. He motioned to Eli's vacant chair. "Have a seat, Clary. Let's talk."

Later that evening, while Clarissa stood at the kitchen sink washing her dinner dishes, a knock echoed along the entry hall. The minute she heard it her spine tingled. She dried her hands on the dish cloth lying on the counter and made her way to the front door. "Who is it?" She knew it wasn't Eli or Paige... or even Archer Hamilton. No answer. Clarissa asked again, "Who's there?"

At that moment, the door burst open tossing the old woman backwards and knocking her to the floor.

"Hello, Clarissa Baker, it's time we had a little chat," Scarlet announced.

Clarissa stumbled to her feet and stood in the middle of the entry hall. "I don't know what you mean."

Scarlet wagged her index finger at Clarissa and clucked her tongue. "You know perfectly well why I'm here." She attempted to cross the threshold. "Well, you are as powerful as we've been led to believe, aren't you?"

"Why are you here?" The old woman stood her ground. She would not show fear to an adversary.

"Allow me to introduce myself, I'm Scarlet Balfour. I've come here tonight as a courtesy, to offer you a *friendly* warning. Do not meddle in the affairs of the coven." All witches held a certain respect for those with exceptional powers, and Clarissa Baker possessed those abilities, which proved evident by the protection spell Scarlet couldn't breach.

"Or what?"

"Or the people you hold dear will start to disappear." Scarlet gave her a smug smile.

"You *will* *not* harm anyone that I love. Do you understand?" Clarissa raised her hand and a bolt of yellow flashed across the entry hall and exploded at the High Priestess's feet.

Scarlet jumped backwards. "Stay out of our business, Clarissa, or there will be consequences." With that said, she dissolved in front of the old woman's eyes.

Clarissa let out the breath she'd been holding and her trembling body folded onto the carved wooden chest beside the staircase. She could still feel the residual darkness of the witch lingering at the open doorway. Thank goodness she had placed a powerful protection spell around her home... one that only she could break.

The telephone on the wall beside the refrigerator jingled, sending a shockwave up her spine and she sprang from the chest. "Oh!" She hurried into the kitchen and snatched the phone from its cradle. "He – hello?"

Eli could hear his grandmother's shortness of breath. "Clary, are you all right?"

"I am now." She let out an exasperated huff.

"Why? What happened?" The sheriff's gut tightened.

"I had a visitor... Scarlet Balfour... the High Priestess of the Circle of the Full Moon coven."

"You're sure you're ok?" Eli got to his feet. "I'm coming over."

Paige gave him a quizzical stare and mouthed, 'what's wrong?'

Eli raised his index finger at Paige, motioning for her to wait a minute.

"There's no need, dear. She's gone."

"But what if she comes back?" Eli paced.

"She came to give me a *friendly* warning to stay out of the coven's affairs. That's all."

"That doesn't mean she won't be back."

"Even if she does she can't come in. I've cast a powerful protection spell around the house only I can break."

"You're sure she can't get inside?"

"She tried and couldn't, so, yes, I'm sure." Clary gave a smile at the thought. The High Priestess had been stunned by the old woman's powers.

"I'll get into the system and see if I can find anything on Scarlet Balfour." Eli crossed the room to the laptop sitting on the dining table.

"You do that, dear. I'm heading to bed. I'll need all the strength I can muster for what's to come."

"Ok. Goodnight, Clary. Be safe."

"I will, dear. Love you. Goodnight."

Paige crossed the room to where Eli had sat down. "Everything all right?"

He glanced up from the computer screen. "The coven's High Priestess paid Clary a visit."

She frowned into his concerned eyes. "That can't be good."

"My thoughts exactly." He logged onto the justice system database. "I'm going to see if I can find anything on her. Surely she's had a parking ticket or some minor misdemeanor at some point in her life. Maybe it will give me something to work with."

Paige sat down on a chair at the side of the table close to him and rested her elbows on top. "Can I do anything to help?"

"Not at the moment, sweetheart. Let me see what I can

find out first." He reached across and rested his hand on hers and gave her one of those heart-stopping smiles she loved. "But thanks for the offer."

"I don't want to think of Clary being alone over there without someone watching out for her."

"She's fine for now. She said she placed a protection spell around the house that not even this Scarlet Balfour could break, so I think she'll be all right for the moment."

"Ok. Well if there's nothing I can do I'm going to bed. I have a date with a book." Paige stood up, leaned in and kissed Eli on the forehead. "Goodnight."

"Goodnight." His eyes moved from the laptop to her. "Love you."

Paige glanced at him over her shoulder. "Love you, too." The book she'd borrowed from the library wasn't for entertainment. She wanted to research witch covens and their powers in the hope of finding something that would help them win the fight against the coven now residing on the border of Moon Grove's boundary.

Once she disappeared along the hallway to their room, Eli snatched his cell from off the table and hit speed dial for Cooper. "Hey, Coop, how's it going?"

"Good. The place is pretty quiet. Nothing out of the ordinary. What's up?" Taylor sat in the passenger seat beside him so he had to be careful what he said.

"Can you do me a favor?"

"Sure, anything. What do you need?"

"Can you run by Clary's place on your rounds? She had an unexpected visitor, which I'll explain later, and I'd like to know she's ok."

"You bet." Cooper did a U-turn and headed in the direction of Clary's house. "On my way now." He cruised along the main street. "Do you want me to call in?"

"Only if something happens. If I don't hear from you I'll know all's well."

"Ok. Have a good night, Eli."

"You too, Coop. And thanks."

"No need. We look out for our own."

"Yeah, we do." He rang off and sat his phone beside the laptop. Would he find anything in the system on Scarlet Balfour? He hoped so.

FOURTEEN

Around midnight, as Eli sat at his laptop sifting through records in the database he realized he'd been wasting his time. He'd discovered nothing. Perhaps it went without saying that supernatural creatures kept a low profile with regard to law enforcement. He also kept a low profile. The human residents of Moon Grove knew nothing of his Lycan tendencies. Even so, it seemed odd that Scarlet Balfour wouldn't have incurred some kind of fine for something during her lifetime. Perhaps she had an alias. Perhaps she only used her real name as part of the coven. He would attempt to get a picture of her on his cell, run it, and see what showed up. She had to have a driver's license.

As his gaze moved from the computer screen to his phone, it rang. He snatched it off the tabletop and frowned at the ID. Archer. *What could he want at this time of night?* "Hamilton, what's up?"

"Need I remind you that we've gotten past the last name calling situation, remember?"

"Yeah, yeah, ok. Sorry. Don't you ever sleep?"

"Vampires do sleep, but right now I've got something more important to tell you. Can you come over to the office?"

Eli's eyebrows rose. "You're still there?"

"Yes. I've been doing some research via the information I received from Carmichael and I think I've found something that could prove useful."

"Can't you tell me over the phone?"

"No, we can't take that risk. The council has eyes and ears everywhere."

"Ok, I'll see you soon." Eli's gaze moved to the hallway. Should he wake Paige and tell her? He figured he should. Getting to his feet, he dropped his cell into the top pocket of his denim work shirt, closed his laptop and crossed the living room. When he reached their bedroom door he stopped. Maybe he should leave a note and not wake her. As he turned around to head back along the hallway the bedroom door opened.

"I'm coming with you." Paige stood in the doorway dressed and ready to go.

"Sweetheart, there's no need both of us losing sleep. Go back to bed. I won't be long."

Paige shook her head. "Not happening. The last time you went off on your own you didn't come back. I'm coming with you, like it or not."

Eli sighed. "All right, let's get going."

Archer's left eyebrow rose when he saw Eli and Paige enter the Tribune office. He'd expected the sheriff to come alone but understood why Paige didn't want to let Eli out of her sight. They'd thought he could be dead while he'd been missing and that had caused a reaction in Paige Archer hadn't witnessed before. "Good to see you both. Have a seat."

"What's so important that it couldn't wait until daylight?" Paige asked as she sat down on one of two chairs in front of the editor's desk.

"Clarissa may be able to create a spell that will counter the coven's attacks on us."

Paige moved forward on her seat. "Is that possible?"

"From what I've been researching it is."

"That's brilliant." Eli smiled, moved around the chair in front of him and sat down.

"Isn't it?" Archer clasped his hands in front of him on the desk blotter. "It's different to the binding spell we spoke about. Should you or should I talk to Clarissa about it?"

"I think we both should. You have the information and I can be there as moral support."

"Good. We'll go see her later this morning. This could be the breakthrough we need to win this fight." Archer leaned back in his office chair and smiled.

Paige wasn't so sure. A coven hundreds of years old would have certain protections in place, otherwise how would they have survived so long? "Do you honestly believe it's that simple? Don't you think, after hundreds of years, they'd be prepared for something like that? Otherwise someone would've killed them off a long time ago." Her gaze moved from Archer to Eli then back to the editor. "And, remember, Scarlet warned Clary off."

"What?!" Archer straightened in his chair. "What do you mean?"

Paige's eyes moved to Eli.

"Yeah, sorry, I meant to tell you Clary had a visitor yesterday. Scarlet Balfour, High Priestess of the Circle of the Full Moon. She warned my grandmother that her loved ones would be targeted if she did anything to stand in their way."

"I'm sorry to hear that, Eli. It must have been frightening for her. Then we can't ask her to do it, it would be too dangerous. We'll have to find another way." The editor had taken a backward step in his quest to help the sheriff and the town.

"What other way?" Eli wanted to know. "This seems like the most expedient course of action."

"I know, but..."

"Clary won't be scared off. She'll help us."

"Doesn't their threat bother you?"

"We're all supernatural creatures who can take care of ourselves. Besides, if I know my grandmother she'll be working on protection spells for all of us."

"Perhaps you should ask her first, Eli."

"And I will when we go to see her."

Scarlet sat in a blue and white striped deck chair on the front porch of the sophisticated log cabin and gazed up at the waxing gibbous moon. She loved the dark hours of the morning before cock-crow, or as the Spanish called it *madrugada*. It was a time for reflection, for meditation, for allowing the mind to be at peace. She believed a clear mind could accomplish anything, whereas a cluttered mind fraught with worry created chaos, and she had to be clear of mind for what would come.

She would lead her witches into battle against Lycan and Vampires, ones not so easy to destroy, despite their own limitations placed on themselves. It would be a battle of wit and skill and the High Priestess knew Eli Blackwood would not relinquish his town easily. He would fight to the death. Remus, a true monster, wanted the wolves, vampires, and other supernatural creatures expedited to Hell so he could rule the town with an iron fist. Moon Grove and the humans that resided in it would be his to do with as he pleased. As a witch who practiced black magic, she could not condemn his actions? He had paid her coven handsomely for their services, set them up in this beautiful home, so best not to bite the hand that fed them.

Scarlet realized her conscience had gotten the better of her. Meditation made you aware of your inner emotions, the ones you kept locked away from others in your life. She stood and walked across to the railing, releasing the uncertainty and fear lodged in her belly. As High Priestess of her coven she would act accordingly. The battle would be won, she had no doubt... but by whom?

FIFTEEN

The next morning, Paige headed into the office early. She had several patients to see throughout the day and she wanted to go over her clinical notes on each one before their appointments. She parked in the alley behind the building and entered through the rear door. The place seemed quiet. Linda obviously hadn't arrived yet.

Paige set her things down on the small kitchen table and wandered along the short hallway to her office and stopped short when she saw her door ajar. She'd remembered closing it on Friday before she left. Stepping up to the door, she eased it back – lucky for her the hinges didn't squeak – and found Linda at her filing cabinet going through the files. Not uncommon, being her administration assistant, but the locked drawers held Paige's private files. Where had she gotten a key?

"Linda, what are you doing?" She stepped into the doorway.

The receptionist spun around, flustered. "I – I…"

Paige raised her hand for Linda to stop speaking. "How did you get a key to my locked files?"

Linda gave a heavy sigh, pushed the drawer closed, and walked over to her boss. "I took a photo."

"When?"

"While you were in the bathroom a couple of days ago. I took the photo on my phone to a locksmith and got a copy made."

Paige frowned into her assistant's eyes. "You're the mole?"

Tears welled in Linda's eyes and she nodded.

Paige raised a hand to her mouth and gasped. "But why? Why would you betray Eli like this?"

"I don't have a choice. Remus will kill me if I don't do what he wants."

Paige folded her arms. "So you were the mole all along and you let us believe it could've been Bobby or Paul or…" She let out an exasperated huff. "You'd better pack up your things. I'm calling Eli."

Linda rushed forward. "Please don't tell him."

"I don't have a choice either, Linda." Paige walked back into the kitchen, fossicked through her purse for her cell and pressed Eli's speed dial. "Hey, it's me. Can you come over to my office? Are you still in town? Because Linda needs to tell you something important. Ok, see you soon."

Linda stood in the doorway. "I'm so sorry, Paige. I didn't have a choice."

"Tell that to Eli when he gets here. Tell him how sorry you are for getting his pack killed. I'm sure he's going to feel grateful that you're sorry."

Tears spilled down Linda's face. "Paige?"

Paige raised her hand again, motioning for Linda to stop talking. She also felt betrayed because she had trusted the woman at her word. "We all have a choice. And I, for one, would never betray Eli's trust." She pointed to one of the two chairs under the table. "Sit. He should be here soon."

Eli arrived fifteen minutes later, parking the Jeep behind Paige's sedan in the alley and entering the premises through the back gate. As he reached the door it opened and Paige stepped aside to let him in.

"What's going on?" Eli asked, closing the door behind him.

"Linda has something to tell you." She motioned to her receptionist. "Go ahead."

"Eli, I want you to know how sorry I am for everything." A single tear slipped down her right cheek and she brushed it away.

"Sorry for what?" Eli frowned into her eyes, not liking where he thought the conversation might be going.

"If I could have done things any other way I would have. You have to believe me."

"What things, Linda?" He could feel the moonstone ring causing his hackles to rise. What had she done?

"Remus made me do it. I didn't have a choice." More tears spilled down her cheeks.

Eli frowned into her eyes. "What do you mean?"

Linda's chin quivered and even more tears slipped down her face. "I – I'm the mole. I'm the one who got your pack killed, among other things."

Eli's intense gaze remained on her for the longest time. He couldn't bring himself to speak for fear of what he might say to her. She'd been working with the council all along. He'd trusted her with Paige's life. What if that had gone horribly wrong? His pack, his friends were dead because of her. Had she been the reason he had been abducted? Obviously.

Paige walked over to him and gave him a tight squeeze, then looked up into his sorrowful, honey colored eyes. "Eli?"

He eased her away from him and stepped closer to Linda. "I'm taking you to the station." He gripped her arm forcefully. "You'll be placed in a cell until I can figure out what to do with you."

"Eli, I…" Linda knew what that meant. He would call a meeting and they would decide what punishment she deserved. Betrayal usually came with a death sentence. She had gotten his wolves killed. She couldn't come back from that. "I had no choice."

"Everyone has a choice and you made the wrong one. You should've come to me. I would've helped you." He escorted her out to his Jeep and sat her in the passenger seat. Paige followed them.

"Eli, are you ok?" She reached up and brushed some stray strands of hair off his handsome, sad face.

"I don't know, Paige. I would never, in a million years, think that Linda would do what she's done. Never."

"I know. It's difficult to take in. I thought we could trust her, too."

"I'll call a meeting later tonight and we'll decide what's to be done."

Paige nodded. "Ok." Lycan protocol deemed betrayal as a serious breach.

He kissed Paige's forehead, rounded the hood, and climbed into the four wheel drive. Pressing the button on the armrest to roll down the passenger window he said,

"I'll call you after… you know." He glanced sideways at Linda sitting beside him.

"Ok." Paige knew he meant after he and Archer talked to Clarissa. She also knew Linda would be entitled to one phone call and Eli wouldn't offer information she could pass on to Remus.

SIXTEEN

Raven eyed Scarlet with a glowering stare. "Why do we have to stay cooped up here? Why can't we go out and have a little fun?" She paced the living room of the elegant wood cabin. "This isn't what we came here for. We're witches. We should be out there doing what we do best… wreaking havoc on mortals."

Scarlet closed the book she'd been reading, set it down on the small, square table nearby, got up from her armchair and walked over to Raven. "We are here for a purpose, and until that purpose is implemented we must keep a low profile. It is for the benefit of us all. To keep us safe."

"That's BS, Scarlet, and you know it." Raven poked her index finger at her High Priestess, her defiant chin raised. "All you want to do is keep us locked away from the rest of the world. Have us all to yourself. Tell us what we can and cannot do."

Scarlet wouldn't dignify the accusation by defending herself. It would make her appear weak. "You will abide by the laws of this coven, Raven, or you will leave." She hadn't meant to say it but she'd had enough of her sister's willful behavior. Undermining her authority in front of her coven would not be tolerated. "There are always witches with similar powers to yours wishing to join the Circle of the Full Moon so it wouldn't be difficult to replace you."

Raven's eyes narrowed. "Are you serious? You'd banish me from our coven?"

"Yes, I would. You have been a disruption for far too long and I will not stand for it anymore. Either you tone it down several notches or *you're out*."

The other witches scattered around the large room watched in shocked silence. Scarlet had always been a fair leader and they knew she hadn't threatened Raven lightly.

Raven gave Scarlet a perceptive grin. "Very well."

"What does that mean, Raven? You're going to abide by the coven's rules or you're happy to part ways and move on?"

Raven gazed at the other faces around the room watching her, waiting for her answer. She knew she had no allies. "I will abide by coven rules." *For now.*

"That's good to hear." Scarlet stepped up to Raven, wrapped her in a tight, sisterly embrace, and whispered into her ear, "Make sure you do. Remember I don't threaten, I act." As the two women parted they smiled at each other… a deception so the other witches didn't catch on to the animosity between them.

Everyone went back to what they had been doing as though nothing had happened.

Raven's gaze moved around the room once more. There would be consequences for this embarrassment. She would make sure of it.

Scarlet knew of her sister's feelings toward her. She couldn't deny she felt the same way and knew she would need to stay vigilant otherwise Raven might attempt to usurp her. Would her sisters defend her honor or her life? She didn't believe so because they were afraid of Raven. She possessed a far greater darkness than all of them combined.

SEVENTEEN

Clarissa's gaze moved from Eli to Archer then back to her grandson. Could she do what they asked? Did she have the power required to perform such a task? Her self-doubt had gotten the better of her. Of course she would do it. She didn't have a choice. "I'll try my best."

"That's all we can ask for, Clary," Eli told her. "If it doesn't work, it doesn't work. We'll have to figure out a backup strategy."

"I have heard of that particular spell, but I've never actually performed it before." Clarissa pressed her index finger to her lips. "I'll consult the cards before I begin. They'll provide the answers I need."

Archer wanted to reassure her. "Don't be concerned by the High Priestess's threat, Clary. We'll all be fine. We can take care of ourselves."

Clary's focus moved from her cup of tea to him. "I don't doubt that, nonetheless I've placed protection spells on each of you, for my own peace of mind. They may not hold indefinitely, but they will for a while at least."

Eli gave the editor a sideward glance. "What did I tell you?"

His grandmother's eyes darted to him. "You know me too well, Eli Blackwood." She gave her grandson a thin smile.

"I knew you'd want to protect the people you love, that's all."

"You'd better go and let me get on with it then," she said, standing and walking around the table to Eli. She pulled his face down to her and kissed his forehead. "I love you."

Eli frowned into her eyes for a moment then said, "I love you, too."

"I'll let you know when I've finished the spell."

"Be careful, Clary," Archer said as he headed for the front door.

"Always. You all be careful too."

Archer and Eli climbed into the Jeep.

"She's worried." Eli couldn't get the look on her face out of his mind.

"Yes, I know. Can you keep her under surveillance?"

"I had the same thought. I wouldn't put it past that High Priestess to come back. She may not be able to get into the house, but I'm sure she could do some damage to my grandmother from the porch if she chose to."

"Mm. Scary thought. Witchcraft can be so insidious."

"I'll place Cooper on surveillance nearby." He pulled the car out of the drive and headed back to the Tribune office to drop off Archer. He had other issues to address.

Back at the station, Rosemarie sat at her desk staring at the computer screen. *How could Linda be the mole? Why would she betray Eli like that?* She gave a heavy sigh and glanced across at Taylor and Rick. *How long will it take before they figure out our town? What will happen once they do? Will they leave? Will they let the authorities know? What will happen to Moon Grove if they do that?*

Rick glanced up and caught her watching him. "Something wrong, Rosy?"

"Huh?" She snapped out of her funk. "Not at all. Just thinking."

"You're sure?"

Taylor's eyes moved from the computer screen to the receptionist.

Rosemarie hated feeling as though she were under a microscope and felt heat rush to her cheeks. "Nothing's wrong. I promise." That sounded lame, even to her.

"Ok. If you need anything you know you can ask, right?" Rick's gaze remained on her.

"Of course. Thank you." She gave him a sweet smile, hoping it would satisfy his curiosity. "What are you all doin'?" She needed to change the topic of conversation.

"Writing up a couple of reports," Taylor said.

"Yeah, me too." Rick went back to what he'd been doing. So did Taylor.

Rosemarie breathed a relieved sigh. She had staved off their curiosity for now. But, as she'd suspected, the new deputies already had their suspicions.

Eli came through the door and rushed across reception to his office, closing the door behind him. Rosemarie glanced over her shoulder. Should she knock and check on him? It had been a blow to them all finding out what Linda had done. They thought they could trust her, and Rosemarie knew how Eli would be taking it.

She rose from her chair, walked over to his office door and knocked.

"Come in, Rosy."

She entered the office and closed the door. "Are you all right, Eli?"

"No, I'm not. This whole Linda situation... I still can't get my head around the fact that she got our pack killed."

"I'm so sorry." Rosemarie crossed the room and sat down in front of his desk. "I know you trusted her... we all did."

"Yeah, and look where it got us."

"Have you decided what you're going to do?"

"I'll call a meeting later tonight so we can vote on an acceptable outcome."

Rosemarie knew that betrayal of the pack meant death. Would Eli allow that to be the final judgement of the committee?

EIGHTEEN

Paige opened the door and stepped into reception only to find it unmanned. Where were Eli and the others? She crossed the office and whacked the domed, silver call bell sitting on Rosemarie's desk with the palm of her hand, the shrill, metallic ding echoing around the room. As she stood, her gaze moved to Eli's glass office, nick-named the fish bowl. Where had everyone gone? Her Lycan hearing pricked up all of a sudden as the sound of voices drifted through the air. Paige pushed through the swinging gate, eased the door back and wandered out to the cell block.

Eli turned around, arms folded, when he heard her footsteps approaching. "Hey, sweetheart, what are you doing here?"

"I didn't have any patients this afternoon so I made an executive decision and closed early for once." She stepped up beside him and gazed at Linda through the cell bars.

Rosemarie poked her head around Eli's large frame. "Hi, Paige, it's good to see you."

Her eyes moved to the receptionist. "Oh, Rosy, it's good to see you too. Where's Coop and the others?"

Eli's honey colored gaze moved to her. "Out on patrol. Why?"

"Did the recruits ask why Linda is locked up here? They must be curious." Paige glanced sideways at her ex-receptionist then back to Eli.

"That's why I got Cooper to take them out. And, yeah, they probably are wondering."

"What are you going to tell them?"

"I'm not sure yet, but I'll think of something." He pointed along the corridor. "Let's head inside."

Paige turned on her heel and walked ahead of him, Rosemarie close behind.

Once back in reception, Eli motioned for the pair to go into his office and followed the women in. "You got my text?"

"Yes," Paige replied. "What do you plan to do with Linda?"

"That's up to the committee."

Paige sat down on one of the two chairs in front of Eli's desk. "Betrayal of the pack warrants death, doesn't it?"

"In most cases, yes." Eli took his seat.

Rosemarie remained standing by the door. "Has Linda told you anything at all?"

Eli shook his head. "She's remaining tight-lipped." He let out a sigh. "She's afraid… and with good reason. If she betrays Remus he'll find a way to eliminate her."

"Could we banish her? Send her away from Moon Grove?" Paige's heart felt conflicted.

"Like I said, it's up to all of us to come to that decision. We'll meet tonight and discuss it."

"Ok." Paige stood up.

Eli gazed up at her. "Where are you going now?"

"I thought I might stop in on Clary."

"I'd appreciate that. She's been working on the spell and I haven't heard from her."

"Then I'll head right over." She made her way to the door. "See you later, Rosy."

"See you later." She waited for Paige to leave. "Eli, you're not going to put Linda to death, are you? There has to be another way."

"It's up to all of us to come to that conclusion."

"We haven't had anything like this happen in a long time." The receptionist's face wrinkled into a worried frown. "As you said, she's afraid and she has every reason to be. Remus is a monster."

"I get that but she made her choice, Rosy. If we don't adhere to the laws everyone will think they can get away with anything. What kind of Alpha would I be if I changed the rules for the people close to me?"

Rosemarie's words were a quiet whisper. "I know. You're right." It didn't make the decision any easier to bear.

Eli got up and walked over to her, resting a comforting hand on her arm. "Maybe Paige's idea is the best option. We'll have to wait and see what the others vote, won't we?"

"I guess so." Rosemarie wrung her hands together. "Matthias and his pack and that other pack won't be there, will they?"

"No. Why?" Eli frowned into the receptionists eyes.

"Because it's our town and we have to make the decision. Not outsiders." A tear slipped down her left cheek and she brushed it away.

"It'll be all right. Whatever happens."

Rosemarie nodded and stepped out of Eli's office. When she reached her desk she picked up her purse, plucked a floral handkerchief from inside and dabbed her moist cheek.

As she sat down at her desk, Cooper, Taylor and Rick came through the door. She sniffed back the urge to cry and pasted a bright smile on her face. "Well, now, there you are," she greeted, resting her hands on the top of her desk. "Have a good patrol? Nothing on the wind out there?"

Rick and Taylor gave the receptionist a curious frown, walked to opposite sides of the office and sat down at their desks. "Nope, everything seemed quiet," Rick said.

"That's good to hear." Rosemarie popped up off her chair. "Would anyone like some refreshments?"

Cooper crossed reception and took his seat at his desk. "Yeah, Rosy, that'd be nice. Thanks."

"Coming right up." She headed out the door and into the kitchen.

"What's wrong with Rosy?" Rick asked, his gaze moving from the open doorway to Cooper.

The deputy frowned. "What makes you think something's wrong?" He wasn't fond of Rick, even though he wasn't sure why, and had a difficult time hiding the fact.

Rick shrugged. "Just a feeling I got when we came in."

"I think you're imagining it." Cooper booted up his computer.

"No, he's not. I felt it too," Taylor added.

Cooper looked from one to the other. "There's nothing wrong. Get on with your reports."

Rosemarie returned to the office carrying a tray and set it down on the small table under Eli's office window. "Help yourself," she said as she poured coffee into a mug for Eli and plated up some choc chip cookies for him as well. His favorite. She picked up the mug and plate and took them in to Eli.

Rick sighed. "I'm telling you, there's something up with Rosy."

"It's your imagination." Cooper's frowning gaze rested on the recruit. Could Rick be picking up the supernatural vibes around the town? He'd have to keep an eye on that.

NINETEEN

P aige raised her hand to knock but the door swung out of her reach and Clarissa appeared in the open doorway. "I knew you were here," she said. "Come on in." She waved Paige into the entry hall. "I baked an apple tea cake this morning and it's still warm. Fancy a piece?" Her smile widened as she ushered her visitor into the kitchen.

"Sure, if you've got coffee to go with it." Paige shrugged out of her jacket, hung it over the back of the chair, and took a seat at the table.

"Of course, coming right up." Clarissa took two mugs from an overhead cupboard and set them on the counter. She cut two wedges of the cake, popped them on the plates and brought them over to the table, then poured the coffee and set a mug down in front of Paige before taking her seat on the other side. "To what do I owe the pleasure?"

"Does there have to be a reason to visit?"

"Eli's worried something will happen to me, isn't he?" She reached across and patted Paige's hand.

She shook her head. "I said I'd come by and he thought…"

"He's worried. I can tell."

"He's concerned over the spell you're working on more so than anything else, I think." Paige picked up her mug and sipped the black brew.

"It is a difficult one. I've been having trouble with it. Even the cards can't offer advice." She sighed. "Oh, I forgot the forks." She jumped up and crossed the kitchen to the drawer, took out two forks and passed one to Paige. "There you go. Can't eat cake without a fork."

Paige stared into the older woman's eyes. "You're worried, aren't you?"

She nodded. "Well, yes, I suppose. Not being able to cast the spell correctly is a concern."

"I have faith in you, Clary. I know you'll figure it out."

"I wish I could be that confident right now." Clarissa sat down, slid her fork into her piece of cake, broke a piece off and took a bite. "Mm, this turned out better than I expected."

Paige scooped a piece of cake onto her fork and popped it into her mouth. "Mm, it's delicious."

"Thank you. At least I got something right today."

"I know you'll work out the spell. You have amazing abilities. You're far stronger than the coven. You just need to believe it."

Clarissa gave Paige a thin smile. "I'll do my best, that's all I can promise."

"And that's all anyone can ask for."

Later that evening, the Moon Grove Lycan committee met in the tall white church on the hill to decide Linda's fate. Betrayal usually required a death sentence, but most of the members, not all, were against it. They had been going around in circles for over two hours and still hadn't come to a decision. Eli stood with hands on hips, his emotions also conflicted, but he couldn't show weakness or his pack and followers would lose respect for him.

Paige's brother, Brent, spoke up. He didn't know Linda so his decision rested solely on Lycan laws. "She betrayed the pack, Eli. She knew the consequences if she got caught."

"We know that, but she's been in Eli's life since they were kids. It's not an easy decision to make," Paige told him.

"Hell, sure it is. She did the deed, she pays the price." He shrugged. "Simple."

"I understand where you're coming from, Eli, but you have to remain strong on this," Abbey reminded him.

"Would you kill me if I did something wrong?" Rosemarie asked, tears welling in her eyes.

"You would never betray the pack, Rosy, so it's irrelevant." Eli paced then turned around. "Maybe Paige's suggestion would be the best option."

"You think sending her out of town will solve the problem with the council?" Cooper stood up and folded his arms.

"No, that isn't easily solved, but Linda is afraid. She feared for her own safety and the lives of the people in her life that the council would've threatened. We can all understand that. And she did help Paige with the council files after I'd been abducted. I believe she tried to make some kind of amends for what she'd done. It would be a permanent banishment. She could never come back." Eli felt the heat of the moonstone ring radiate up his finger. His eyes moved to the glowing milky stone and he stuck his hand into the pocket of his jeans to hide its effect.

Archer glanced around the group before speaking. "I think Brent and Abbey are right, Eli. She got most of your pack killed by handing over information to Remus. And Paige nearly died at the hands of Gregor, don't forget. Linda knew what the consequences of her actions would mean."

Eli frowned at the editor. He didn't want to admit it, but he knew Archer made a valid point. He gave a heavy sigh. "So what's the verdict? Those who believe Linda should suffer her fate raise your hands."

Abbey, Brent, Archer, his brother and his friends raised their hands. That made five votes for the death penalty.

Eli's gaze moved to his deputy. "Cooper?"

"I – I don't know. I agree with what's been said here, but death seems so final."

"I need your vote. You can't sit on the fence."

Cooper let out a huge sigh and raised his hand, the grief he still felt for the loss of Bobby and the others nudging his decision.

"Ok. Then that makes six to three."

"Oh, Eli." Rosemarie burst into tears. "This is too hard. I'm going home."

Eli stopped her. "Not in your current state of mind you're not. Take a seat over there and I'll come talk to you in a minute or two. Ok?" He couldn't allow her to drive herself home in such a distressed state.

Paige got up, walked over to the receptionist and sat down beside her, taking her hand in hers. "Eli has to go along with the decision of the committee, Rosy, no matter how he feels. You know that, right?"

Rosemarie nodded and sniffled, dabbing at her teary eyes with a handkerchief. "I know. But it's so hard. Linda has lived in Moon Grove her whole life. She's been a part of Eli's life for most of that time."

Paige wrapped her arms around her and gave her a tight squeeze. "I know."

Eli crossed the chancel and sat down on the other side of Rosemarie. "Rosy, look at me."

The receptionist turned her tear-filled eyes to him.

"You know my hands are tied on this, don't you?"

She nodded and a single tear slipped down her right cheek.

Eli brushed it away with his thumb. "I wish things could've been different, but we live by laws to keep us safe. Linda... Linda did the wrong thing and got innocent people killed. If I don't adhere to the decision of the committee..."

"I know," Rosemarie whispered. "You have to go along with the unanimous vote."

"Then we're good?"

She nodded again. "I know this must be difficult for you and I'm sorry for that."

He leaned in and kissed her forehead. "Thank you."

Paige motioned with her head for them to move away from Rosemarie for a moment.

He nodded at her then turned his concerned gaze back to the receptionist. "You stay put for a bit. I don't want you leaving until you're feeling better. Ok?"

Rosemarie nodded and scrunched her handkerchief between her fingers. "All right."

He followed Paige over to the altar. "What is it?"

"Do you have to do it?"

"As Alpha, yes, I do."

Paige reached out and gripped his arm, tears stinging the backs of her eyes. "Oh, Eli."

"Who else is there?"

"You're right, I know."

"What's on your mind, Paige?" He frowned into her tear-filled eyes.

She lowered her voice and glanced around the hall. Most of everyone had gone. "What if Linda managed to escape? Would the committee order her to be found?"

His frown deepened. "It would be up to all of us to vote again."

"What if she simply... vanished?"

"Are you suggesting what I think you're suggesting?"

She nodded.

"Paige."

"Eli, it's better than the alternative, isn't it? Do you want to stick a silver dagger in her heart?"

The thought hadn't crossed his mind. But, no, he didn't. "So you want me to…"

She shook her head. "I'll do it."

"Where is she going to go?"

"I have friends in Washington who'll help her out. I only have to give them a call."

"Washington?"

"Yes. It's far enough away from Moon Grove and the influence of Remus and the council."

"Let me think it over."

"There isn't enough time. Doesn't the sentence have to be carried out tomorrow night? The night of the full moon?"

Eli hadn't been keeping track of the moon's cycle; he'd been too preoccupied with the Coven of the Full Moon and the town's current predicament. "Hell! You're right."

Paige held out her hand. "Give me the keys to the station."

"You're not doing this alone, Paige."

"And, as the Alpha and Sheriff of Moon Grove, you can't come with me."

"You do realize this would be considered a betrayal to pack law."

"I know what it is. Just give me the damn keys."

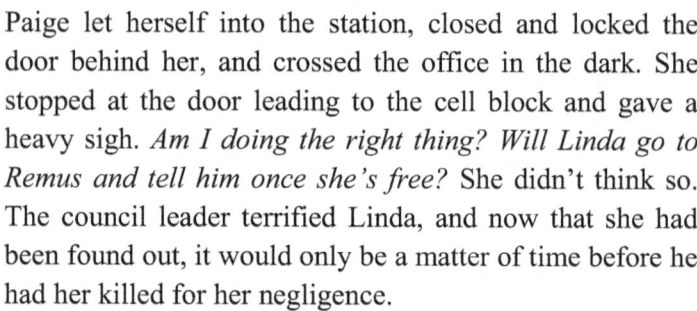

Paige let herself into the station, closed and locked the door behind her, and crossed the office in the dark. She stopped at the door leading to the cell block and gave a heavy sigh. *Am I doing the right thing? Will Linda go to Remus and tell him once she's free?* She didn't think so. The council leader terrified Linda, and now that she had been found out, it would only be a matter of time before he had her killed for her negligence.

She turned the handle, opened the door and headed out back. When she reached the cell block her eyes widened. The heavy metal door had been ripped from its hinges and the barred cell door hung skewed at a peculiar angle. Linda had shifted and escaped. Paige tugged her cell phone from the pocket of her jeans and pressed speed dial for Eli. "Hey, it's me. Linda's gone."

Eli came through the exit and stepped into the cell block, his eyes roaming the devastation. "What the hell?"

"She had to escape. What other choice did she have?"

Eli ran his gaze around the block then turned and looked at the broken exterior door. "None, I guess."

"Well, that solves the problem." Paige crossed the block to him.

"Does it? What if she goes to Remus?"

"She seemed genuinely afraid of him so I don't think she will. Besides, if she told him we discovered what she's been doing wouldn't he kill her?"

"We don't know the nature of their relationship, so we can't be sure of anything." He frowned at the mangled door. "I'll have to get Fred out here pronto to secure this place." He shook his head. "What a mess."

Paige frowned at him. "What is it?"

Eli's gaze moved to her. "What do you mean?"

"You've got something on your mind."

"It's all too convenient, don't you think? What if the council had a hand in it?"

Paige's eyebrows rose. "You mean staged it to look as though Linda broke free?"

"Anything's possible. They have spies everywhere."

"Then that means they have her. But we still don't know where they are."

Once again, Eli wouldn't divulge that he did know where they were. It would remain his secret until the right time presented itself. "Mm." He stood with hands on hips, his eyes moving around the room. "Well there's not much we can do tonight. We may as well head home."

"I guess you're right. See you there." She brushed past him and headed along the corridor.

"Paige."

She turned around. "Yes?"

He held out his hand. "The keys."

"Oh, sorry. Here you go." She tossed them across to him.

He caught them mid-air. "See you at home."

She smiled and headed out the door.

Eli studied the damage. Could the council have made it look like Linda had escaped? It wouldn't be that difficult. They had the opportunity and resources. If they had her would they kill her? He suspected they would because she had been discovered. Would he do something to stop it? Not unless he wanted his secret of knowing where they were revealed. Linda had chosen her path and she would have to deal with the consequences.

TWENTY

When Eli arrived home he went straight to the floor safe to retrieve the items the mayor had hidden away in the safety deposit box. He tugged the bag out of the safe and took it into the living room. Among the items – a worn, leather ancient tome. He plucked it from the bag and sat down at the end of the table. Would there be something inside that would rid Moon Grove of Remus? He opened it to the first page but didn't recognize the archaic language. He knew some Latin but this wasn't it. Perhaps the book would turn out to be a puzzle they couldn't decipher.

Paige came into the room from the kitchen with two mugs of coffee. "What are you doing?"

He sighed. "I had hoped to find something in this that would help us get rid of Remus… once we find him."

Paige set a mug down in front of Eli and sat on the chair closest to him. "Is there?"

"It's written in a language I don't understand."

"May I?" She made a gesture toward the thick tome.

He slid the book across the table.

"Mm. It looks like a form of Latin but it's not something I've seen before."

"I wonder if Archer would know." Eli whipped his phone from the pocket of his shirt and keyed in the editor's number.

Paige placed a hand on his arm. "Wouldn't he be sleeping?"

"He never sleeps."

The phone rang for a long time before Archer answered.

"Hey, did I wake you?" Eli asked.

"Not a problem. What's up?" He said in a sluggish tone as he attempted to wrench himself from the clutches of immortal repose.

"I have an ancient book here that might give us a way to get rid of Remus but I can't understand the language. Paige thinks it's Latin but…"

"You want me to come take a look?"

"Would you mind? It might even offer a way to deal with the coven."

"Ok. I'll be out at your place as soon as I can."

"Thanks, Archer. I appreciate it."

"No problem. I'll see you soon." He rang off.

"Is Archer coming out here now?" Paige sipped her coffee.

"Yeah, he is."

"How old do you think Remus is?"

Eli shrugged. "Don't know. Older than a thousand, maybe."

Paige's eyes widened. "Wow. That old."

"Yeah. He's been around long enough to find ways to

protect himself. Who knows what he has up his sleeve."

"You think he took Linda, don't you?"

"The thought crossed my mind."

"If he did she'd be dead." Paige gave a heavy sigh.

"I know."

"Why make it look like she escaped? That's what I don't understand."

Eli frowned. "None of us could know what goes through Remus's mind. He's a psychopath."

"Maybe she did escape."

"Maybe. I guess we'll never know unless her body turns up."

Paige cringed. "That's a horrible thought, Eli."

He reached across and rubbed her arm. "I know, but it's the truth."

"I hope she did escape."

"Yeah, me too." Eli understood Linda's fear even though she had betrayed him and his pack.

Paige stood up, dressed in pajamas and robe. "I'd better go and dress before Archer gets here."

"Good idea." He gave her a thin smile and watched her head down the hallway. His eyes moved back to the book. An ancient tome. What secrets did it hold? Eli wondered how Ross Redmond had gotten his hands on it. A question that would never be answered.

Archer arrived at Eli and Paige's half an hour after the sheriff's call. He climbed the front porch steps but before he could knock the door opened and Paige stood in the doorway. "Hi, come on in." She motioned for the editor to step inside and closed the door behind him.

Archer crossed the living room to the table and sat down. "Is that it?" His head tilted toward the book on the table.

Eli's gaze moved from him to the ancient tome. "Yeah, it is."

The editor pointed at it. "May I?"

"Sure."

"Thanks."

Paige sat down opposite Archer, her eyes on him as he perused the pages. "Can you decipher it?"

"Unfortunately, no." It's older than I am." His gaze turned to Eli. "Could I photocopy some of these pages and send them to Carmichael? I'm sure he'll be able to help us with it."

"I've got a photocopier in my office. Follow me." Eli stood up, strutted down the hall and opened the first door on the right. "Once we know what language it is maybe we can find a way to end Remus. Alistair seems to think with him out of the way he'll be able to control the other members of the council."

"Do you think he can?" Archer asked, stepping into the room.

"I hope so, because if he can't we'll be up against them as well as the coven for the death of Remus. All hell will break loose if that happens."

"I'm counting on Clarissa to create that spell. It's the only way we can all be protected against the powers of the coven."

Eli's serious stare met the editors. "Even so, we need a solid backup plan. We can't only rely on my grandmother."

Archer nodded. "I know. And we won't. But if she can pull it off..."

"Like I said, let's ensure we have a backup plan."

Paige came to the door. "Want some coffee?"

Archer glanced over his shoulder. "None for me, thanks."

"I'm good," Eli said as he slid the open book onto the glass.

"Ok, then, I think I'll head to bed and leave you to it. Goodnight."

"Goodnight, Paige," Archer said with a smile.

"Night, sweetheart, I won't be long."

Paige gave him a smile and disappeared down the hall.

Eli passed the photocopied pages to the editor. "How soon do you think we'll get something back?"

"I'll get these off tonight as soon as I go home and I'm sure Carmichael will be in touch ASAP."

"Good. The sooner we have a plan in place the better I'll like it." He walked Archer out to the front door. "Be careful. We have no idea who we can trust right now. Don't let anyone else see those." He pointed to the A4 sheets of paper in the editor's hand.

"I won't. I'll let you know when I hear something." He headed to his car.

"Archer?"

The editor turned around. "Yes?"

"Thanks."

"No problem." He climbed into his Mercedes.

Eli waited for Archer to drive off before closing the door. As he headed down the hallway, his mind turned to the council leader. There had to be a way to rid Moon

Grove of Remus and create a peaceful environment to live in for all residents. The vampire had had control of their town for far too long. It had to come to an end, once and for all.

TWENTY ONE

Over breakfast the following morning, Eli made Paige an offer she couldn't refuse. While sitting across from her, watching her eat, he'd come up with the solution to her current receptionist problem. "I think Rosy should come and work for you for a while."

Paige glanced up from her bowl of oatmeal. "You'd loan her to me?"

Eli nodded. "Sure I would. You need to keep your practice running and that'd be difficult without someone on the front desk. You can't do two things at once."

Paige came around the table and hopped onto his lap, wrapping her arms around his neck. "I appreciate the generous offer, Sheriff Blackwood, and I accept. It'll be nice having her around."

"Good. Glad that's settled." He leaned in and planted a gentle kiss on her lips before easing her off his lap. "We'd better get going. I've got a full day ahead."

"Me too. When will Rosemarie be starting?"

When Paige entered the office, seeing Rosemarie behind the desk working at the computer surprised and elated her. She hadn't expected Eli to initiate his offer so quickly. "Good morning, Rosy. It's lovely to have you here."

The plump, pink-cheeked receptionist smiled up at her. "Mornin', Darlin', it's nice to be here." She stood up. "Can I get you anything? Coffee? I made a batch of cookies last night so they're in the kitchen on the table any time you feel a little peckish."

"Well I appreciate that. Coffee would be great. Can you bring it into my office?"

"I certainly can." She turned and headed down the short hallway to the kitchen.

Paige smiled as she wandered down to her consultation room and stepped inside. She'd have to watch the cookies or she'd gain fifty pounds by the time Rosemarie returned to the station.

Later that morning, Paige crossed the road and headed over to the Tribune office. She'd have to place another want ad to find a new receptionist. As much as she loved having Rosemarie around, she couldn't stay with Paige indefinitely, and besides, it wouldn't be fair of her to keep the woman any longer than she had to. Eli needed her.

As she entered the office, Archer walked up to her. "Hey. To what do I owe the unexpected pleasure?" His handsome smile widened.

"Hey. Do you still have that ad I placed for a receptionist?"

"Of course. It's in your file." He led Paige down to his desk. "Have a seat."

"Thanks." Paige removed her jacket, dropped it over the back of the chair and sat down. "Eli's lent me Rosy for a while, but I don't want to keep her too long. He needs her at the station."

"It's good that you've got someone in the interim, though." Archer pulled up Paige's file on the computer.

"Yes, it is, and I'm grateful for it, but I know she does an awful lot around the station and Eli will be lost without her there."

"I'm sure he can handle it." He hit the enter button. "There, all done. It'll run in tomorrow's paper and the ensuing classifieds for as long as you need it."

"How much do I owe you?"

Archer raised his hand. "No charge. It's on me."

"I can't…"

"Yes, you can. Now say thank you."

Paige gave him a serious stare for a moment, then smiled and said, "Thank you. I appreciate it."

"There, that wasn't so hard. Besides, I run the place so I can do what I like."

"You're incorrigible, you know that, right?"

"Of course I do. I wouldn't be a vampire if I wasn't."

At that moment, the door opened and a woman stepped into the office.

"Will you excuse me for a few minutes?" Archer stood up and came around the desk.

"Sure." Paige swiveled on her seat, her gaze following the editor along the office to the attractive woman standing inside the closed doorway.

"Can I help you?" Archer asked as he stopped in front of the woman.

"Yes, I think you can." A smug smirk crossed her attractive face as she raised her hand and a bolt of light hit the editor in the chest.

Paige screamed, "Archer! No!" Her eyes changed to a honey glow and she shifted into wolf form, bounding along the office at maximum speed.

The woman's eyes widened and she threw open the door, rushed outside and disappeared along the sidewalk.

Paige couldn't follow her naked. She lowered herself onto her knees and raised Archer's head off the floor. *Is he alive?* As vampires didn't breathe she couldn't tell.

After a tense couple of minutes, he opened his eyes and gazed up at her, his eyes widening when he noticed she wasn't wearing any clothes. "What… what happened?" He climbed to his feet, took off his jacket and wrapped it around Paige.

"Thanks." She slipped her arms into the sleeves and buttoned the front. "That must've been Scarlet or one of the other witches from the coven."

"That's a rather brazen move, coming in here like that. It appears they're going to try and pick us off one at a time to give them the advantage."

An icy chill ran the length of Paige's petite frame and it had nothing to do with her being naked beneath Archer's coat. "We need to let Eli know."

"Yes, we do." His eyes roamed Paige's jacket-clad body. "But, first, I think I need to drive you home so you can change."

Paige gazed out of Archers' Mercedes Benz windshield, her mind somewhere else. The editor noticed and reached across and touched her arm. She jumped and her eyes moved to him. "I had a thought. Why didn't whatever that witch did to you kill you? I'm so grateful that it didn't, of course, but, still, it makes you wonder, doesn't it?"

"I'd say Clarissa had something to do with that. She told Eli and me that she cast a protection spell over the people who are important to her, and, thankfully, I'm included otherwise I'd be dead."

Paige rested her hand on his shoulder. "Thank God she did or who knows what would've happened back there. She might've killed me too." Her stomach did a sickening flip flop. Both she and Archer could've been dead right now.

"At least Eli's calling an emergency meeting to warn everyone, especially those who aren't protected. We can't lose anyone else. We need all the help we can get." The hybrid vampires would arrive any day, but even so, they still needed an army to fight the coven of thirteen. Max, Archer's brother, and his friends, had been injected with the serum and seemed to be handling it well. They had that on their side.

When they turned off the highway and onto the dirt road leading out to Eli and Paige's, the sky grew dark, threatening rain.

Paige gazed out of the passenger window at the gray, pendulous clouds rushing across the afternoon sky. "That can't be good." She swallowed the wad of nerves lodged in her throat.

Archer slowed to a crawl, leaned over the steering

wheel and gazed up at the darkening sky through the windshield. "No, it can't." He stepped on the accelerator, dirt and gravel spraying behind the convertible and sped along the road. "We need to get inside."

Up ahead, the coven of witches appeared out of nowhere, blocking their path.

As the editor slammed the gear lever into reverse, spinning the back wheels, the car lifted off the ground into the air, flipped over and hurtled into the nearby trees.

TWENTY TWO

After the continuous ring, Paige's phone went to voicemail. Eli pulled his cell from his ear and frowned at the screen. *Why isn't she picking up?* He crossed his office, dropped into his desk chair and decided to call Rosemarie. "Hey, Rosy, is Paige with you? She's not picking up."

"No, Darlin', she went across to the Tribune to place a want ad."

"Thanks, I'll give Archer a call."

"All right. Talk to you later. Have a good day." Rosemarie frowned at the digital phone she'd returned to its cradle. It wasn't like Paige not to answer her phone, especially when Eli called her.

Eli pressed speed dial for Archer and waited. No answer. Voicemail. His gut tightened. Something didn't feel right. He lurched out of his chair and stalked into the office. "Cooper, keep an eye on things till I get back."

"Sure, Eli. Something wrong?"

"I'm not sure. I'm going to check it out before I sound any alarm bells."

"Ok. Anything I can do?" Cooper stood up behind his desk.

"Yeah, keep an eye on our new deputies." He glanced at his watch. "They should be back any minute. Don't let them go out again until I return."

"So something is up?"

"Maybe. Let me go into town and see what I can find out." He headed for the door and as he opened it Taylor and Rick appeared on the porch. "You two stay here until I get back. Understood?"

Both deputies nodded and waited for Eli to step out of the office before going inside.

Rick gave Cooper a curious frown. "Do you know what's going on?"

"Not your concern. Just do what Eli told you."

The deputy frowned at him. "What's your problem, man? You've been hostile with us since the first day we arrived."

"I don't have a problem."

"Yeah, you do." Rick stood with hands on hips. "And I'd like to know what it is."

Taylor stepped up beside her partner. "He's right, Cooper, you've been riding us the whole time. I get that you lost your team and your friends, but that isn't our fault. We're here doing our job and trying to get along. Why can't you see that?"

Cooper's dark gaze rested on the pair. "You have no idea. You should pack up and leave before…"

Rick's right eyebrow arched. "Before what? Is that some kind of threat?"

"No, it's not a threat. But you'd be wise to get out of Moon Grove while you still can."

"What does that mean?" Taylor's blood chilled in her veins. Cooper's words frightened her and she remembered Eli saying there were undertones to the town.

"If you stay you'll find out."

"Stop already." Rick had had enough. "Why don't you get whatever it is off your chest instead of playing cryptic games with us?"

Cooper came around his desk and stood in front of the pair. "Are you sure you want to know?"

"Yeah, we are."

Cooper laughed in Rick's face. "You couldn't handle it."

"Try me." He folded his arms and stepped up to the deputy.

"Leave while you can. That's the best advice I can offer." He crossed the office, pushed open the swinging gate and headed to the kitchen.

Taylor trembled. She had turned a gray shade of white.

"Are you ok?" Rick asked, a look of concern on his face.

"No, I'm not." She huffed out a nervous breath. "Cooper scared the crap out of me."

"He's trying to push our buttons, that's all. Don't pay any attention to that little performance."

"Well it worked. I feel like packing up and going home." Taylor walked over to her desk and plonked herself into her seat. "There's something wrong with Moon Grove. Remember me saying that to you when we first got here."

"Yeah, I remember." Rick turned his head and stared along the corridor leading to the kitchen, his gut tightened. *What the hell is his problem?*

When Eli entered the Tribune office and found it empty he wondered where Paige and Archer were. Wandering down to the back door, he peered into the small office Archer used for privacy. Empty as well. He frowned. Continuing through to the print room, he spotted Neville. "Do you know where Archer is?"

The man nodded over the noise and pointed back along the hallway. Eli followed him into the office. "Yeah, he took Paige home."

"Do you know why?"

"Sorry, no." He shrugged. "Is there anything else? I have to get back to work."

Eli eyed the guy for a moment then said, "No. Thanks."

"No problem." He headed back to the print room.

Eli decided to take a drive out to his house. His gut squeezed into an even tighter knot of nerves. *Something's definitely off.* He headed for the street, turning the closed sign around, before locking the door on his way out. No point in leaving the place open if Archer wasn't there. He crossed the street and climbed into his Jeep. Before turning on the engine, he gave Paige's cell another try. Still no answer. His hackles went up. He needed to get out there fast. He flipped the switch on the dash and the siren squealed, red and blue strobe lights flashing across the roof of the wagon, as he took off along the main road heading for the highway.

TWENTY THREE

Remus pressed the heavy, antique telephone receiver to his ear in anticipation of hearing the High Priestess's voice on the other end of the line. He had forfeited his immortal repose to learn what had taken place. Could his scheme be working? Would he finally be free of the meddling Sheriff Blackwood and his dogs? He hoped so. "What news do you have for me?"

"I paid a visit to the witch. She is more powerful than I expected and has managed to remain unattainable so far. But I *will* find a way. You have my word. We set a trap for Paige O'Connell and her vampire friend. They should be out of commission for a while, which gives us an advantage." Her glossy black lips spread into a satisfied smile. "I'm initiating the next phase of your plan. I will inform you once I have more news."

"Excellent, Scarlet. I am delighted with these turn of events. Keep up the good work."

"I will. The more players we can knock out of the game the easier it will be to finish off the rest."

"I admire the way you think. Keep me informed." He rang off and dropped the receiver into its solid base.

"Who were you talking to?" Alistair asked as he entered the living room.

"Scarlet, the High Priestess of the Circle of the Full Moon coven. Everything is going according to plan. Even better than I anticipated."

"How so?"

"She is implementing a plan of elimination. Knocking certain players out of the game to ensure we win the battle." Remus clasped his hands behind his back and crossed the room to Alistair. "Why the sullen expression? Are you not pleased with the excellent news?"

"Of course, my Lord. More than pleased. Once we have total control of Moon Grove we can return home. Something I most fondly look forward to."

Remus rested a hand on his comrade's shoulder. "Yes, as do I." He gave Alistair an odd smile then turned on his heel and walked out of the living room.

Alistair knew he had to get word to Eli as soon as possible. Once the sun set, he would call the sheriff and make a time to meet. Which players, as Remus had referred to them, had been knocked out of the game?

TWENTY FOUR

Eli swung the Jeep onto the dirt road, the heavy tread of the tires throwing up gravel and other debris as he sped along the narrow laneway. His eyes widened and his heart hammered against his ribs as he spotted Archer's upturned, mangled Mercedes in a dense cluster of trees. He screeched the wagon to a halt, threw open the door and leapt from the vehicle. "Paige? Archer?" he called frantically, jumping the wire fence and racing to the passenger door. No one inside. Eli's ragged breathing intensified and his anxious eyes roamed the surrounding hazy trees. *Where are they?*

He spotted something in the tall grass and bent over to pick it up. Paige's phone. The screen had been shattered and when he pressed the button it wouldn't turn on. That's why she hadn't answered his call. What had happened out here? He rushed back to his car, climbed in, spun the wheels and headed to the house. Could they be there?

Eli pulled up short, turned off the engine and raced around the back of the car to the front porch. He pushed the key into the lock and flung the door open. "Paige, Paige are you here?"

No answer.

He stalked down the hallway, throwing open every door.

Neither she nor the editor were in the house.

He raced back to the front door and out onto the porch, his heart thundering inside his chest. "Paige?" he called again.

His Lycan hearing picked up a sound. He leaped off the decking and headed around back.

Both Paige and Archer were sitting on a large tree stump near a pile of firewood.

Eli rushed up to Paige, pulled her into his arms, and held her tight. "I thought…"

"We're ok, but Archer's car isn't."

"Yes, I saw it on my way here. How did you get out of the wreck in one piece?"

Archer stood up. "I think we have your grandmother to thank for that."

"The protection spell." Eli breathed a relieved sigh. "I thought the coven had captured you."

"We thought that too, but they disappeared once they caused the crash." Paige pressed her body even closer to Eli's, if that were possible. She'd thought the coven would kill them. "I'm so glad you came looking for us."

Eli raised her face up to meet his gaze. Her forehead and cheeks were scratched and bruised. "They won't get away with this."

"The other vampires will be here in a day or two. Then we'll have reinforcements." Archer walked over to the pair. Max and his friends are hybrids now, too, so we're in a good position to fight."

"Not if those witches keep attempting to eliminate us." Eli eased Paige out of his embrace. "We need to see Clary to find out how that spell is coming along."

"She's been having difficulty with it," Paige told him. "She's worried, Eli."

"We still need to be sure. If she can't make it work we'll have to find another way."

"What other way?" Archer folded his arms. "The coven is powerful and they're proving that by catching us off guard."

"At least they can't kill us." Eli couldn't have been more grateful that his grandmother's powers surpassed that of the coven witches. Something he never knew until now.

"Yes, but for how long?"

"That's what we're going to find out. Come on." Eli took Paige by the hand and headed back to the front of the house.

Archer followed.

By the time Eli pulled the wagon into the driveway of his grandmother's home the sun had almost set. He climbed out of the car, came around the hood and opened the passenger door for Paige. They had dropped Archer off at the Tribune office on the way because he'd told them he needed to make contact with Carmichael.

When Eli and Paige stepped onto the porch the front door opened. "Hello, you two." Clarissa smiled at them until she noticed Paige's wounds. A deep frown formed on her weathered face. "What happened?" She stepped out onto the welcome mat, gripped the young woman's face with gentle fingers and turned it to either side. "I've got something that'll fix those right up."

"To answer your question, Clary, the coven upturned Archer's car with he and Paige inside."

A dark expression crossed Clarissa's face. "They did, did they?" She ushered the pair inside and banged the door shut behind them. "They won't get away with that. But, first, let's get those scratches and bruises taken care of." She motioned for Paige and Eli to go into the kitchen. "Have a seat."

The pair sat down in their usual places.

Clarissa went to an overhead cupboard, pulled down a tray with an assortment of small bottles inside and brought it over to the table. "Now, let me see." She ran her gaze around the selection. "Ah, here it is." She plucked a small, green glass bottle from the collection, popped out the dropper, dripped two drops onto her fingertips and dabbed the lotion onto the scratches and bruises on Paige's face.

"What is that?" Paige asked.

"A little concoction of Aloe Vera, Witch hazel, Knitbone and some other bits and bobs. These should be all healed by tomorrow."

"Thank you, Clary." Paige smiled at the old woman. "I appreciate you doing this."

"Nonsense." Clarissa waved off the comment. "Can't have you going into the office looking like you've been in a boxing match, now can we?" She gave Paige a conspiratorial wink, pushed the dropper back into the bottle and set it down on the table. "Tea?"

"Sure, tea would be good," Eli said.

"Coming right up." Clarissa returned the tray of potions to the cupboard then switched on the kettle.

"How's the spell coming along?" Eli's eyes followed her around the kitchen.

"I am working on it and I'm sure I'll be able to sort it out with the help of the cards. They've been most enlightening so far."

"Things are becoming dangerous. It seems the witches are trying to pick us off one at a time so they'll gain the advantage. Archer and Paige were lucky this time. But who knows who'll be next."

Clarissa carried the tray with teapot and teacups over to the table, set it down in the center and poured the tea. "The protection spell I've placed on you all should hold."

Eli reached across and stopped her for a moment. "But what if it doesn't?"

The old woman passed around the cups then sat down opposite the pair. "I'll double up so that it will."

"The coven uses dark magic. They're bound to find a way to break it sooner or later."

Clarissa's mind sifted through the archives in her brain of every spell she knew. Could there be something that would prove more sustainable? "Leave it with me. I'll figure something out."

"I hate to put pressure on you, Clary." Eli could see the worry etched into the lines on his grandmother's face, even though she wouldn't admit it.

"You're not. I offered to help... and I *will*."

Archer unlocked the door under the staircase at the Tribune office, stumbled into the dark space and closed the door behind him. He hadn't let on to Paige and Eli that he'd been injured during the crash. His black sweater had camouflaged the blood seeping into it. He lifted the soggy, blood-soaked hem of his sweater and inspected the incision in his skin. A piece of jagged glass had lodged itself in his left side below his ribs when the windshield imploded, the searing pain now radiating up his torso and into his armpit. He flipped up the lid on the cooler, tugged a blood bag from inside, twisted the blue cap and shoved the tube into his mouth. He'd need to fortify his strength before removing the intruding piece of shrapnel from his body. If he didn't he would pass out from loss of blood, the same as anyone would.

It would take around twenty four hours for the wound to heal completely, and in the meantime he'd need to rest, unless his newfound hybridism intensified his recovery. Only time would tell.

A sharp rap on the door caused him to swing around, the glass tearing at his flesh, the pain traveling further up his body.

Max opened the door outwards and stepped inside. "Hey, bro, you look like you could use a hand."

"Thanks for coming," Archer told him, his words choppy. "I'll need you to pull this out once I've had a couple more of these." He reached into the cooler and tugged another blood bag from inside.

"No problem. Those witches need to be taught a lesson. They can't mess with us and think they can get away with it."

"I agree. But we have to tread carefully where they're concerned otherwise we could all end up dead. They have powers beyond what we're aware of. Apparently, they can kill a person with a look."

"What?!"

"Yes. Clarissa Baker is working on a spell to suppress the coven's ability to do that, but she told Eli that the High Priestess wouldn't lose those powers completely."

"Hell."

"Precisely."

"Still, they need to know they're not playing with just anybody."

"Agreed. But until we know exactly what we're up against we need to be cautious."

Max's eyes moved to the piece of glass protruding from his brother's side. "Ready to do this?"

Archer nodded and braced himself against the table behind him.

"It's gonna hurt like a mother."

TWENTY FIVE

Rick and Taylor cruised the quiet, tree-lined streets of Moon Grove in the patrol wagon, the spotlight on the roof doing a thorough sweep of the surrounding houses and businesses as they traveled along the deserted main road. An eerie silence enveloped the town and it seemed odd to the two deputies that there were no people milling around the streets at seven o'clock. "I wonder where everybody is," Taylor said, giving Rick a frowned, sideward glance.

"Beats me." He swung the cruiser around the next corner. "Nothing's open, either. Not even the Jade Dragon. I love their food."

"Something's going on. Can't you feel the vibe in the air?" Taylor's body gave an involuntary shiver.

"Maybe it's us, Tay. We came from a big city to a poky little town and…"

"No, that's not it." Taylor's gaze moved back to him. "There's something else."

"Like what?" Rick did a U-Turn and headed back along the dark dead-end street toward the main shopping hub.

Taylor shrugged. "I'm not sure, but there's definitely something up with this place. *And* remember what Cooper told us? Or didn't tell us. He's meant to be my partner but now you and I are teamed up, even though Eli said we wouldn't be."

"I don't think the two things are related."

They turned onto the main drag, heading back toward the station.

"Well I do. He's been acting weird since we got here. You said so yourself."

"I said he's had a problem with us since we got here. Two different things, Tay."

"No they're not. I think they're connected to whatever's going on around here." She could feel it in her gut. Even Eli had been secretive with them regarding certain aspects of the town. "And what happened to the woman that had been in the cell block? Where did she go?" Too many unanswered questions were circling Taylor's mind and it unnerved her.

"I don't know. Maybe she…"

As they reached the street to the station something hurtled out of the trees and whipped across the road in front of the patrol car.

Rick slammed on the brakes and screeched to a stop. "What the hell was that?!"

Taylor couldn't answer. Her heart had lodged itself in her throat, its beat so fast she thought it would burst through her chest.

Rick's gaze moved to her then back to the road, and again he said, "What. The. Hell. *Was*. That?

Taylor shook her head and breathed, "I don't know." Her words were choppy, her heart still knocking against her ribs. "A - A dog, maybe."

Rick gave her an incredulous frown. "You think that looked like a dog? Are you kidding me?"

Taylor shrugged and threw her hands up. "I don't know what it looked like. Maybe… maybe a wolf?"

"There are no wolves around here."

"How do you know that? There might be."

"There aren't." Rick flung open the door, stepped out onto the road and ran his gaze along the street. Nothing. He swiveled the spotlight on the roof of the patrol in the direction the animal had taken. No sign of it. He let out a sigh. "Well, whatever it was it's long gone."

"Rick, get back in the car. It's not safe out there with that thing running around."

"It's gone, Tay." His eyes roamed the street once more then he climbed back into the driver's seat and closed the door. "Let's keep this to ourselves."

"Why?"

"Because Eli'll think we've lost our minds if we tell him we think we saw something. Besides, what did we actually see?"

Another shiver ran through Taylor. "I wish I knew." But did she really want to know?

Alistair emerged from the shadows as Eli approached the police station door. They no longer kept the office open all night every night because there didn't seem to be a need for it, but the patrols still did their rounds. He unlocked the wood and glass door, swung it back, and motioned for the vampire to step inside ahead of him, then closed and locked it again before ushering Alistair into his office. "Have a seat."

Eli rounded his desk and dropped into his chair. "What's so urgent that you had to meet me here at midnight?"

"I have to be careful I am not discovered slipping away from the property. Remus usually retires early these days, but I have to wait until I know he's sleeping before I can leave. He received a call from Scarlet earlier this evening. She informed him they were knocking players out of the game so that they would have the advantage."

"Yeah, we figured. Archer and Paige have already been on the receiving end of their dangerous tricks."

Alistair's eyes widened and he leaned forward. "Are they all right?"

"Yeah, they are. They were lucky this time." Eli clasped his hands across his abdomen and eyed the vampire with caution. He wouldn't offer any information Alistair could take back to his leader. Clary's protection spell would remain their secret. He could be a double agent for all he knew.

"Remus has implemented another strategic move, although I am unaware of what it is at the moment. You need to warn everyone you have on your team and tell them to be extremely careful."

Eli's right eyebrow arched. "You'll let me know when you find out what that is, won't you?"

"Of course I will. I am on your side in this war, Eli."

The sheriff wasn't so sure. Alistair had his own motives, but if he could extract information from the vampire to assist their cause he would. "I appreciate that."

"We both want the same thing. To be rid of Remus and to restore Moon Grove to its former glory, before he lost control."

"And you believe the other council members will adhere to your new leadership once he's gone?"

"I know they will. Some of them have already expressed their concern."

"Well, then we need to work together to achieve the outcome we all want."

"Oh, absolutely. I am at your disposal." He stood up. "I must go. I can't have Remus wondering where I have been if he wakes and finds me gone."

"I'll hear from you?"

"You will."

Eli walked Alistair to the door and saw him out before returning to his desk and opening his laptop. Archer had sent him a message earlier saying he would send the translated pages via email once he got them back from Carmichael. Had he?

On his way home, Eli decided to stop by the Moon Grove Tribune. He wanted to talk to Archer. Would he still be there? As the editor rarely slept, he may have been catching up on some work. The sheriff hoped so. He pulled the wagon into the curb, his gaze moving to the newspaper office's window. No lights. Not surprising, considering vampires had nocturnal vision.

He climbed out of the Jeep, crossed the sidewalk and peered inside. No movement. He stepped into the alcove and knocked. Perhaps Archer *had* gone home to sleep, after all. As Eli turned around to head back to his car the door squeaked open and Max appeared in the doorway. "Hey. Lookin' for my brother?"

"Uh, yeah, is he here?"

"No. He went home. He needed to rest."

Eli's right eyebrow arched. "Oh? Why?"

Max stepped out of the office and closed the door. "He got injured in the car crash." He frowned. "He didn't tell you?"

"No, he didn't. What happened?"

"A large piece of windshield glass lodged itself in his left side and he lost a lot of blood."

"I wish I'd known so I could've helped him sooner."

"How could you? He never let on." Max locked the door behind him then turned around to continue the conversation. "I'm heading home now."

"Would you ask him if he's heard anything from Carmichael?"

"Are you referring to the pages he sent to him?"

"Yeah." Eli frowned at him. "He told you?" Archer had promised to keep the pages confidential so why tell Max?

"Yeah. There isn't much Archer doesn't tell me." He tugged his car keys from the pocket of his jeans. "I'll be sure to ask him to give you a call when he can. Tonight, he needs to rest and rejuvenate."

"Of course. If he needs anything let me know, ok?"

"Thanks. We will. Goodnight." Max passed Eli and headed along the sidewalk to his car, climbed in and drove away.

Eli ran his gaze along both ends of the main road as far as he could see. Not a soul on the street. But, then again, what could he expect after midnight. He pressed the remote key to his Jeep and opened the door. Someone called his name and when he turned around, he found a young woman standing in the middle of the deserted road. His gut tightened. She had to be one of Scarlet's coven. What did she want?

"Can I help you with something?"

She gave him a shrewd smirk and strutted over to him. "No, but I believe I can help you."

"How?" Eli's eyes roamed the surrounding buildings. Could this be a trap? He returned his gaze to her – short blonde hair, elfin features, slight build and quite beautiful with emerald green eyes.

"You need a way to defeat the coven, in particular Scarlet, and I want to be rid of her."

"So you can lead it, you mean?"

"Maybe. There are others older than me who covet the power… but, yes, perhaps I could." Her mischievous grin widened. "Your witch is powerful. She has been searching for the talisman using her ancestor's cards, but she won't find it."

"Why not?" Eli folded his arms.

"Because it's not of this realm."

"Where is it?"

"That is for me to know, for the moment. Do you want my help or not?"

"What do you want in return?"

"What I want is for you to dispatch Scarlet." She licked her glossy pink lipstick. "Think you're up for it?"

"How do I know you're telling me the truth?"

"You don't. But if you want to win this war you'll need to do everything you can to eliminate the competition."

"And what happens with the other witches?"

"Once Scarlet is out of the way they won't fight. She is the most powerful witch in our coven. Without her they'll know it's too dangerous." It wasn't entirely true, but he didn't need to know that. Raven wanted Scarlet gone and would do whatever it took to make that happen. She extended her hand. "Do we have a deal, Sheriff Blackwood?"

"Can you get the talisman from wherever it is?"

"With some difficulty, yes. So do we have a deal?"

Eli's gaze moved to her outstretched hand then back to her face. "Let me think it over."

Raven lowered her hand. "You have forty eight hours. After that the offer is off the negotiation table and you face the coven on your own."

"Fair enough. How can I contact you?"

"When you have made the decision I will be in touch with you." She gave him another devious grin and vanished before his eyes.

TWENTY SIX

Paige heard Eli's Jeep pull into the front yard. She glanced at the bedside clock. 2:27 AM. Where had he been all this time? He'd phoned earlier to tell her he'd be home soon, so what had happened between then and now? She threw back the covers, climbed out of bed, pulled on her robe and padded barefoot along the hallway to the living room. "Hey, what took so long?"

Eli closed the front door, tossed his Stetson onto a hook on the coat rack and shrugged out of his police issue jacket. "I had a visit from one of the witches. Raven. She wants to help us."

"And you believe her?" Paige folded her arms and frowned at him.

"I didn't say that. She said the talisman doesn't exist in this realm, so there's no way for us to find it."

"Does she know how to get it?"

"She didn't elaborate on that, but I'm assuming she does."

"Why would she want to help us, Eli?"

"She wants to take control of the coven."

"Of course she does. What other motive could she possibly have? Is there no loyalty anywhere?"

Eli walked over to her and pulled her into his arms. "Of course there is. We had that in our pack. We still do."

She looked up at him. "Did we? Linda isn't loyal."

"Linda's not part of our pack."

"But she had been once."

"Yes, that's true, but she left and started working for Ross Redmond. I guess being exposed to a variety of underhanded situations and people changed her perception of right and wrong."

"So what does this *Raven* want you to do?"

"She wants me to kill Scarlet."

Paige pulled free of Eli's embrace. "And how does she expect you to do that? From what Clary has told us Scarlet is the most powerful witch of their coven."

"She plans on getting the talisman from wherever it's being kept."

"And she's going to give it to you?"

"If she wants to eliminate Scarlet from the equation then I would assume so."

Paige gave him an incredulous stare. "You know you should never *assume* anything."

"And I don't, but I'll wait and see what happens with her." He walked into the kitchen, took a mug from the overhead cupboard and poured himself a coffee. "Oh, by the way, I ran into Max at the Tribune office. He told me Archer had been injured in the accident."

Paige's eyes widened. "How badly?"

"A large piece of windshield glass lodged itself in his left side and he'd lost a lot of blood. Max said Archer needed to rest up to rejuvenate so that's why I haven't heard back from him."

"If he'd said something we could've helped him. I wonder why he didn't."

Eli shrugged. "Don't know. Maybe he didn't want to worry you. You were injured too."

"Yes, but not as bad as him, obviously."

"Why don't you give him a call in the morning and see how he's doing?"

Paige stepped up to Eli and wrapped her arms around his waist, resting her head against his firm chest. "I will. He shouldn't keep things like that from us. We're all in this together."

"Yeah, we are."

The sleek black convertible turned onto the dirt road, its tires leaving a dust cloud behind it. When it reached the fence line the car slowed to a crawl and pulled in behind the Jeep parked in the front yard. The driver stepped out and ran her gaze around the familiar tree-lined property. It had been many years since she had been in Moon Grove or had seen Eli Blackwood, and she wondered what he would say when he saw her at his door.

She climbed the front porch steps. *At least someone's awake, the light's still on in the living room.* She raised her hand to knock but pulled back. *Will he be pleased to see me? Only one way to find out, I guess.* She gave two sharp raps on the door.

Brightness from inside spilled into the dark and

Eli's tall frame appeared in the open doorway. "Ruby? What are you doing here?"

"I came to help." She gave him an unsure smile.

Paige stepped up beside him. "Who's this?"

Eli's gaze moved from the witch on his doormat to his girlfriend. "Uh, this is Ruby. Ruby McLaren. She used to live in Moon Grove."

"Oh." Paige ran her gaze over the woman. Quite attractive with green eyes, full mouth, perfect skin and almost the same colored hair as Paige.

Eli moved aside to allow Ruby to enter the house. "Come in." He and Ruby had had a brief liaison after his wife had been killed, due to grief. It had been a mistake and they had both realized it, but it still didn't make seeing her again any less uncomfortable. "You said you're here to help?"

"Yes. I thought Clary could use some extra witch muscle."

He wasn't surprised Ruby knew of their current predicament. She'd always had a sixth sense when danger threatened Moon Grove. "She's working on a spell and hasn't been able to perfect it so far."

"Mm. I'll go see her later today and see if we can figure it out together."

Paige stood with arms folded. She had the distinct feeling Ruby had been a part of Eli's life in more ways than only a witchy friend. Her eyes remained on the pair as they talked and she hoped the obvious attraction between them wouldn't become an issue. Jealousy reared its ugly head. Eli belonged to her and she to him and she wouldn't allow anyone to move in on her man. "It's late. Are you staying at the Inn?"

"Yes." Ruby's gaze moved from Eli to Paige. "I suppose I should go." She walked over to the front door.

Eli followed and opened it for her.

She looked up into his honey colored eyes. "I'll see you later." She smiled and stepped out onto the porch.

"Sure. See you then." Eli waited until Ruby had driven away before closing the door.

"Is she going to be a problem?" Paige asked, stepping up behind him.

Eli swung around. "What do you mean?"

"You seemed to be quite taken with her."

He frowned into her eyes. "You think I…"

"She seemed to be interested in you, too."

"Paige. There is nothing between Ruby and me."

"Maybe not now, but once, right?" She folded her arms.

Eli huffed out a sigh. "We had a brief… encounter after Michelle passed away. We both knew it'd been a mistake and that it happened because of the grief I felt at her loss."

"And now she's back."

Eli pulled her close and stroked her silky hair. "I love you. And only you."

Tears stung the backs of Paige's eyes and she blinked them away. She would not allow Ruby to come between her and the man she loved. "I love you too, Eli, and I trust you. It's her I don't trust."

"Ruby's here to help Clary, nothing more."

Paige wasn't at all sure what the witch's intentions were.

TWENTY SEVEN

Rosemarie gave Paige a cheerful smile as the psychologist stepped into the office. "Good morning, Darlin'. It's getting a bit chilly out there. Can you believe winter's already on its way?"

"No. And before we know it it'll be Christmastime again."

The receptionist waved the comment off. "Oh. Don't even go there."

"I have to say, I love winter with the snow and the holidays. It's a lovely time of year. Cold... but lovely, nonetheless."

"I guess you're right. I do love the holidays." Rosemarie stood up. "Can I get you anything before your work day begins?"

"Coffee smells good. Would you mind bringing a cup into my consultation room?"

"Of course not. Coming right up." Rosemarie turned on her heel and headed to the kitchen.

Paige removed her gloves and knit cap and stuffed them into her purse, then stepped behind the reception desk to check her schedule. She'd have a patient arriving in fifteen minutes, enough time for that coffee to kick in. She wandered down the hallway to her office, hung up her jacket and purse and sat down behind her desk.

"Here you go," Rosemarie said, setting the mug down with a plate of cookies. "Enjoy."

"Thanks, Rosy, I will." As she and Eli had been up until almost sunrise she'd need it.

Paige booted up her laptop and loaded the file for her first client, nibbling on a cookie as she read over their previous session notes.

Rosemarie appeared in the doorway. "Your appointment called to reschedule."

"Ok. Well that gives me ample time to enjoy my coffee." She smiled.

"But there is someone here to see you."

"Oh, who?"

"Me." The familiar voice said from behind the receptionist.

"Thanks, Rosy. You can head back out front now."

Ruby remained in the hall.

"Why are you here?" Paige couldn't hide the tightness in her tone.

"May I?" Ruby motioned through the doorway.

"Sure. And, please, close the door." Paige's lighthearted mood sank into the pit of her stomach. She hated confrontations.

"I wanted to make peace." Ruby eased her curvy frame into one of the two chairs in front of Paige's desk.

Paige frowned. "I don't understand."

"I think you do." She clasped her hands in her lap.

"Ok. If you want honesty, why did you come here?"

"I came here to help. I know the Coven of the Full Moon is here."

"Yes, Eli mentioned you have a sixth sense when it comes to the town."

"I don't want to see anyone I know die at the hands of those witches. That's the reason I came back. Once the war is won I'll return home."

"Why would you risk your life for a town you haven't lived in for...?"

"Seven years. Regardless of where I live now this is still my home. I grew up here, and I'll be damned if I let anyone destroy it."

"And Eli?"

"Eli is a *friend*. Nothing more." She gave Paige a thin smile.

Paige wasn't sure she believed everything the witch had said, but she knew how desperately the town needed help. "Good to know. I have a client coming in soon."

Ruby stood up. "Then I'll be on my way. I'm glad we had a chance to talk. To clear the air."

Had they cleared the air? Paige wasn't so sure.

Archer entered the police station around 10:15 AM, his gaze moving to Eli's office. The sheriff was at his desk. The editor walked across to the swinging gate, pushed it back and wandered over to the door. "Where is everyone?"

"Out on patrol. Come in. Have a seat." He motioned for the editor to sit down. "How are you?"

"Good as new. Max mentioned he told you what

happened." Archer sat in the first of the two chairs closest to the door.

"Why didn't you say something?"

"I didn't want to worry either of you. I knew I'd be fine."

Eli leaned back in his chair. "That's what I thought. I'm glad you're ok. You heard from Paige?"

"Yes, she called earlier. I appreciate both your concern."

"That's what friends do."

Archer's left eyebrow rose. "So you consider us friends?"

Eli gave him a sheepish look. "Of course I do. We've been through a lot together."

"Good to know." The editor smiled.

Changing the subject, Eli asked, "Have you heard anything from Carmichael?"

"Not yet. Perhaps the language is so old it's going to take some time to decipher."

"Well let's hope they can. We need to find out why Ross Redmond had that book and what information it holds."

Archer nodded. "Understood. How's Paige doing? She said she's fine, but…"

"She's ok. Clary used one of her potions on Paige's face and by this morning the scratches and bruises were gone."

"That's good." Archer waited a beat, then "I wanted to ask you something." He gave Eli a serious stare.

"Ok. What is it?" Eli straightened in his chair.

"Do you know where the council is hiding?"

"Why would you ask me that?" Eli tried to maintain a poker face.

"I've had a feeling you do. I understand you didn't want to share the information because you weren't sure of the identity of the mole, but now you are."

Eli sighed. "Yes, I know where they are. But I'd still prefer to keep it to myself for now."

"Ok. At least we have an advantage. Any word on Linda's disappearance? Do you think the council abducted her?"

"Yes, I do. It seemed too… staged for my liking."

"Do you believe she's dead, if that's the case?"

"Don't you? You know how Remus operates. He wouldn't want any loose ends."

"What if she did escape?"

"It's too convenient."

"Is it? The committee voted the death penalty. Why wouldn't Remus sit back and allow the pack to administer the punishment? He knows Lycan law."

Archer had a point.

TWENTY EIGHT

Ruby knocked on Clarissa's door and waited, her stomach doing nervous flip flops beneath the waistband of her jeans. Would the older woman be happy to see her? Would she want her help? She swallowed hard and cleared her throat in anticipation of the greeting she would utter when the door opened. It didn't. She tugged her cell phone from the pocket of her black wool coat and checked the time. 12:07 PM. Eli had said his grandmother would be home.

She tucked her phone back into her pocket, wandered along the porch to the side steps and around to the gate. Stepping into the yard, she made her way to the back door. She knocked. No answer. She closed her eyes, inhaled a deep breath and let it out slowly, then used her witch hearing. A heartbeat. Ruby raised her hands and said, "Ianua patentibus." The lock popped open and she rushed inside. "Clary? Clary, where are you?"

Racing into the entry hall, she noticed the open cellar door under the stairs. She peered into the gloom. Why wasn't the light on? "Clary, are you down there?"

A feeble moan echoed up the staircase and Ruby flew down the wooden treads into the dark space beneath the house. She whipped her phone out of her pocket and flicked on the flashlight. Clary lay unconscious on the floor in front of her spell table. Ruby knelt beside the old woman and lifted her head off the floor. "Clary, Clary, what happened?"

Clarissa gasped, "The... spell reversed itself... and knocked me out cold."

Ruby raised Clary into a sitting position, her back against the bench. "You know you should never try to do that kind of spell alone."

The old woman nodded. "I know, dear, but we're running out of time and I didn't have another witch to assist me."

"Well, now you do."

Clarissa frowned. "Does Eli know you're here?"

Ruby gave her a thin smile. "Of course he does. We've already spoken. That's how I knew you'd be home."

"Oh." She waited a moment, then said, "You've met Paige?"

"Yes." Her left eyebrow arched.

"Ok. Good. Now help me to my feet."

"I'm not here to cause any issues, Clary. I came because I knew Moon Grove needed my help."

"Glad to hear it, because if you are you can turn around and head back out of town."

Ruby frowned at Clary and raised two fingers in a Boy Scout oath. "I give you my solemn word as a law-abiding witch... I am not here to come between Eli and Paige."

"Very well, then, we have work to do."

Later that afternoon, a charcoal colored van pulled into the curb outside the Tribune office and four people emerged. Two men, two women dressed in black. The curious gazes of onlookers followed the intimate group as they crossed the sidewalk and entered the building.

Archer left his seat and stepped around his desk as the four moved closer. "I've been expecting you," he greeted, hand extended.

"Yes, Carmichael informed us of what's happening here and we are more than happy to assist," the first male said. He turned to his companions. "This is Isabella, but most call her Izzy. That's Constance, but she prefers Connie. He's Oliver and I'm Tristan."

"It's good to have you here. I've made reservations for you at the Inn down the road. Once you get settled in we'll head over and I'll introduce you to Eli Blackwood, the town sheriff."

"Sounds like a plan." Tristan glanced at the others then returned his gaze to the editor. "We'll meet you back here, say, in an hour?"

Archer nodded. "Yes. Just tell reception the booking's under my name."

"Thanks. We appreciate it."

"I'll see you in one hour." He smiled.

"You will."

The group headed back out to the street, climbed into the van, Tristan behind the wheel, and drove down the main street to the Moon Grove Inn.

"Quaint," Izzy said, running her gaze over the two story building.

"That's not the word I'd use," Connie said, folding her arms with a huff.

Tristan peered between the front seats. "Hey, we're here to help so let's make the best of it. Ok?"

"Whatever." Connie shrugged.

"Come on, let's get settled in." Tristan climbed out of the van and walked around to the back door. He handed the others their luggage then pulled his case out and followed them to the front porch.

"It's not that bad," Oliver said, climbing the steps and pushing open the multi-paned glass door. "In fact, I find it charming."

"Yeah, me too." Izzy stepped inside behind him.

Tristan waited for Connie to go in before entering the lobby.

"Hello, I'm Leanne, how can I help you?" The young reception desk clerk offered.

"Hi. We have reservations under Archer Hamilton," Tristan told her.

She ran her gaze over the list on the laptop. "Oh, yes, we've been expecting you. Your rooms are ready. Let me give you your keys." She reached around behind her and tugged four keys from their hooks. "Here you go. You're at the end of the hall. Two rooms on the right and two on the left. Lunch is between 12 and 2 and dinner is between 6 and 8. If you need anything at all don't hesitate to ask. We hope you enjoy your stay with us."

"Thanks." Tristan handed around the keys. "I'm sure we will." He gave the young woman an enigmatic smile before picking up his suitcase and wandering up the stairs behind his companions. He glanced over his shoulder and his and Leanne's eyes met. She gave him a coy smile and turned her gaze back to the laptop in front of her. Vampires had that kind of effect on humans, especially women. She could be an easy distraction, but that wasn't the reason for him being in Moon Grove.

Taylor and Rick pulled into the station parking lot and Rick turned off the engine. The pair had spotted Eli on the front porch talking to the Moon Grove Tribune editor and four other people. "I wonder what's going on there," Taylor said.

Rick shrugged. "Who knows?"

"Let's go around and find out." Taylor unclipped her seatbelt and stepped out of the patrol wagon.

"Tay, wait." Rick came around behind the Jeep. "You don't want to make Eli mad at us."

"We're heading inside. If we happen to hear something…"

"Don't say anything. Ok?"

"I can say Hi can't I?" She glowered at him.

"Yeah, of course. But don't ask any questions."

"I didn't plan to."

The two deputies wandered past the dark van and Eli's Jeep and stepped onto the porch. "Hey, Eli," Taylor offered with a smile.

The group stopped talking.

"Hey. Back already?" Eli gave the pair a stern stare.

"Yeah, we've finished our rounds for now." Rick ran his eyes around the strangers standing with Archer

Hamilton then returned his gaze to Eli. "Anything you want us to do?"

"Not at the moment. Why don't you go in and have something to eat. There's coffee and donuts in the kitchen."

Taylor scrutinized the group as she continued past and into the station. Cooper wasn't there. She breathed a relieved sigh and waited for Rick to follow her inside and close the door. "What do you make of the four standing with the editor?" She motioned to the back of the door with her head.

"Nothing much. We didn't get the gist of what they were discussing so…"

"Didn't you think they looked kind of anemic?"

"To be honest I didn't notice." He shrugged.

"The editor gave me an odd look, too. I wonder why."

"Are you sure you're not imagining things, Tay?" Rick stepped through the swinging gate and headed toward the kitchen. "Come on, let's grab a coffee and a donut. I'm starved."

Taylor blew out a frustrated breath and followed her partner along the corridor. "Your mind is always on your stomach. Don't you think we have bigger things to concern ourselves with right now?"

Rick picked up a jelly donut and took a large bite, red jelly running down the left side of his chin. He ran his index finger up his chin and scooped the jam into his mouth. "Like what?"

"Like what we saw the other night." Taylor folded her arms.

"You mean what we didn't see, don't you? Neither of us had time to get a good look at it."

"Exactly."

Rick turned over two clean mugs. "Want coffee?" He glanced at her over his shoulder.

"Sure. If it'll make you happy."

"Tay, I'm not saying there isn't something going on but until we have some actual proof there isn't much we can do."

"Then we'll get proof. There's something wrong with this town and I *will* find out what it is."

"Ok. But don't say I didn't warn you. So far, we've got nothing to go on."

"That's not true. We have a few things."

"Yeah?" He gave her a skeptical stare. "Like what?"

"The church for one. Why is it locked? You were the one who said that's odd... and you're right. We did see something the other night. And after having some time to process it, I know it wasn't a dog. And who's the group in dark clothing out front right now? They don't look like regulars to me."

"Ok, so we may have some stuff to look into."

A smile spread across Taylor's face. "So you're going to help me?"

Rick picked up another donut. "Sure, why not."

TWENTY NINE

As the hush of evening enveloped Moon Grove, Scarlet stepped out onto the front porch and sat down. She needed some quiet time to think. There had to be a way to dissolve Clarissa Baker's protection spell, but how? She glanced up at the clouded moon as if it would speak to her and provide the answer she needed. But, of course, it didn't. Mother moon observed the earth in silent reverence. She gave an involuntary shiver, stood up and walked over to the railing. Winter would settle upon the town and soon snow would fall. The season wasn't one of her favorites as the cold often played havoc with spellcasting, making it difficult for spells to travel through the frigid atmosphere.

The door creaked open behind her and Raven came out onto the porch.

"Do you need to see me?" Scarlet asked, turning to look at her sister.

"No, I needed some air." She crossed the porch to Scarlet. "Chilly night. Winter will arrive soon."

"Yes, those were my thoughts too." She studied Raven for a moment. "Are you sure you don't want to speak to me?"

Scarlet had a sixth sense where her coven sisters were concerned. Raven disliked her for that reason because she often picked up on things that should remain secret. "What makes you think I do?"

"A feeling, that's all."

"With the impending battle looming, sister, I wondered if the talisman is secure."

Scarlet's right eyebrow arched. "You need not concern yourself with such things. I can assure you it is quite safe and unattainable."

"Good to know. It would be our undoing if it were to fall into the wrong hands."

"Only I know the incantation to enter the shadow realm and retrieve the talisman. You can be assured no one can get their hands on it."

"At least we can rest easy on that score." She gave Scarlet a thin smile, turned on her heel and headed back into the house.

Scarlet's curious gaze remained on the closed door. *There has to be a reason for Raven's questions. What is she up to?*

THIRTY

Paige and Eli woke up with a start at the same time, both sets of eyes darting around the smoke-filled room, both coughing as they flew out of bed. Eli rushed to the door and placed the palm of his hand on the wood. Hot! His anxious gaze moved to the floor, flames were licking the bottom of the bedroom door. "We'll have to get out through the window."

He threw the sash open and helped Paige climb out. Before climbing out himself, he grabbed clothes from off the armchair sitting in the corner and his cell phone from off the bedside table. Once outside, he and Paige dressed quickly then stood and watched everything they owned go up in flames.

"The coven's getting desperate," Eli said, heaving a huge sigh as his family home began falling in on itself. He knew the items inside the hidden, heavy duty safe would be protected. Tugging his phone from the pocket of his shirt, he keyed in Archer's number. "Hey, it's me. Can you come out here? Someone set our house on fire."

Archer sprang up in bed. "What?! Are you ok?"

"Yeah, we're fine. It's lucky we woke up when we did or we might not have been."

"Hell! I'm on my way. I'll call the fire brigade in Bellehurst."

"Thanks. But I don't think there'll be much left by the time they get here."

"I'm sorry, Eli. It had to be the coven that did this." He pulled on his black sweater.

"Yeah, exactly, which means they're getting desperate. Scarlet must realize that Clary will complete that spell."

"Then why didn't they burn her house down?"

"Protection spell, remember?"

"Yes. Then how is your house burning to the ground?"

"The spell she placed on us is personal, although if we'd been caught in the fire I don't think it would've saved us."

"I'm glad you're both ok. Who'll be next?"

"Good question. I'll call a meeting so we can discuss actions to take to protect ourselves. Maybe Scarlet found a way to diminish the spell Clary placed on us. Who knows?"

"I'm heading out now. See you soon." Archer raced out of the door, around the hood of the Ford Transit and climbed in. It would take a few days for the insurance company to clear him for a new car. In the meantime, he'd utilize the Tribune van.

Eli pushed his phone into the pocket of his shirt. "Archer's coming out to pick us up." The keys to his Jeep were in the burnt out living room.

Paige wrapped her arms around him and they stood in silence watching the remains of their home crumble.

Archer's white van stopped short behind the police Jeep and he jumped out and rushed around the hood. "Oh, Eli, I'm so sorry." His eyes roamed the smoldering devastation. "You can both stay with me if you need to, until you figure out what to do next."

"Thanks, I appreciate that, but Paige and I have been talking. We're going to stay at her place. That way we'll be close to Clary as well."

"You've lost everything. What can I do to help?"

"Be safe. The coven's already tried to kill you twice."

"I think they were toying with us, initially, but it looks like they're getting serious now."

"Yeah, it does."

The shrill sound of a siren in the distance echoed on the chill breeze. Too late. A glowing pile of orange embers were all that remained of their home. Once the heat diminished, Eli and Paige would see what they could salvage from the rubble. From what Eli could discern, it wouldn't be much.

"Do you want me to drive you over to Paige's?"

Eli gave a heavy sigh. "Yeah, as soon as the firies have finished here."

Archer ran his gaze over Paige's ashen face. "Do you want to sit in the car?" he asked.

She looked at him with tear-filled eyes. "I want to stay with Eli. We both nearly lost our lives tonight."

The editor stepped up to her and rubbed her arm. "I know. But you're safe now."

"Are we? While the coven is in Moon Grove none of us are safe."

The fire truck pulled up behind Archer's van and three firemen climbed out. Eli walked over to the trio. "Thanks for coming. There's not much left, unfortunately, but there are still some live embers."

"Sorry, Eli. It's a shame this has happened. I know you've lived here your whole life." Chad Vincent had been a resident and fire chief of Moon Grove during Eli's teenage years but had moved over to Bellehurst when he landed the job at the firehouse there.

"Thanks, Chad. Yeah, it's hard right now. I'm kinda numb, you know?"

"Understandable." He motioned to the other two men to douse the remains. "If there's anything I can do don't hesitate to call. Ok?"

"I appreciate that. Thank you."

Chad gripped Eli's arm in a compassionate gesture of camaraderie before joining his men.

Paige walked over to Eli. "Do you want to leave now? We should go see Clary."

Eli's gaze moved from the burnt out remains of his family home to her. "Sure. Yeah. You're right, we should."

She held him tight for a long moment. "I'm so sorry you lost your home, Eli." Tears stung the backs of her eyes and she blinked them away as she looked up into his sad face.

"I've been thinking… maybe they didn't mean to kill us only weaken us."

"What do you mean?"

His eyes moved to the editor then back to Paige. "Like Archer said a moment ago, they were toying with us. Maybe they still are."

"You think they're doing this to cause pain?"

"Yeah, I do. While we're grieving over the loss of, say, Archer's car or our house our minds are not on the impending battle."

"Sounds like something Remus would orchestrate," Archer said.

"It does. As long as we're ok that's all that matters. We have to keep our heads in the game otherwise they'll defeat us."

By the time the firies left, the sun had risen over the distant horizon. A new day had begun. Archer pulled the van into Clary's driveway and Eli and Paige got out. "Thanks, Archer, I'll talk to you later." Eli closed the door, took Paige by the hand and they climbed the front steps. He had called to let his grandmother know they were on their way.

Clary opened the door the moment they stepped onto the porch. "Eli, I'm so sorry you lost the house, but I'm glad you're both all right." She wrapped her arms around the pair and held them tight.

Eli eased himself out of her embrace. "Thanks, Clary. It's hard losing all of those memories."

"I know, dear." She took his arm and led him and Paige inside. "I'll make us some breakfast."

"Thanks, coffee would be good right now." Eli sat down next to Paige.

"Coffee it is then." Clary scooped coffee into the coffee maker, took three mugs from the cupboard and sat them on the counter before crossing the kitchen and sitting down opposite the pair. "What are you going to do now?"

"We're staying across the street for the time being. And we'll figure out the rest as we go." Right at that moment, Eli felt devastated but knew he had to keep it together or the witches and Remus would win. "Would we have died in that fire, Clary?"

"I'm afraid so. It appears Scarlet has found a way to weaken my protection spell. If only I'd thought to place one around your home, Eli. I'm so sorry." She blinked back tears.

"You couldn't have known they would do something like this. Don't blame yourself." Eli sat straight up on his chair and frowned into his grandmother's eyes. "Will the spell here hold?"

"That's a different kind of spell, my boy. She can't break it, only I can."

Eli breathed a relieved sigh. "Good to know. Can you place one on Paige's house?"

"It's already done." She gave him a shrewd grin. "When you called I went across the street and cast the spell. I had a feeling you might want to stay there."

"Thanks, Gran."

Clary got up and poured the coffee. "The coven is playing dirty. I assume Remus has everything to do with it."

"Yeah, we do too." Eli's gaze moved to Paige then back to his grandmother. "He's determined to rid Moon Grove of me and every other supernatural creature that lives here."

"Well he won't get away with it. Ruby and I have been working on the spell to stop the witches from killing anyone by sight."

"How's it going?"

"There have been a few bumps... but we're getting there."

"I hate to put pressure on you, Clary, but the sooner the better."

"I know, dear, I know."

THIRTY ONE

W hen Eli and Paige pulled into the yard in Clary's 1956 blue and white Chevrolet, Eli made a beeline for the space where their bedroom had been to rummage through the debris for the safe. It wasn't there. He climbed over charred rubble searching through the ruins in case it had been pushed elsewhere by the force of the water when the firies doused the house. Nothing. *It has to be here somewhere.* He continued to pick up and toss blackened pieces of wood out of the way in an effort to find it.

Paige had been searching the living area of the home in the hope of finding anything to salvage from the wreckage. Everything had been burnt beyond recognition. She turned and glanced over her shoulder at Eli and wandered over to him. "Where's the safe?"

"Good question." Eli continued to fossick through the burnt remnants of furniture and other items before he stood up and turned around. "It's not here."

"Who knew you had it?" Paige frowned at him.

He shrugged. "Nobody. Only us."

"Well someone obviously did or it would still be here." Paige stood with hands on hips staring at the space where the safe had been.

"You're right. But who?"

"Are you sure you haven't mentioned it to anyone? Archer perhaps?"

"I don't think so." Eli's serious gaze met hers. "Find anything?"

She shook her head. "No, there's nothing left." A single tear slipped down her right cheek.

Eli pulled her into his arms. "I'm sorry, sweetheart."

Paige eased back and looked up into his honey colored eyes. "You don't have to be sorry, Eli, this isn't your fault. It's the coven's and Remus's."

"What if they burnt down the house to get to the safe?"

"That's a bit extreme, don't you think?"

"Is it? Whoever took it has the book and other items and who knows what that will offer them? If they know how to use them."

The thought of Remus having that book terrified her. "Did Archer get those pages back from Carmichael yet?"

Eli gave a heavy sigh. "I'm not sure. With everything that's been going on lately I forgot to ask him again. He said he'd let me know when he did, so I guess we wait until he does."

"Or we could go ask him." Paige ran her eyes over the remains of their home, Eli's family home where he grew up, and tears stung the backs of her eyes. "Let's go. There's no point in staying here any longer."

"Yeah, I guess you're right." He took Paige's hand and walked back to the classic, two-toned sedan. "We'll head into town and talk to Archer. He may have something by now."

The closed sign displayed on the door of the Tribune office seemed odd at 11:20 in the morning. Eli peered through the glass. The editor wasn't behind his desk or anywhere else he could see. He turned to Paige and frowned. "I wonder where Archer is."

"Yes, it's not like him to play hooky on a work day." Paige glanced up and down the street on the off chance he'd been out buying coffee or some food. Vampires did their best to appear human in the mortal world, so buying a coffee or something to eat would seem normal to the people he interacted with who knew nothing of the supernatural aspect of the town.

Eli tugged his cell from the pocket of his shirt and hit speed dial for Archer. Voicemail kicked in, "Hey, leave a message after the tone and I'll get back to you."

"Archer, it's Eli. Paige and I are at your office. Where are you? Give me a call when you get this." He looked into Paige's concerned eyes. "We'll probably get a call back any minute."

She huffed out a sigh. "I hope you're right." Her solar plexus told her otherwise. A horrible thought crossed her mind. *Could Archer have taken the safe? Is that why he's not here? But why would he?*

"Maybe he had something else to do before coming in today."

Paige attempted to shrug off the unsettling feeling. "Maybe."

"Why don't we wander down to the Inn, have a coffee, and wait for his call?"

"Ok." She slipped her hand into his. "But what if he doesn't call?"

"Then we'll head out to his place and see if he's there."

Paige nodded. "Good. I'm worried."

Eli frowned into her eyes. "Why?"

"I don't know. I've got a bad feeling, that's all."

"You think something's happened to him?"

She shrugged. "I can't say for sure, but the coven has made two attempts on his life already. That's a concern in itself." The chill air sent a shiver up Paige's spine. Winter would arrive in a couple more weeks. How quickly the year had flown by. It would be her second Christmas in Moon Grove. Her mind wandered back to the day Stephanie, her best friend, had been attacked in the Ghost Train at the Winter Wonderland Carnival by Eli's demented, werewolf father. He had meant to stab *her* because he didn't want their wolf bloodlines intermingled. The incident had affected Stephanie so badly she ended their friendship. They had been friends for years and Paige still missed her every day.

Nonetheless, she hadn't made any new friendships, not anyone she could call a best friend, since moving to the town. Rosemarie had become the closest person to her, apart from Eli and Clary, but she didn't think they'd be besties. She missed that close connection with someone. Someone who knew the real her and wanted to be her friend anyway.

Eli pushed open the Inn door and ushered Paige into the warmth of the café. They found a table by the window and sat down, Eli shrugging out of his police issue jacket and hanging it on the back of his chair. "What would you like?"

"I think a cup of hot chocolate would be nice."

"Hot chocolate it is." He headed over to the drinks counter. Being the sheriff of Moon Grove had certain perks. He could come into the Inn at any time during opening hours and help himself to a coffee or other beverage on the house. He could even order a meal if he wanted to.

Betty Rogers stepped into the dining room from the kitchen and spotted the sheriff. "Eli, how are you?" She came over to him and wrapped her arms around him in a friendly hug. "It's been a while." She stepped back and gave him a pained look. "I heard about the fire out at your house. I'm so sorry, hon."

"Thank you, I appreciate it." He picked up the mugs of hot chocolate.

Betty noticed. "Is Paige here with you?" Her gaze roamed the room and when she spotted the young woman sitting by the window she waved. Her eyes moved back to Eli. "Are you hungry? I could fix you both some brunch, if you'd like."

"We're good, Betty, but thanks."

"If you change your mind you know where to find me." She gave him a warm smile and headed back into the kitchen through the louvered, wooden saloon doors.

Eli set a mug down in front of Paige then took his seat opposite. "It's been fifteen minutes since I left the message on Archer's cell. I think we'd better head out there once we have our these and find out what's going on."

Paige nodded. "I agree."

Eli pulled the Chevrolet up behind the Tribune van and turned off the engine. "It looks like Archer's home." He stepped out of the car, came around the long hood, and opened the door for Paige.

"I wonder why he didn't call you back." She ran her gaze over the elegant wooden house with wall-sized windows.

"Let's go find out."

The pair stepped up onto the front porch and Eli knocked. The home looked empty. "Doesn't appear to be anyone here."

Paige glanced over her shoulder at the white Ford Transit. "Then why is the Tribune van parked over there?"

"Good question. Let's head round back." He leapt off the front steps and made his way to the left side of the house. Paige followed.

The pair peered inside through the huge panes of glass. No one.

"I wonder where he could be."

"Perhaps Max picked him up and they went somewhere together... Bellehurst maybe."

Paige frowned into Eli's eyes. "But that still doesn't account for why he hasn't called you back. You know he would as soon as he got your voicemail message."

He sighed. "I have no idea."

"I think something's happened to him, Eli. My gut is telling me something is definitely wrong."

"I have Max's number in my cell. Let me give him a call." He slid his phone out of his shirt pocket and found

Archer's brother's number in the address book. "Hey, Max, is Archer with you? He's not, huh. Any idea where he might be? No, he's not there. The office is closed. We're here at the house and he's not here, either. I left a message on his phone but he hasn't called me back yet. Yeah, I know it's not like him. Sure. We'll head back to town now. Ok, see you there." Eli turned to Paige. "He hasn't seen him."

"I knew it."

"Max is meeting us at the Tribune office." The pair climbed into the car, the rear wheels spinning as the Chevy sped down the drive, heading for the freeway.

THIRTY TWO

Matthias couldn't shake the antsy feeling. His body twitched as he sat in front of the roaring fire, his serious gaze focused on the legion of tall pines outside the window. He hadn't been on a run for the past few days and needed to get out of the cabin into the fresh air and autumn sunshine or he'd go stir-crazy. And as Alpha of his pack he couldn't allow that to happen, he had to set a prime example for his Lycan brethren. Unable to contain the urge any longer, he ripped the clothes from his muscular frame, shifted into wolf form, and bounded into the woods. It felt good to be free of his human skin. He could breathe again.

He whipped through the trees at a hundred miles per hour, everything around him a blur, white plumes of frosty air escaping his muzzle, early signs of winter settling upon the town. He slowed his pace as he came upon a cabin tucked into the woods and moved closer to it, remaining hidden among the trees. Being a supernatural creature, he could see and sense certain magical vibrations in the atmosphere. This cabin had a cloaking spell attached to the extension added to accommodate the thirteen witches residing within it. *So this is where they're hiding out.*

Matthias darted from one tree to the next, moving to a better vantage point. The door opened and a woman stepped out onto the front porch. He could feel the dark magic radiating from her elfin frame. The High Priestess of the coven held that kind of power. He watched her walk across to the wooden railing and gaze up at the cloudy autumn sky. His Lycan eyes remained on her longer than they should – beautiful and threatening – a dangerous combination.

He turned and bounded away, heading back home. He would let Eli Blackwood know he'd found the coven's secret location.

THIRTY THREE

Max was on the sidewalk outside the Tribune office when Eli and Paige pulled into the curb. The worried look on Archer's brother's face caused Eli's gut to clench. He stepped out of the Chevy and crossed the pavement, Paige close behind. "Have you heard anything from Archer?"

"No, and I'm concerned. It's not like him to disappear and not tell someone where he's going."

Eli stood with hands on hips. "When did you see him last?"

"Yesterday. Here." Max glanced over his shoulder through the office window.

"Let's go inside and take a look around." Eli pointed to the locked door.

"What good will that do?" Max's frowning gaze returned to the sheriff.

"If he's been abducted it may have happened here. We need to do a search of the premises to rule that out before taking the next step."

Max's eyebrows rose. "You think he's been abducted?"

"It's possible. I'm sure your brother filled you in on the tricks the coven has been playing with us all. And they've attacked him twice already. Who's to say they didn't orchestrate this?"

Archer's brother tugged the key from his jacket pocket and unlocked the door. "Let's check it out then. We need to find him."

Eli closed the door and followed Max and Paige down to Archer's desk. "Is Archer's cell phone here?"

Max shrugged. "I – I don't know. Is it important?"

"It might be. If it's here then something's happened to your brother. If it's not then he could've gone somewhere and not let anyone know." The disappearance of the safe at his house popped into his head. *Has Archer taken it? Is that the reason why he's missing?*

"I'll check the other office." Max turned on his heel and marched along the short hallway.

"What are we looking for, Eli?" Paige gave him a worried frown.

"Signs of a struggle." He ran his eyes around the room. There didn't appear to be any.

Paige's eyes followed his direction. "I don't see anything."

"Neither do I."

Max came back into the office holding up a phone. "Found this lying on the floor in the other office."

"Then I think your brother's been abducted."

"Wouldn't there be signs of a struggle. I know Archer wouldn't give up without a fight and nothing in there indicated any kind of altercation." Max roamed the room with his vampire eyes. "Nothing out here either."

"I had hoped there would be so we'd know for sure. Maybe they took him by surprise. He often works here alone late at night."

"We have pretty acute hearing. He would've heard if someone had broken in."

"I've come here at night and the front door has been unlocked." Eli rummaged through papers on the editor's desk, not sure what he was looking for.

"Ok. But he would've had time to get out the back if someone came through there." Max pointed to the windowed door.

"Not if they came in from both directions at the same time."

At that moment, the door opened and Matthias stalked along the office. "I know where the Coven of the Full Moon is hiding out."

Eli came around the desk to him. "Where?"

"You know that cabin that sits off Peak's Ridge trail?"

"They're there?"

"Yeah. And dark magic is oozing from the place." Matthias folded his arms. His gaze roamed the office and beyond. "Where's the vampire?" The Alpha's eyes moved to Max.

"My brother's missing." He came around the desk and stood next to Eli.

Matthias's eyebrows rose. "Seriously?"

"Yeah. We think the coven took him." Eli mirrored the Alpha's movements.

He gave Eli a skeptical frown. "Why would they?"

"As you know they've been trying to pick us off one at a time. This could be their way of making sure our numbers are depleted. Archer being taken might be the first in a line of other abductions." Eli perched on the corner of the editor's desk.

"So what are you planning to do?"

"Find out where they've taken him and get him out."

"Do you think he'd be at that cabin?"

"No, I think they would've taken him to Remus."

The color drained from Matthias's face. "And you want to go charging in there to rescue a bloodsucker?" His sheepish gaze shot to Max again then back to Eli.

"He's a *friend*, Matthias. Of course I do." Eli stood up.

"You can count me out. I'm not risking my pack for the likes of him." The Alpha turned on his heel and headed for the door.

"You said you'd help," Eli called after him.

"With the battle. I'm not daft enough to raid Remus's residence and expect to get out alive. Good luck with that." He opened the door and stalked along the sidewalk to his four wheel drive.

Max folded his arms. "The guy's a jerk. He knows what's going on and chooses not to get involved."

"Matthias has his reasons for not wanting to confront Remus. His pack has managed to stay under the council's radar for years and he wanted to keep it that way. I honestly didn't expect he'd help us when I asked him and it wasn't until Paige talked to him that he changed his mind. So cut him some slack."

"Maybe you shouldn't. He's Alpha of a powerful pack of wolves and it's his duty to participate in every aspect of this war, even if it means storming the council's hideout."

"Look, I get where you're coming from. You want your brother back, and so do I, but we can't push people into doing what they won't do. Remus is Matthias's Achilles heel and there's nothing we can do to change that. He'll be there when we need him most. We have enough help and we'll make it work to get Archer back."

Max gave Eli a doubtful look. "I hope you're right."

THIRTY FOUR

Eli swung his gaze from the computer on his desk to the woman standing in his office. He crossed the room and snapped the blinds closed. "Can't you use the front door like any normal person? Why are you here?"

"I believe you've made your decision." She gave him a shrewd smirk. "You want to retrieve the talisman."

"Yes, I do." He sat on the corner of his desk and folded his arms. "You'll keep your word and help me get it out?"

"Of course I will. But there is one thing you need to know first." She stepped up to him.

"And what's that?"

"I cannot go into the shadow realm. You will have to do it."

"What?!" Eli bounced off his desk and frowned into Raven's eyes. "I thought you said you'd get it."

"Yes… I am sorry I misled you. Scarlet is the only one who knows the incantation to get into the realm so I have to use other means to get you in."

Eli's frown deepened. "And it's dangerous, right?"

"It is not without risk."

He sighed. "Perhaps this is your High Priestess's way of getting rid of me. Maybe she sent you? How do I know you won't trap me in there?"

"I want to be rid of Scarlet and I'll do anything to make that happen. You can trust me on that."

Eli gave another heavy sigh. What other choice did he have? "When?"

"I will be in touch. I have to work on a way to open the portal. It won't be easy."

"Ok. And one more thing, next time use the door like a normal person. You can't come popping in here whenever you feel like it. I have deputies working for me that know nothing of Moon Grove's supernatural undertones and I want to keep it that way."

Raven gave a nod. "Of course. As you wish." With that said she faded out.

Eli walked across, opened the blinds, and returned to his desk.

Taylor's gaze moved from Eli's office window to Rick. "I wonder why Eli closed the blinds. It's not like he had someone in there."

Rick shrugged it off. "He's allowed some privacy when he wants it, Tay. No harm in that."

"Yeah, I know. Of course he is. But there has been some strange stuff going on around here lately. Like those four we saw talking to him the other day. Something about them seemed off to me."

"Like I said, I think you're reading too much into it."

Taylor gave a frustrated huff. "I thought you were going to help me with this."

"Yeah, yeah, I am. But someone has to keep a logical head. We can't go making unsubstantiated assumptions that will land us in hot water."

"I guess." She turned her gaze back to her computer screen.

"Besides, what do we actually have right now?"

"That creature we saw for one thing."

"We don't even know what we saw. It could've been a wild dog or something."

"When *I* said *dog* you didn't think so."

"I know. But now that I've had time to process it... what else could it have been?"

"That's what we're going to find out. There is something wrong with this town. I can feel it."

Eli arrived at the church around nine o'clock to find everyone waiting inside. He'd called an emergency meeting to discuss a plan to rescue Archer. There had still been no word from the editor and that only made the abduction theory more plausible. Where else could he have gone?

Paige stood in front of the altar talking to Max. Everyone else, minus Matthias and his pack, were seated in the pews awaiting the sheriff's arrival. Paige stepped away from Archer's brother and addressed the group. "Everyone, everyone. Eli's here." She took a seat on the front pew, Max sitting beside her.

"Thanks. I called you here tonight because we have a situation. We believe Archer Hamilton has been abducted and could be imprisoned at one of the council's other residences in Bellehurst."

Daniel raised his hand. "Are you sure of that?"

"No. At this point it's a theory. We found his cell phone at the Tribune office and he hasn't made contact with his brother or anyone else by any other means."

Rosemarie wrung a handkerchief around her fingers. "But we don't know where Remus and his cohorts are."

Eli gave her a sheepish glance. "Actually, I do."

The hall fell silent.

He inhaled a deep breath and let it out. "When we had the mole situation I thought it best to keep the information on a need to know basis until we discovered the identity of the informant. I had planned to tell you all eventually."

Paige stood up, a questioning frown on her face. "You couldn't tell me?"

"I couldn't tell anyone at that point."

She gave him a disgruntled stare and sat down.

Eli knew he'd have to smooth things over with her once they had Archer back, but right now that had to wait. "Ok. We have no idea whether Remus has guards or other vampires with him and his cohorts so we'll be going in blind. Anyone who wants out should leave now."

A voice echoed down the nave. "But I do." Linda strutted down the aisle and walked up to Eli.

"Linda!" He stared into her honey colored eyes.

"I want to help you, Eli."

"Then start by telling us if Remus has Archer."

"He does. And he plans to kill him."

"When?"

"Soon. There's something else you should know."

"What's that?"

"Remus has your safe. Archer went out to your house to make sure no one else got their hands on it. The council has eyes and ears everywhere in this town as you know. Someone saw him with it and told Remus."

"How did Remus know?"

Linda gave him a furtive glance. "I told him." She raised defensive hands. "While I still worked for him, before Paige discovered the truth."

"How do we know we can trust you now? How do I know this isn't some kind of setup?"

She stepped up to him, tears welling in her eyes. "I'm so sorry for everything I've done. Remus tried to kill me but I managed to escape with the help of Alistair. He's on your side, as am I, Eli. Please give me a chance to redeem myself."

Eli's gaze moved to Paige. She nodded.

"All right. But if you do anything to jeopardize the pack again it will mean your life."

Linda nodded and a single tear slipped down her left cheek. "I understand." She looked across the chancel at Paige. "Thank you." Turning back to Eli she said, "There isn't much time. Remus knows Archer received information from Carmichael and once he extracts it from him Remus won't need him anymore."

"We need to move on this as fast as we can." Eli looked at Linda. "How long do you think Archer has?"

"A couple of days at best."

Eli knew Archer wouldn't hand over the information willingly and hoped his grandmother's spell would continue to protect his friend. Depending on the method Remus chose to obtain the information from him, the spell might not hold and Archer would die.

THIRTY FIVE

Clarissa and Ruby were in the cellar of the old woman's home working fanatically on the spell to repress the death stare the thirteen witches possessed. So far, all of their attempts had failed. Clarissa felt exasperated and couldn't concentrate any longer. She let out a frustrated huff. "I need a break." She turned and headed for the stairs.

Ruby's gaze followed her. "But, Clary, we need to finish this. Eli and the others are counting on us."

Clarissa spun on her heel. "You think I don't know that," she spat. The angry look on her face softened. "I'm sorry. I didn't mean to take it out on you. It's a difficult spell at best and it's one I've never attempted before."

"We all have to learn new tricks some time." Ruby gave Clarissa a thin smile and a shrug.

A smile spread across the older woman's face. "Yes, you're right. But, right now, I need a cup of tea and time to seek guidance from the cards."

"Ok. Why don't you let me make the tea while you go do that?"

"All right. I'll be in the living room." Clary climbed the steps, crossed the carpeted entry hall, and stepped into the room, while Ruby headed to the kitchen.

The younger witch fingered through a selection of teas in the overhead cupboard. "Ah, this one should do the trick." She took the packet of Dragonwell off the shelf and scooped three heaped spoonfuls into the china teapot, poured in the boiling water, and breathed in the aromatic fragrance. "I've made Dragonwell, Clary. It should help with inspiration," she called.

Clarissa appeared in the doorway. "I forgot I had that. Good choice."

Ruby sat two mugs on the table then carried the teapot over and the jar of organic honey.

Both women took their seats.

Ruby poured tea into both mugs and passed the honey to Clarissa.

"Thank you, dear. I do hope this helps because I'm fresh out of ideas. The spell is trickier than I thought it would be."

"I'm sure it will," she offered, stirring honey into her tea. "Even if we can reduce the intensity of the death stare it will be better than nothing."

Clarissa looked across at the young witch sitting opposite and frowned. "No, that's not good enough. Those witches need to learn their place in our supernatural society. They cannot think they can go around killing people willy-nilly and get away with it. I won't let them."

Ruby set her mug down on the table, reached across and took the old woman's hand. "They're dangerous, Clary. Don't forget that. They've been hurting the people we love already. If you antagonize them who knows what they'll do?"

"Their High Priestess already paid me a visit to warn me off…"

"That's exactly what I mean."

Clarissa let out an exasperated huff. "We must stop them. Somehow."

"And we will. But with caution."

The older woman sighed. "Why did Remus bring them here?"

"Because he wants total control over Moon Grove and Eli's determined not to give in to him. But at what cost?"

Clarissa's right eyebrow arched. "So you think we should give in?"

"No, no, that's not what I'm saying. I think that whatever we do, we need to do carefully so Remus doesn't hear of it."

"He has eyes and ears everywhere in this town, Ruby. He's bound to find out sooner or later." Clarissa sipped her tea.

"Better later rather than sooner. When we have everything in place."

A knock on the front door startled both women.

Clarissa glanced over her shoulder then turned to look at Ruby. "I wonder who that could be at this time of night."

Ruby shrugged and stood up, the twitching nerves in her stomach playing havoc with the tea she'd swallowed. "Maybe you shouldn't answer it."

Clarissa got up from her chair, the anxiety on her face disappearing. "It's all right, dear. I think it's Eli." She headed into the entry hall and called out, "Who is it?" before opening the door.

"Clary, it's me."

The older woman breathed a relieved sigh and glanced back at Ruby. "See, it's only Eli." She opened the front door. "What brings you here so late?"

He stepped aside to reveal Raven standing behind him.

Clarissa's warm, grandmotherly expression hardened. "Why have you brought her here?"

"We need your help."

"We?" Clarissa frowned at her grandson.

"Raven knows where the talisman is. It's in the shadow realm. She can't go in to get it and…"

"And she wants you to go in to retrieve it instead?"

"It's the only way to stop the coven… and Remus."

Clarissa's perceptive gaze studied the witch standing beside Eli. "And why would you want to help us?"

"I want to be free of Scarlet, so if helping you will accomplish that then I'm in."

Clarissa's eyes moved to her grandson. "You believe her?"

"I don't have a choice. There have been some new developments."

"What kind of developments?"

"Archer's been abducted. Remus has him and something that's far more dangerous to our town."

"That's definitely not good."

"No, it's not. Will the protection spell you placed on him hold?"

Clarissa pressed her fingers to her lips. Would it? "I – I hope so. It all depends on where he is."

"What do you mean?"

"Well... if he's in a basement for example the spell might not hold true. Being underground tends to diminish its potency."

"Then we need to get that talisman so we can counteract whatever Remus has planned and stop the coven as well."

"All right, but I'm not inviting her in." If she let the witch enter her home the protection spell she placed on it to keep the coven out would be weakened. "Wait there." Clarissa turned on her heel, took Ruby by the arm, and walked back into the kitchen. "I don't trust that witch... not in the slightest. She's up to something. But we do need to help Eli. Remus is deranged and anything he devises is going to destroy Moon Grove and the otherworldly residents who live here."

"What do you want me to do?"

"Help me create a spell to open the shadow realm's portal, but once it's open I'm going to make sure Raven goes in with Eli."

"How?"

"I have my methods." She gave the young woman a shrewd smile, turned around and headed back into the entry hall. "All right, we'll do what we can. I'll let you know when we're ready."

Archer came to lying on a table in a pitch black room. He ran his gaze around the dark space and allowed his nocturnal vision to widen, taking in his claustrophobic surroundings. He appeared to be in a small basement. But where? And how long had he been here? A slithering sensation curled through his solar plexus. Remus had sent his adherents to abduct him from his office and the council leader now had the book and accompanying artifacts from Eli's safe.

Panic washed over him as he realized the ramifications of what could happen and he tugged at his metal restraints. He had to get out of here, somehow, and warn Eli. Now that the vampire had those items the town and its supernatural residents were in serious danger. Who would Remus eliminate first? Archer knew the answer. He tugged and tugged to no avail. An anxious thought crossed his mind. *Will the protection spell keep me safe?* He hoped it would.

THIRTY SIX

Cooper sat across the station tapping his pen on the desk top while his serious stare focused on Rick. They were on late shift together. Having humans working as deputies in Moon Grove could be a dangerous business, and a risky one. He knew he'd been human once and he also knew what it meant to be loyal, now that he belonged to Eli's pack, and he wouldn't let anything jeopardize that.

Rick's frowning gaze moved from his computer screen to Cooper. "Would you mind? I'm trying to get some work done over here."

Cooper dropped the pen onto his desk, stood up, and crossed the room. "What are you doing?" He peered around the monitor then straightened up and folded his arms.

"Writing up some reports." Rick pushed his office chair away from the desk and stood up, mirroring his colleague's posture. "Why do you need to know?"

Cooper shrugged. "No reason."

"What's with you? Why do you have a problem with Taylor and me?"

"Because you don't belong here."

"Look, I get that you miss the people who died. I do. It's hard. I understand that. But you have to move on. The town needs a police presence and…"

"It has one."

"Well, it obviously isn't enough otherwise we wouldn't be here. Although I don't understand why that is when nothing ever happens in this town. Nothing worth reporting, anyhow." Rick plonked himself back into his chair with a sigh.

Cooper gave him a derisive smirk. "You think so, huh? You don't know the half of it."

Rick's eyes darted to him. "You've said that before. What do you mean?"

The deputy let out a humorless chuckle. "If I told you I'd have to kill you."

"That's a dick move, Cooper. Don't say something and then not follow through."

"You think? If you knew what went on in this town you'd be on the first bus outta here." He hoped he'd scare the crap out of Rick and both deputies would consider leaving. More for his and Taylor's sake before something happened to them that couldn't be undone. He didn't particularly like them, well, not Rick anyhow, but he wouldn't want to see anything happen to either of them. It wouldn't be fair, considering they had no idea what they'd walked into.

Rick sprang from his chair. "Why don't you just spit it out and get it over with? Tell me what you're hinting at instead of playing cryptic crosswords with me."

"Let me ask you a question. Have either of you seen anything unusual?"

"No, why?" The night he and Taylor had encountered that animal on the street popped into his head. But they had made a pact not to say anything until they had some proof.

"You answered that way too fast."

"What? So now there's a time limit on how fast or slow I answer your dumbass questions?"

"Tell me."

"There's nothing to tell."

"I don't believe you."

"Go to hell, Cooper. You're not my boss." Rick returned to what he'd been doing before Cooper's interruption.

"I'm trying to help you."

"Sure you are. You want us out of here. That's all."

Cooper crossed the office and took his seat. "Don't say I didn't offer."

Rick glared at him. "Offer? You haven't offered anything. If you had one shred of care factor for Taylor and me you'd tell me what it is you're hinting at."

Cooper ran Rick's comment around his Lycan brain for a moment then said, "If you want to be honest with me maybe I'll let you into the secret of Moon Grove."

Rick's eyes narrowed. "And why would I do that?"

"Because it might save your life." Cooper leaned back in his office chair and folded his arms. "You have no idea what lies beneath this town."

Rick remembered the pact he'd made with Taylor. She'd be pretty ticked if he broke his word, but he wanted to know what Cooper knew. "What if I give you something then you give me something?"

Cooper leaned forward, resting an elbow on his desk, and smirked at Rick. "All right. Whenever you're ready."

Rick didn't like the smug look on Cooper's face, it riled him. "Forget it. I think you're just trying to rattle me… and Taylor."

Cooper shrugged. "Believe what you like. But don't come crying to me when something happens. I tried to warn you."

THIRTY SEVEN

Paige was at the kitchen sink when Eli came into the room. She'd already prepared breakfast and wanted to wash up the utensils before sitting down to eat. She glanced over her shoulder. "Morning, breakfast is ready. Would you mind pouring the coffee while I finish this?"

"Sure." Eli crossed the kitchen to the coffee maker and poured two mugs of steaming black coffee then set them down on the table and took a seat.

"You got in late last night," Paige said, sitting opposite him.

"Yeah, I know. Sorry I woke you." He took a cautious sip of his coffee.

"That's ok. So what happened?" Paige picked up a piece of toast and spread lashings of butter across it. She loved buttered toast: her only indulgence, well, apart from Rosemarie's cookies.

"Clary's going to work on a way to get me into the shadow realm. She said she'll call once she and Ruby have figured it out."

Paige gave Eli a concerned frown. "I wish you wouldn't go. Anything could happen to you in there."

Eli reached across the table and took her hand in his. "I'll be careful. Promise."

"You can't make that kind of promise. We have no idea what that place is like. It could be fraught with danger. Why doesn't Raven want to go? Have you asked yourself that question? What's she hiding?"

"She told me she can't enter the shadow realm. Scarlet has an incantation in place that prevents other witches from going in."

"And you believe her? She's a witch, Eli. One that came here to kill us." She eased her hand out of his and picked up her knife and fork. "I wish you'd reconsider."

"We're running out of time, Paige. We need the talisman now that Remus has the book and artifacts. It's the only way to stop him and the coven from destroying our town. And it might also be the only way to get Archer back."

Paige let out a heavy sigh. "I know that, but…"

"There are no buts. We have to do it now before all hell breaks loose in Moon Grove." He reached across and once again took her hand in his. "You trust me, don't you?"

"You know I do."

"Then let me do what needs to be done to protect us." He stood up, walked around the table, pulled Paige into his arms and kissed her gently. "I promise you I won't let anything happen to me."

A knock echoed into the entry hall startling the pair and their gazes moved toward the sound.

"I wonder who that could be," Paige said, easing herself out of Eli's embrace. She glanced at the wall clock on her way to the front door. 6:57 AM. *A bit early for visitors*.

"Wait. Let me open it." Eli brushed past Paige and reached for the handle.

Paige's brother, Brent, stood on the welcome mat. "Hey, I wasn't sure you guys would be here."

"Come on in," Eli moved aside and Brent stepped into the entry hall.

"Hi, sis."

"Hey, yourself. Want some breakfast?"

Brent stuffed his hands into the pockets of his hoodie and gave his sister a mischievous grin. "Sure, seeing as you're offering."

The three headed into the kitchen.

"Why the early visit?" Eli asked, taking his seat.

"Oh, yeah. Mom had to go outta town for a couple days. She said she knows someone who might be able to help us."

"Do you want to stay here while she's away?" Paige scooped scrambled eggs and bacon onto a plate, brought it over to the table and set it down in front of her brother.

"Thanks for the offer but I'll be ok. I'm a werewolf, remember?" He gave her a cheeky wink.

"Nonetheless, a lot of dangerous things are taking place here and no one knows who'll be next. If you're on your own you're an easy target."

"I appreciate the concern, sis, but I'll be fine. I can take care of myself. And, besides, I don't wanna cramp your style."

"You wouldn't be," Eli offered. "If you want to come and stay you're more than welcome."

"Thanks. But I like my own space." He gave Paige a sheepish glance then picked up his cutlery and dug in. "Mm, this is great."

"Do you know who your mom went to see?" The cop in Eli wanted to know.

"She didn't mention it. She said someone who might be able to help."

"Someone supernatural, you mean?"

Brent shrugged. "Well, yeah, I guess so."

Eli leaned back against his chair and folded his arms. Had Abbey done a runner like before? Or could her trip be legit? "Stay safe out there, ok?"

"Like I said, you don't have to worry. I'll be fine."

Eli wasn't so sure. As Paige had said anyone alone would be an easy target. Look at what happened to Archer. "You're part of our pack now so I'll always be concerned for your safety."

"I know, and thanks. The other reason I came by... I wanted to ask when we're going to get Archer."

"I'm waiting on some information and then we'll go."

Brent frowned. "What kind of information?"

Eli didn't want to get into the whole talisman situation with Brent. "I may have found a way to deal with Remus and the coven at the same time. If that's the case, we'll go get Archer as soon as I have what I need."

"How do we know they haven't... you know... already?" He didn't want to say the word *killed*. He knew Eli and the editor were friends.

"Linda said Remus is trying to extract the book's information from him and he won't kill him until he gets what he wants. So we have a small window of time. And if

210

I know him at all, Archer won't hand over the information willingly."

Eli pulled the Jeep into the curb, leaned across and kissed Paige before she climbed out. "Have a good day, sweetheart. I'll pick you up around six."

"Thanks. You too. I'll see you tonight." She gave him a smile, closed the door and crossed the sidewalk, giving him a wave as he drove away.

The door opened before she reached it. "Oh, good morning, Rosy."

"Morning, Darlin'," she greeted, stepping aside to allow Paige to enter the office.

"Any new appointments today?" Paige crossed the comfortable space and headed to her consultation room. Rosemarie followed.

"No. Not a one. I'm starting to worry. If we don't have clients the business isn't going to do well."

"It's only been recently, Rosy, and I think it's the current in the air that's keeping people away. The supernatural ones, at least." She set her purse down on her desk, shrugged out of her burgundy coat and hung it on the coat rail behind the door. "Once we get this whole mess sorted, and I know we will (although she wasn't as certain as she'd like to be), I'm sure business will pick up. People are scared... and with good reason."

"It's a frightening time, what with the coven and Remus attacking from both sides."

Paige walked over to Rosemarie and rubbed her arm. "Yes, it is. The sooner we can get this situation under control the better." She gave a thin smile. "Would you mind making some coffee?"

"Already done. I'll go get you a cup. I also brought in some homemade oatmeal cookies to go with it."

Paige patted her flat stomach. "If I keep eating like this I'll gain ten pounds overnight."

Rosemarie chuckled. "Never. You're so petite I doubt a couple of cookies will do anything to your figure." With that said she disappeared out the door.

The buzzer went off in the office. Someone had come in. Paige set her phone down on her desk and headed along the hallway. "What are you doing here?"

Linda stepped up to the reception desk. "I know how to get Archer out of Remus's clutches."

"Eli's already working on it." Paige couldn't help feel the heat of betrayal wash over her. Linda had fooled them all. And even though Paige had nodded to Eli to give the woman another chance there would always be some doubt. "Why don't you tell him your idea?"

"Because if we don't do something now Remus *will* end him. It's only a matter of time. Time your friend doesn't have."

A flicker of anxiety curled through Paige. She couldn't let anything happen to Archer. "What's your plan?"

Rosemarie heard the door close as she set the coffee and cookies down on Paige's desk. She walked along the short hallway and stepped into an empty office, her gaze moving through the window to the street. Paige had gotten into a car with Linda. Where were they going and why hadn't Paige said anything to her before leaving?

The musical tone of Paige's cell startled the receptionist. She turned on her heel, marched into the consultation room, snatched the phone off the desk and stared at the screen. Eli. A queasy feeling of apprehension curled its way through Rosemarie's belly – Paige had forgotten to take her phone with her. *That's not good.* "Hello, Eli."

"Oh. Hi, Rosy. Is Paige around?" Rosemarie's voice on the line surprised him.

"Uh, no, she's not right now." The receptionist didn't know whether to tell Eli Paige had gone off with Linda or not.

"Where is she?"

"I'm not sure."

Eli could sense something in Rosemarie's tone. "What's going on, Rosy?"

"Nothing. Well, at least I don't think there is."

"Where's Paige?" he asked again. "And why did she leave her phone?"

"I don't know. All I know is I heard the door close and when I came into the office Paige was leaving in a car with Linda."

Eli straightened in his chair. "And Paige didn't tell you where they were going? She didn't leave a note or anything?"

"I don't think so." Rosemarie walked back into the office to check the desk. Nothing. "When I heard her phone it bothered me right away because we have no way of contacting her."

"How long have they been gone?" Eli headed out of the station. "Cooper, hold the fort."

"Maybe five minutes.

"Which way were they heading?"
"Toward the highway."
"Thanks, Rosy. I'm on it."

THIRTY EIGHT

Abbey stood on the sidewalk of the small, rural township and ran her gaze around the faces of people waiting for passengers to step off the bus. He wasn't among them. *Where could he be?* He'd given his word he'd be there to meet her when she arrived. Her anxious thoughts were interrupted by the bus driver. "Hey, lady, are ya gonna get your bags or what? I'm on a tight schedule." He tapped the watch on his wrist and gave her a frustrated grimace.

Her eyes moved to him. "Oh, sorry, I'm looking for my ride." She walked over, tugged the duffle bag off the ground and slung it over her left shoulder. "Thanks."

"Yeah, yeah." The driver slammed down the luggage compartment doors and climbed back into the bus, the vehicle hissing as it pulled away from the curb.

Abbey gazed up and down the busy road. Why hadn't he kept his word? She gave a heavy sigh as she spotted a café across the street. She'd find a quiet corner, order a coffee, and give his cell a call. Maybe he'd been delayed. But, then, why hadn't he contacted her?

She pushed open the door and the warmth and delicious food aromas of the café wrapped itself around her. She wheeled her suitcase along to a booth at the end of the store and took a seat, picking up the menu and perusing the selection. A waitress came over to her table.

"What can I get for you?" She offered a pleasant smile.

"Coffee. And a serving of bacon and eggs. Over easy, thanks."

"Toast with that?"

"Yes, thanks."

"Sure. Won't be too long." The young woman tore the note paper off the pad, walked behind the counter and punched it onto a spike sitting on the server. "Bacon and eggs over easy. Toast on the side."

Abbey tugged her phone from the pocket of her jacket and keyed in his number. She made a mental note of it rather than adding it to her address book. Safer that way. When the call connected a phone went off in the café. *Could it be him?* Her eyes roamed the other booths and tables in the cramped space.

A tall, slim, dark-haired man, dressed in black, sidled out of a booth two tables down, turned around and headed toward her. Eldridge Crane. She recognized him immediately.

Abbey watched him as he came closer, his pale blue eyes reaching into the depths of her Lycan soul. A handsome figure of a man with dark, wavy short hair and chiseled jaw, he stood at six feet and had a certain air of worldly sophistication to him.

He made a gesture toward the vacant seat opposite her. "May I?"

Abbey nodded. "Yes, of course. Please."

"You said you needed my help. That it's a matter of life and death. Would you care to elaborate now you're here?"

"You know of Moon Grove and of Remus?"

He gave one sharp nod, the expression on his face changing to one of awareness.

"He has brought the Coven of the Full Moon to our town and…"

Eldridge raised a hand motioning for her to stop speaking. "What do you think I can do against such dark forces?"

"I've heard things. And from what I've been told, you are the most powerful warlock on the planet. Surely you wouldn't want innocents to die because Remus has lost his mind?"

"Remus may be many things, Ms. O'Connell, but mad is not one of them. Devious, yes. Cunning, most definitely… but never mad."

"Will you come with me and help Eli Blackwood rid the town of Remus's hold over it?"

He inhaled a deep breath through his nostrils and let it out slowly. "If I were to do as you request what's in it for me?"

Abbey's eyes widened. She never dreamed he would expect anything in return. "The satisfaction of knowing you saved Moon Grove from the demented clutches of a maniac. Isn't that reward enough?"

A thin smile spread across his handsome face. "Very good, Ms. O'Connell. I see you've done your homework."

"You mean you were testing me? What if I *had* offered you money or something more?"

"Had that been the case, I would have declined."

"So you're coming with me?"

"Of course. I'm up for a good witch fight."

THIRTY NINE

The town seemed different during daylight hours: picturesque, quaint, pretty, were words that came to Taylor's mind as she gazed out of the passenger window of the patrol Jeep. Moon Grove had a bygone era charm to it and, even though she wasn't at an age to remember that time period, she could appreciate the old world beauty of the place. She remembered what Cooper had said. They had no idea what lay beneath the rural township. A shiver ran the length of Taylor's spine and her thoughts wandered back to the night she and Rick had encountered that animal whipping across the road in front of their car. What had it been and where did it go? Would they see it again? She wasn't sure she wanted to see it again even though they were doing some investigating of their own.

Rick gave her a sideward glance. "You ok?"

Taylor let out a huge sigh. "Why does the town seem so unassuming during the day and so ominous at night?"

He chuckled. "Everywhere seems more ominous at night, Tay. It's the nature of the beast. Nighttime is scary."

"Yeah, I know but…"

"But what?"

"Cooper's words keep popping into my head."

"Like I said, he's just trying to push our buttons. He doesn't want us here and if he can scare us away all the better for him."

"I get that, but there's something else. I've felt it."

"Look, we'll do some surreptitious digging around and see if we can come up with anything. That's all we can do. If we find something, great, if not…" He shrugged.

Rick pulled the Jeep into the curb. "Let's grab some lunch at the Inn while we're in town. Might as well, it's on the house."

"Sure, why not."

He picked up the radio mic and pressed the button. "Eli, you there?"

"Yes, go ahead."

"Taylor and I are taking our lunch break."

"Copy that."

When the pair reached the front door it swung open and the four strangers Taylor and Rick had seen at the station house were in the open doorway. Taylor's eyes widened when she spotted the group, but they didn't pay any attention to either of them and continued on their way out the door.

"What do you make of that?" Taylor asked.

Rick shrugged. "What do you mean?"

"They didn't acknowledge us."

"Why should they? We didn't talk to them at the station."

"I know but seeing as we work with Eli…"

Rick held the door open. "I still think you're making too much out of it." He waited for her to step into the Inn but she didn't.

"I'm not. There's something about them I can't put my finger on. But I will eventually. That's a promise."

"Are we going in?"

Taylor glanced over her shoulder at the four climbing into the dark gray van. "No, let's follow them and see where they go."

"Come on, Tay, let's eat first. I'm starved."

Taylor's gaze moved to him. "This is our chance to see what they're up to." She glowered at him and folded her arms. "You said you'd help."

"And I will. Not at lunch time though. We need to keep up our strength, you know."

She let out a frustrated huff and held out her hand. "If you won't come with me I'll go alone. Give me the patrol keys."

Rick frowned into her eyes. "No. You can't go running off on your own. It could be dangerous."

"Well, it's obvious your stomach is more important than my safety so give me the keys." She wriggled her fingers at him.

Rick gave a heavy sigh. "All right, I'll come with you. But after we check them out we're coming back for lunch. Deal?"

"Deal." Taylor gave him a satisfied smile.

The pair raced down the path and climbed into the Jeep. The others had a minute head start and they'd have to catch up to them. Rick pulled the patrol out onto the main road and headed in the direction the group had taken.

"There they are." Taylor pointed through the windshield. "They're turning the corner up there."

"I can see, you know." Rick waited a couple seconds then swung the Jeep around the corner. "I wonder where they're going."

"They're heading for the church." Taylor's heartbeat ticked up a notch. "Why would they go up there?"

"Good question." Rick pushed the gas pedal down, turned onto the steep, narrow road, and made sure to keep some distance between the Jeep and the van. He stopped on the right-hand shoulder.

"What are you doing?" Taylor asked.

"Giving them a couple minutes to get out and go inside. We don't want to be seen, do we?"

"No, but we need to get up there to see who else is at the church."

Rick's right eyebrow arched as he stared into Taylor's eyes. She had a point. "Ok." Dirt sprayed from the back tires as he jerked the Jeep onto the road. "It's too open up there. If they're waiting outside they're going to see us."

"It's a chance we'll have to take."

When the Patrol came over the rise, the pair spotted the four being ushered inside by a young guy.

"Hey, isn't that Paige's brother? What's his name? Brent?" Taylor pointed at the group entering the church, then whipped her phone out of her shirt pocket and snapped a couple of photos.

Rick eased his foot onto the brake and stopped the four wheel drive in the center of the narrow road. "Yeah, you're right."

"Why would he be up here with them?"

Rick shrugged. "Maybe they wanted to pray or something."

"That may be, but why would Brent be letting them into the church? It's not like he's a minister or anything.

"Yeah, that does seem strange."

When the front doors closed, Rick continued along the drive and parked out of sight at the far left back corner of the tall, white steepled structure. "Let's take a look around."

Taylor climbed out of the Jeep and followed Rick along the side of the church.

When he came to the first side door he tugged on the brass handle. Locked. He and Taylor moved to the second door. Also locked. He turned to her. "This makes no sense."

"I know, right?"

"Let's go round the front and try those doors." Rick took a determined step toward the front of the church.

Taylor grabbed his arm. "Wait. What happens if the doors are unlocked? We can't go inside."

Rick frowned at her. "Why not?"

"Because we don't want Brent and the others to know we've seen them. We need to get something solid first."

Rick let out a sigh. "So what do we do now?"

"We keep a record of this – date, time, location, who's here."

"And then what?"

"We create a file."

"You know, so far we've got nothing. Like I said, maybe those guys came up here to offer worship."

Taylor gave him a skeptical frown. "You think so?"

"I don't know what to think. This really doesn't give us anything. We have no idea what they're doing here."

"Not yet. But, eventually, our digging will turn up something. I guarantee it."

FORTY

The lock snapped back on the solid wood door, the metallic click echoing around the rocky walls. Archer's gut wound itself as tight as a piano string. He widened his nocturnal vision to see the person entering. When the door swung outward and Paige rushed inside he thought he was dreaming. "Paige? Is it really you?"

"Yes, it's me."

Linda followed her into the pitch black space and pulled the door closed so that nothing looked out of place if someone came to check on their captive.

"What are you doing here?" Archer still thought he might be hallucinating.

"We came to rescue you." Paige held up her cell phone flash light to examine the restraints on his wrists and ankles. Solid steel similar to police issue handcuffs, but much stronger.

"How did you get in here?"

Paige glanced beside her. "Linda."

"Wait. How did Linda get you in? Isn't anyone upstairs?"

She shook her head.

"I've been here alone the whole time?"

"Yes." Paige wrestled with the cuffs on his wrists.

"Does Linda have the keys for these?"

"No. We'll have to improvise." Linda came around the other side of the table.

"How do you know someone won't come back?" Archer had a foreboding feeling.

"We don't, but Remus and the others are in Bellehurst. It's possible they could have someone checking on you but I haven't seen anyone so far." Linda used her Lycan strength in an attempt to fracture the shackles holding him down. They wouldn't budge.

"You've been watching the place? Where am I?"

"Yes, I have," Linda replied. "Can't be too careful. And to answer your second question you're at the mansion."

Archer realized Remus had planned to leave him here to starve to death, not interrogate him about the ancient book and information Carmichael had sent.

Paige moved around the table to Linda. "How are we going to get these off?"

"I have an idea." Linda crossed the room to the door. "I won't be long."

Paige swung around, her anxious eyes meeting Linda's. "You're…"

"Yes, I'm coming back." She opened the door and stepped into the corridor.

"Does Eli know you're here?" Archer asked.

"No, I didn't want to worry him. And, besides, I am capable of doing some things on my own."

"I never doubted it for a second." He gave her a grateful smile.

"Good." She smiled back. "I'm so glad you're ok. I thought Remus planned to interrogate you for information about the book."

"I don't think so. I think he planned to leave me here."

"But why? He brought you here because you had the book and artifacts."

"Then perhaps he's biding his time... because the coven's in town."

"Or he already knows how to use them."

"That's a worrying thought. Let's hope not."

The door creaked open and Linda stepped into the room, followed by Eli.

Paige gave a small gasp. "How did you know we were here?"

"I called your cell and Rosemarie answered. She told me you'd left with Linda."

"And you followed us over here?"

"Of course I did. I wouldn't risk you being in a dangerous situation alone."

Paige wasn't sure whether or not she should be annoyed or pleased. She chose the latter, knowing her safety meant everything to him meant so much to her.

Linda folded her arms. "So you thought I brought Paige here to trap her, is that it?"

"Right now, I'm working on the trust issue. You're actions haven't given me any other option so far."

Linda couldn't argue with that. "I guess that's fair. But I am doing my best to redeem myself. You can trust that."

Eli crossed the room to Archer. "Let me get a look at those." He checked the restraints, then tugged a small wad of keys from his pants pocket and fingered through them.

Pushing one into the lock of the wrist cuff, he twisted it and the metal catch snapped open.

"How'd you do that?" Paige asked.

"Most handcuff keys are universal." He unlocked the second cuff on Archer's wrist then moved to the editor's ankles. "Although, these ones are different."

Linda held up a blow torch. "That's why I went to get this."

As the sun slid into the distant crimson horizon on the outskirts of Moon Grove, Scarlet stopped in the center of the main street and ran her gaze over the stores and businesses lining the quaint shopping hub. It would be easy for her to cast a spell and suspend everyone in the town, including Eli Blackwood and his wolves, but what would be the fun in that? The coven had been summoned here to eliminate the supernatural inhabitants Remus believed undermined his authority, and that is what they would do just as they had done in many other towns similar to this one all over the world. It would not be much of a battle because she and her sisters possessed the upper hand. They were, after all, powerful black magic practitioners.

She wandered along the sidewalk, taking in everything and anyone around her. The pedestrian traffic appeared sparse. Could it be due to the noticeable dark current in the air? A thought crossed her witch mind, *What if I suspend the human residents of the town for one night? What would happen then? All hell could break loose and they'd be none-the-wiser.* The idea caused a devious smile to spread across her pretty face. Should she? Perhaps the battle would be over sooner than expected if she did.

Eli spotted the unknown woman walking past the Tribune office window. *Is that Scarlet Balfour?* From what his grandmother had described, she could very well be. Tugging his cell phone from the pocket of his shirt, he left Paige with Archer and stepped out onto the street to follow the woman, hoping to get a photo of her he could run through the justice system database. When she stopped outside the Inn and glanced back over her shoulder, he ducked into the flower shop alcove. Her wary gaze remained on the store for a few moments, then she turned around and continued along the sidewalk to a silver Chevrolet Express van. As she turned her head in his direction to check the road for traffic, before stepping off the curb, Eli snapped a couple of pictures of her and one of the vehicle license plate. He'd upload them into the system as soon as he got home.

Paige set a mug of coffee down in front of Eli and took a cautious sip of her own as she watched him load the information into the police database. When the photo of the woman Eli had followed appeared on the screen Paige gasped.

Eli's eyes moved from the laptop to her. "What's wrong?"

Paige sat her coffee mug on the table, turned and headed down the hallway. "I'll be right back."

While he waited for Paige to return, Eli finished loading the photos of the woman and the license plate number into the system in the hope something would pop up.

Paige came back into the living room with one of the books she'd been researching. "Here, take a look at this." She passed the heavy, open volume to him and pointed to a painted portrait above a couple of paragraphs. "Isn't that her?"

Eli ran his gaze over the face of the woman in the picture. Although the painting would be hundreds of years old there could be no mistake. The solemn gaze of Scarlet Balfour stared back at him from the page. His eyes moved to the information below the portrait. "It says she lived in Scotland and was tried for being a witch in 1594. They tortured her to get a forced confession then executed her not long after."

"Executed?" The hairs on the back of Paige's neck stood static.

Eli looked up at her. "That's what it says."

"Then how is she alive?"

He closed the book and sat it on the table. "Witchcraft, obviously."

A shiver ran the length of Paige's body. "She's more powerful than we realized."

"It would appear so. I'll talk to Clary in the morning and see what she can tell me about witches returning from the dead. I also need to find out how the incantation is going to get me into the shadow realm."

Paige stepped up behind his chair, leaned in and wrapped her arms around his neck. "I still wish you wouldn't go. It's far too dangerous going in there without backup of some kind."

"I understand your concern, sweetheart, but I don't have a choice." He eased her around the chair and sat her on his knee.

"What if it's a trap? What if Raven is working with Scarlet to get you out of the way?"

"I'm not putting any trust in Raven's promise to help. I'm not that foolish. You have to trust *me* on this."

"I do, but…"

"We're running out of time, Paige. I have to go in to retrieve the talisman. Without it, Moon Grove is at the mercy of Remus and the coven. And we can't let them win."

FORTY ONE

The sleek black sedan cruised along the deserted main street of Moon Grove, the occupants heading in the direction of Paige O'Connell's house. The stillness of the town had an eerie feel to it at midnight, as though the darkness hidden beneath it had somehow acquired a means of seeping into the atmosphere during the witching hour.

Although supernatural creatures themselves, a shiver of apprehension poured over the passenger, causing a rash of goosebumps to spread across her skin. The sinister secrets of the town ran deep, giving it a murky aura obvious only to the otherworldly inhabitants.

The car pulled into the driveway of the double story, gray and white timber clad home and the driver turned off the engine and headlights. "Should we wake them?" he asked.

"Yes, time is of the essence," his passenger said.

The pair left the vehicle, walked up the path and onto the front porch.

"You're sure this cannot wait until morning?"

She shook her head. "No, it can't." She raised her hand and knocked.

No movement inside, as far as they could tell.

"Perhaps they're not here."

"They're here." She knocked again, louder this time. "Paige, it's me."

An interior light flashed on, the amber glow radiating through the glass side panels and curtained door.

The door opened. "Mom? What are you doing here at this hour?" Paige asked.

"I've brought someone with me that can help us." Abbey motioned to her companion. "This is Eldridge Crane the most powerful warlock on the planet."

Eli moved to the open doorway. "Come in."

"Thanks." Abbey stepped into the entry hall followed by Eldridge.

Paige yawned. "This couldn't have waited till morning?"

"We just got back and I thought we should come right over. I didn't want either of you getting the wrong idea about why I left." Abbey shrugged out of her jacket and hung it on the coat rack beside the front door. "Did Brent come and see you?"

"Yes, he did," Eli replied.

"Let me make some coffee." Paige headed to the kitchen, Eli, Abbey, and Eldridge following her.

"Have a seat," Eli offered.

"Thank you," Eldridge said, with a tilt of his head.

Abbey sat on the other side of the table next to him and Eli took his usual seat, raising his fist to his mouth to stifle a yawn. "We appreciate you coming here, Mr. Crane."

"Please, call me Eldridge. After what Abbey has relayed to me it would have been remiss of me not to come. There is no doubt you need my help against Scarlet Balfour and her coven."

"You've had dealings with her before?" Eli leaned back on his chair and folded his arms.

"Not directly, no. But I know others who have."

Paige brought the mugs of coffee over to the table and set them down in the center. "Help yourself." She took a seat next to Eli.

"We believe they have the power to kill with a look. Do you know if that's fact?"

"It is true."

"My grandmother and her assistant have been working on a spell to counter that ability. So far it has been unsuccessful."

"She won't need to. I will sort it out." Eldridge reached over and slid a mug of coffee across the table toward him. "You've been approached by one of the witches?"

"How did you…?"

"She offered up the talisman?"

"Yes, but…"

"Just go with it," Abbey told him. "Eldridge is incredibly knowledgeable and powerful. Tell him what he needs to know."

Eli's gaze moved from the warlock to her. "I want to know more about your companion before I put total trust in his abilities."

"And rightly so." Eldridge took a sip of his coffee. "What can I tell you?"

"How do you two know each other?"

"We didn't until Abbey contacted me."

"That seems odd to me. Why would you want to help someone you don't know?" Eli's frowning gaze remained on Eldridge.

"I practice safe magic, most of the time, but I have the ability to use dark magic even though I choose not to. I've been in similar situations to this before and word has traveled through the circles of magic. I don't hide from the supernatural world. I can be found quite easily, if you know the right people to ask. That's how Abbey came to find me."

"So you're going to use dark magic to help us win the fight against the coven and Remus?" Eli straightened on his chair.

"If need be, yes. Does that bother you, Eli Blackwood?"

"It depends."

"On what, exactly?"

"On whether or not you're here for the right reasons."

"I can assure you I am."

"Eli, what are you doing?" Abbey asked, a disgruntled frown crossing her face.

"I'm doing what's necessary to keep the people I care about and the town safe."

Eldridge raised his hand. "It's fine, Abbey. I'm happy to tell the sheriff whatever he wants to know."

"Do you know Remus?"

"I know of him, yes. I know he's a dangerous psychopathic vampire who will stop at nothing to acquire what he wants. And, from what I've learned, he wants you dead, along with anyone else that stands in his way."

Eli had a gut feeling Eldridge Crane had come to Moon Grove for other reasons and he would need to find out what they were. "So how do you plan to help us defeat him?"

"Before we get to that, I want to ask you something."

"What's that?"

"Do you still want to go into the shadow realm to retrieve the talisman?"

"Do I need to now you're here?"

"It forms a protective barrier around Scarlet and the coven. If we had it in our possession we would most assuredly win the battle."

Eli's wary gaze studied the warlock's face for a moment. *Could the talisman be the reason why he's here? Could there be more to it than being a protective device for the coven?* "Can you get me in?"

"I can do better than that. I'll accompany you."

FORTY TWO

When Ruby stepped out of Clarissa's house she crumpled onto the front porch, her twisted body writhing in agony. Scarlet stood on the lawn, left hand raised, with a smile of satisfaction. Clarissa rushed to the door, the look of anguish on her wrinkled face, but didn't dare step across the threshold. If she did, Scarlet would surely kill her. "Stop!" she shouted. "Ruby has no quarrel with you or you with her. Let her go."

Scarlet's dark gaze moved to the old woman. "Ah, but she does. She has been helping you perfect a spell to inhibit our abilities. That makes her an enemy of the coven as well."

Clarissa's eyes darted from the High Priestess to her agonized apprentice then back to the witch. "Please, don't do this."

"If you step outside the confines of your place of protection I will stop."

Clarissa's anxious mind tried to think of a way to prevent her own death. What could she do? Her gaze moved across the street to Paige's house. A light shone through the window. Could she infiltrate Paige's thoughts and let her know she needed help?

A shrill scream escaped Ruby's lips and, before Clarissa could initiate her telepathic ability, Paige's front door flew open and Eli and a man she recognized as Eldridge Crane raced across the road.

Eldridge thrust out his left hand, a spray of black particles showering the witch as he called out, "Obligaverit potestates," to bind Scarlet's powers. The spell wouldn't hold indefinitely, only long enough for them all to get into Clarissa's house and secure their safety.

Scarlet stood rigid on the spot.

"Get inside, quickly," Eldridge commanded.

Eli scooped Ruby up into his arms, pushed past his grandmother and set the young woman down in an armchair. Eldridge whipped the front door closed, chanting an incantation, before he turned and gave Clarissa a discerning stare. "You were right not to set foot outside. Scarlet would have ended your life if you had."

"Thank you for coming to our rescue, Eldridge."

"It is my pleasure, madam."

Clarissa rushed into the living room to check on Ruby. "I'm so sorry, hon, I…"

Ruby's grimace subsided. "It's ok, Clary. I understand. We can't afford to lose you. I'm expendable."

"No! No, you're not. I planned to let Paige know using telepathy but before I could…"

"We heard the scream," Eli told Ruby.

"I'm grateful. Thank you."

"Can I get you anything?" Clarissa asked her.

Ruby reached out and took the old woman's hand. "No, thanks, I'll be ok in a few minutes."

Eldridge peered through the curtained front door. "It appears the witch has gone."

Eli stepped into the entry hall, opened the door and checked outside. "Good. But I'm sure it won't be the last time she tries something like this."

"Undoubtedly." Eldridge's astute gaze met Eli's. "Now the coven knows I am here they will be far more cautious. Underhanded is a word that comes to mind. You will all need to be on your guard."

A knock echoed into the hallway and everyone's gaze moved toward the sound.

"It's me," Paige called through the door.

Eli opened it. "Come in."

Paige and Abbey entered the house. "So that's Scarlet Balfour?" Abbey asked.

"Yes. She is a very powerful witch. It is fortunate that I am more powerful otherwise Ruby," he said, turning his gaze toward the young woman sitting in the armchair, "might not be with us now."

Another knock on the front door caused everyone to swing around.

"Who could that be?" Paige asked.

"Let me get it," Eldridge offered.

"Why?" Eli frowned into the warlock's eyes.

"Because it may very well be trouble."

Eli followed him over to the door.

Raven stood on the porch. When she saw Eldridge her eyes grew wide.

"What are you doing here at this time of night?" Eli asked, his frowning gaze meeting her shocked one.

"I – I came to find out if your grandmother has found a

way into the… into the shadow realm. We need to move quickly."

Eldridge spoke up. "There is no need. I will accompany the sheriff into the realm."

Raven's eyes widened even more. "You – you can get him in?"

"Yes. I can." He gave her a shrewd smirk knowing she would wonder how he would do it.

Her eyes moved to Eli. "Then our arrangement is null and void? You won't be helping me with my problem?"

Eli opened his mouth to speak but Eldridge answered her question instead. "If you mean eliminating Scarlet from the equation – I may be able to help you with that task."

"You can?"

"Possibly. We will discuss it when Eli and I return."

Eli watched the interaction between the witch and the warlock. Her reaction to Eldridge struck Eli as odd. She seemed afraid of him. Could there be a reason for that?

Raven's gaze returned to the sheriff. "I release you from our agreement." With that said, the witch disappeared before their eyes.

"Well, I am glad that is sorted," Eldridge said, closing the front door.

"You're going to kill Scarlet Balfour?" Eli's frowning gaze remained on the warlock.

"Yes. Without her the coven is defunct. Isn't that what you want?"

"What I want is to defuse the situation with the least amount of deaths."

"But did you not agree to dispatch Scarlet in order to get into the shadow realm?"

"I didn't actually say I would, I only allowed Raven to think I would. There's a difference."

"Deception is a dangerous affair. Be careful who you make promises to. With war comes death, Eli Blackwood. You should be well aware of that fact." Eldridge turned on his heel and walked back into the living room.

Eli's eyes followed him. There was more to Eldridge Crane than what he had shared with them. Could being a self-confessed, black magic practitioner pose more problems than they needed?

FORTY THREE

Eli called a morning meeting at the church for 7 AM, before the business day began. He needed to introduce Eldridge Crane to those who hadn't yet met him, and to also set in motion ways to keep everyone safe, especially the human adherents such as Rosemarie, and the two new deputies. The coven would stop at nothing to weaken their resolve, as they had already proven, and it was time to be prepared for what they'd attempt next.

Eli had a large army now. More than he could have ever hoped for, thanks to Matthias for joining them in their time of need, and Brent for bringing Daniel and his pack to Moon Grove. He also appreciated what Archer had done by arranging for hybrid vampires to fight alongside them. Something, in the past, he might not have accepted. He had learned a lot from the editor and it had made a difference to his previously biased opinion of vampires.

They were waiting for Matthias and his pack to arrive. He always turned up when he pleased and it frustrated Eli. He knew it was Matthias's way of telling him he'd always be Alpha of his own pack. Eli walked up the nave and stood outside the front entrance, spotting the group emerging from the tall pine trees nearby. When they came closer Eli asked Matthias to wait.

Once the others were inside, Matthias gave Eli a dubious frown and asked, "What's going on?"

"I wanted to have a conversation with you about your relationship with Remus and the council."

Matthias stood with hands on hips, his scowl deepening. "There is no relationship with the bloodsucker. Why are you asking me this?"

"Someone told me that you used to work for him. Is that true?" Eli folded his arms.

He didn't answer. A look of disgust crossed Matthias's rugged features and he diverted his gaze.

"Matthias, I need to know I can trust you."

The Alpha's dark eyes darted back to Eli. "You know you can."

"Do I? The information is correct, isn't it?"

"Yes, ok, I did work for him... a *long* time ago."

"Do you want to tell me why?"

Matthias let out a heavy sigh. "You might find it hard to believe but I loved a woman once. Genevieve. We were planning to get married. She knew about me and loved me nonetheless."

"So what happened?"

"*Remus* happened. He threatened to turn her if I didn't do what he wanted. So I did."

"What did he want you to do?"

Matthias frowned into Eli's eyes. "Do I have to tell you that?"

"Look, whatever it is it's in the past. I just need to know I have your full cooperation and that there isn't going to be any issues."

"There aren't going to be any issues, Eli. I owe nothing to Remus. He didn't keep his word."

Eli's eyes widened. "What do you mean?"

"Remus turned her and I had to kill her. She came to the cabin ravenous, hungry for blood, and attacked one of my pack. I didn't have a choice."

"What happened to your pack member?"

"He died a slow and agonizing death. Not something I'd wish on my worst enemy."

The shock revelation turned Eli's heart to lead. "I'm sorry, Matthias."

The Alpha folded his arms. "Yeah, well, as I said it was a long time ago."

Eli rested a hand on his companion's shoulder. "It's something you never truly get over. Losing someone you love. I know."

Matthias had heard what had happened to Eli's wife all those years ago and realized an understanding had formed between them. "Yeah, you're right. You don't."

The pair walked into the church hall together, Matthias taking his seat with his pack, and Eli stepping onto the chancel. "Can I have your attention, please?"

The hall fell silent.

"Thank you. I'd like to introduce Eldridge Crane, a warlock who has offered his assistance with our fight against the coven. Abbey traveled to Wilmette to ask for his help and he agreed." Eli motioned for Eldridge to stand up.

The warlock bowed slightly. "Thank you, Eli. I am happy to be here at this time. Let us hope for a satisfactory outcome to the current predicament." He ran his gaze over the group before taking his seat again.

Rosemarie raised her hand, her gaze moving to Eldridge. "No offence, Mr. Crane, but how do we know we can trust you?"

"Fair question, madam." Eldridge stood up, but before he could answer Abbey popped up off the pew and turned to glare at the receptionist.

"Eldridge is a well-respected magic practitioner who has offered his help in other situations similar to this with remarkable success, and you insult him with that kind of question?" Her frowning gaze met Rosemarie's.

Rosemarie stood. "I think it's important to know all the facts before placing our trust in someone we don't know, regardless of his credentials. Our town... our lives are at stake here."

Eldridge glanced at Abbey. "It is fine. I am happy to answer any question." He turned to the group. "I want you to know I am an ally not an adversary. My powers surpass that of the coven and will assure the variance between winning and losing. And I plan to help you win."

It had been decided that no one would be left alone at any given time. Now that Scarlet knew Eldridge had come to help she would find insidious ways to attack individual members of their team.

As Eli and Cooper drove through Moon Grove, heading to the station, they noticed the eerie quietness of the town.

Where were the human residents? The town comprised of a ratio of more human inhabitants to supernatural ones, so why weren't they on the streets? The hackles on Eli's neck rose. Something was wrong.

"The town seems awful quiet this morning, don't you think?" Cooper observed.

"Yeah, my thoughts exactly. Something doesn't feel right."

Cooper's gaze moved from the road to him. "Do you think the coven has done something?"

"It's a distinct possibility. Let's get to the station."

When the pair pulled into the parking lot Taylor and Rick's cars weren't there. They should've been on duty already.

Eli and Cooper frowned at each other and stepped out of the patrol.

"Where's Rick and Taylor?" Cooper ran his gaze around the parking lot and surrounding streets.

"Good question." Eli headed for the front porch.

Cooper followed.

Once inside, Eli picked up the digital phone and called Archer. "Hey, it's me. Yeah, I have noticed. What do you think is going on? Ok. I'll see you when you get here." Eli keyed in another number. "Abbey, it's Eli. Are you still with Eldridge? Can you bring him to the station? Good. I'll see you soon."

"Should we do a sweep of the town and check in on the humans?"

"Let's talk to Eldridge first. He may have an idea of what's going on."

"Ok." Cooper crossed the office and took his seat behind his desk, his gut churning, his hackles up.

Eli paced. "I think this is the beginning of the war. With the human residents out of the way the coven can do whatever they want to us and no one will be any the wiser when it's over." He heard a car drive into the gravel parking lot, walked over to the front door and stepped out onto the porch. "Thanks for getting here so quickly."

"Do you have any idea what's going on?"

"Yes, I do. I think this is the beginning of the battle. I think Scarlet has done something to keep the human inhabitants of Moon Grove out of the way while the war takes place."

Archer swallowed hard. "Then I need to round up Max and the others." He tugged his cell phone from the pocket of his pants and hit speed dial. "Max, can you round up the others and come to the police station? I'll explain when you get here. Ok, see you soon." His gaze returned to Eli. "What about Paige and Rosemarie?"

"Hell, I didn't think about that." He keyed in Paige's office number. Rosemarie picked up. "Hey, Rosy, everything all right there?"

"Hello, Darlin', what do you mean?"

"Can you and Paige come to the station as soon as you can?"

The receptionist's stomach went hollow. "Is something wrong, Eli?"

"I'll tell you when you get here. Just lock up and leave right away."

"Ok. We'll be there in a little while."

Eli breathed a relieved sigh and looked at Archer. "Whatever's happened to the other humans in town didn't happen to Rosy."

"Perhaps that's because she was at the meeting in the church with the rest of us."

"You could be right about that. There is a certain immunity there."

"Or the other possibility is Rosemarie is supernatural and either she doesn't know it or doesn't want to reveal it."

Eli's right eyebrow arched. "I've never given that idea any thought."

Archer shrugged. "Some supernaturals don't know they are. She could be psychic or have another ability she isn't aware of. Perhaps that's why she fits in so well."

The door opened and Abbey and Eldridge stepped into the office.

Eli walked over to them. "Thanks for coming." His gaze moved to the warlock. "Do you have any idea what's going on?"

"It would appear Scarlet has placed the human residents of your town in a kind of suspended animation."

"What?"

"As I said, she is a very powerful witch. She has, shall we say, knocked out the humans of Moon Grove so that they will have no knowledge of what takes place here during the fight."

"Unbelievable." Eli stood with hands on hips. "So what do we do?"

"There is nothing we *can* do. And it's probably best they are out of it. We would not want innocents killed in the war, would we? They will return to their normal lives once the battle has been fought. In the meantime, we have bigger things to be concerned with."

FORTY FOUR

The sky grew increasingly dark overhead, thick charcoal clouds forming an ominous halo above them, as Paige and Rosemarie traveled toward the station. A wind picked up, sending leaves and other debris swirling along the road ahead of them. A shiver tumbled down Rosemarie's spine as she gazed through the windshield. "Something's definitely not right."

"I'm thinking that too, Rosy." Paige pressed her foot down on the accelerator. They needed to get to the station pronto. "Did you notice how quiet the town is? It's like everyone has vanished."

"I didn't until after I got the call from Eli." She had been busy on computer doing her daily tasks.

"I'll be glad when we get to the station." Paige increased the pressure on the accelerator, her stomach doing nervous flip flops underneath her black pants. She swung the car off the road into the parking lot, skidded to a stop and turned off the engine. The wind had picked up even more. "Come on, let's get inside."

Both women dashed onto the front porch and headed to the door, Eli opening it as they reached it and they rushed inside.

"It's turning nasty out there. What's going on?" Paige asked, shaking off the anxiety she felt as she shrugged out of her coat and hung it on the rack by the door.

"Yeah, it is. Has to be the coven's doing." Eli pulled her into his arms. "Are you both ok?" His concerned gaze moved to Rosemarie.

"I'm scared, Eli," the receptionist told him.

He reached out and pulled her to him, holding both women in his comforting embrace. "It's going to be all right."

Eldridge walked over to Eli. "Can we talk in your office?"

Eli eased the women out of his arms and frowned at the warlock. "Sure." He gave Paige and Rosemarie a reassuring smile and said, "Won't be long."

Eldridge held the swinging gate on the partition open and motioned for Eli to step through ahead of him, then followed the sheriff into his office and closed the door.

Eli folded his arms. "Why the secrecy?"

"Because what's happening is only going to get worse. If you want to go into the shadow realm and retrieve the talisman now is the time to do it."

"Do you think it will do any good?"

"As I mentioned to you when we met, it will ensure our success. Without its protection, Scarlet and her witches are vulnerable."

"Ok, then let's do it." Eli's gaze moved through the window of his office to the woman he loved and the other people he cared for. "Can you guarantee that we'll get back safely?"

"There is always an element of risk, Eli, but I will do my best to return you to the people you love."

"What do we need to do?"

Eldridge raised his right hand, index finger extended, and chanted an incantation as he drew a large invisible ring in the air. A swirling circular portal opened up and he pulled Eli into the dark with him.

When Paige noticed the flash of light she raced across reception, flung open Eli's office door and gasped. The pair had vanished.

Cooper came up behind her, followed by Archer, Rosemarie and Abbey. "Where's Eli and that warlock guy?" the deputy asked.

Paige glanced at him over her shoulder, her face pale. "I have no idea."

When Max, his friends, and the vampire hybrids Archer had arranged to come to Moon Grove arrived Paige made an executive decision to move everyone from the police station to the church. To her mind, it seemed the safest place for them. And, as Eli had said many times before, it seemed to be a place of immunity. She had sent out text messages to Matthias and Daniel asking them to meet her there. They would already be aware of the situation by the atmospheric conditions that had whipped up out of nowhere.

Lightning now accompanied the blustering wind and the thick charcoal clouds drifting across the sky had amalgamated into a blanket of blackness above them.

Everyone sat in silence inside the church hall, their faces creased with expressions of worry. Daniel and his men arrived before Matthias and sidled into the pew behind Max, Blake, Chris, Abbey, Clarissa, Ruby, Linda, Cooper and Rosemarie. Archer sat with the hybrid vampires on the other front pew.

"Thanks for getting here so quickly," Paige said.

"We figured the battle had started by the conditions outside and we were on our way over when I got your message," Daniel told her, glancing over his shoulder at the bright flashes of static light radiating through the multi-colored stained glass windows, the rumble of thunder causing the floor to shudder beneath their feet. His eyes roamed the church hall. "Where's Eli?"

Paige wasn't sure what to tell him. "He – he's gone to get something that can help us win the fight against the coven and Remus."

"What about the warlock, Eldridge Crane, where's he?"

"He went with Eli for protection."

Daniel frowned at her. "Where'd they go, Paige?"

"Into the shadow realm."

"What?!"

"It's necessary. Trust Eli's judgement. He knows what he's doing."

"You're sure about that guy? Do you think he's trustworthy?"

"We don't have a choice, Daniel. Without his help we're doomed."

At that moment, Matthias and his pack stalked down the nave and sat behind Archer.

"Thanks for coming," Paige offered.

"Yeah, well, with what's going on out there where else would we be?" Matthias gave her a stern stare. His eyes also roamed the church hall in search of Eli. "Where's the sheriff?"

"As I explained to Daniel, he's gone to get something that will help us."

"Oh? What?"

Paige let out a heavy sigh. "The coven has a protective talisman. It's hidden in the shadow realm. Eli and Eldridge have gone in to retrieve it."

Matthias sprang to his feet. "You let him go into the shadow realm with a warlock no one knows well enough to know if he's here to help us or the coven?"

Paige thought about that for a moment. His words rang true. *What if Eldridge has abducted Eli? What if he's working with Scarlet?* Her eyes moved to her mother. "Mom, what do you really know about Eldridge Crane?"

"I know he's a man of honor. There hasn't been any word that he is anything more than that. He has used his power to protect other towns from the likes of the coven, and we should be grateful he came here to help us."

FORTY FIVE

Matthias remained on his feet, his serious gaze still locked onto Paige. He'd had enough of waiting around for something to happen. "Why don't we preempt this situation by going out to that cabin off Peak's Ridge trail and ambushing the coven? If they don't know we're coming they'll be unprepared."

He had a point. Paige ran the idea around her mind for a moment before offering a response. "I think we should wait for Eli and Eldridge to return with the talisman. If we can reduce the protection around the coven it will give us the advantage we need to win this battle."

The Alpha couldn't help state the obvious. "But what if they don't come back? What if I'm right in my assumption about the warlock? What if he took Eli to get him out of the way?" He glanced over at Abbey then returned his brooding gaze to Paige. "I know your mother feels he's an ally but we don't know that for sure. None of us know anything about him."

The tangle of anxious nerves in Paige's solar plexus sank into the uneasy sea of doubt in the pit of her stomach.

She didn't like the feeling. *Could Matthias be right?* "Look, Eli would want us to stay put. We're safe here."

Matthias folded his arms. "Are we? We're sitting ducks being here in one place together."

Again, he made perfect sense.

Archer stood up and looked across the chancel at Clarissa. "Clary, can you place the same kind of protection spell around the church that you used on your home?"

The old woman gave his suggestion some thought. "I – I'm not sure. It's a complex spell that adheres to the occupant of the property." She glanced at Ruby sitting beside her.

"I think if we do it together we can make it work," the young woman said. "Strength in numbers." She reached across and squeezed Clarissa's wrinkled hand.

Archer moved his gaze to Matthias. "Rather than us all being massacred out at the cabin by forces we can't possibly foresee, would you be willing to remain here if Clary and Ruby can secure the church to keep us safe?"

The Alpha let out a heavy sigh. To his mind, if they planned to fight then they should fight. Nothing good could come from sitting back and waiting for the war to come to them. "I think we should strike first, while we can. If we're able to knock out some of the witches from the fight and reduce the number of the coven it would benefit us and definitely give us the advantage. We have the manpower now." He motioned around the hall at the other wolf pack and the new vampire hybrids sitting near Archer. "Why not get it done?"

Paige crossed the chancel to where the two were standing. "Eli would want to be part of the battle and, as I said, we need the talisman to weaken Scarlet and her coven. It's the only way."

"I think you're wrong." Matthias stood his ground.

"It's not your call to make, Matthias, and I'd appreciate your cooperation. It's important we remain a united front otherwise the whole situation will come crashing down around us. Eli asked you to trust him... can you do that... *please*?"

Matthias gave her a dark stare. "If Eli was here, maybe, but I think I'm willing to take my chances out there. It seems to me you're afraid to act. You're waiting for the warlock to step in and take control and he might not return. What do you plan to do then?"

Paige tried to maintain a cool composure as she frowned into his wolf eyes. *What would I do then?*

As the pair roamed the streets and Eli's Lycan vision expanded to allow him to see more clearly, he couldn't believe what he saw. The shadow realm resembled a darker version of Moon Grove... similar to an 80's horror movie set. The Halloween series came to mind as he ran his gaze around the hazy town. He caught up to Eldridge. "I can't believe what I'm looking at. How does this place even exist?"

"It has existed for as long as time itself."

"Why does it look like Moon Grove?"

"It adapts to the individual itinerant. If someone came here from, say, Washington that is what they would encounter." He continued walking. "I must warn you.

You'll see and hear things that will undermine your sanity. Don't trust anyone or anything you meet."

Eli swallowed hard and his gut tightened. "What do you mean, exactly?"

"We are likely to meet people we've known on earth, ones that have passed on. It is not uncommon here. Sometimes, you could come upon people you love... or... even yourself."

"What?!" Eli grabbed Eldridge's arm to stop him. "You mean I could see my mother, my best friend or my wife? Even Paige? But that doesn't make sense."

"It doesn't have to. The shadow realm will do its utmost to weaken your defenses to keep you here."

Eli's taut gut released into a rolling wash of nausea. "I thought you said..."

"What I said was I would do my best to get you back to the people you love. You must be vigilant and trust nothing you see here." He shrugged out of Eli's grasp and ran his gaze around the dimly lit street. "Now, where do you suppose the talisman is?" Eldridge stepped into the fog bank in front of them and disappeared from sight.

"Eldridge?" Eli called, following him into the mist. "Eldridge, where are you?"

No answer.

"Eldridge?" He kept moving in the direction the warlock had taken and came through the miasma to the front yard of his house. "What the...?"

A young boy, no older than seven ran up to him. "Hello."

Eli stopped in his tracks. Why did the child seem familiar to him? "Hello." He ran his gaze around the yard and the front of the house. "Are you alone here?"

The boy shook his head. "My mom is inside. Want to come meet her?" He gave Eli a strange smile.

"Thanks, but no. I'm looking for someone." He continued to roam the yard with his eyes.

"You mean the man you were with?"

Eli's gaze snapped back to the boy. "Yes. Have you seen him?"

The boy pointed into the trees behind the house. "He went through there."

Eli knew the woods at home like the back of his hand, but here… a different story. His focus returned to the boy. "What's your name?"

"Elijah. Mom says it's my dad's name." He smiled again.

Eli lowered himself in front of the boy and ran his eyes over his young face. A voice behind him caused him to spring to his feet and spin around.

"Hello, Eli."

"Michelle?"

"It's so good to see you."

Eli felt dazed, his head foggy. "This can't be."

"But it is." She came up to him and brushed his cheek with her fingertips. Glancing at the boy beside him, she said, "This is your son."

Eli shook his head and stepped backwards. "No. This isn't real."

"I was pregnant when that wolf killed me. I had planned to tell you, but…"

"The Doc would've told me when he did the autopsy."

"When I found out I asked him not to say anything and he kept his promise."

"No, it's not true." With his heart thundering in his chest, Eli turned on his heel and rushed back into the fog. "Eldridge, where are you?" The thought crossed his mind that the warlock had abandoned him. When he emerged out of the haze, Scarlet stood in the middle of the street ahead of him.

"Hello, Eli Blackwood." A smile of satisfaction spread across her face. "We meet at last."

The moonstone ring on Eli's finger radiated a sensation of warmth along his hand and up his arm. Eli glanced down at it and saw it begin to glow. "You're here to try to stop me from finding the talisman, aren't you?"

"I can assure you it is well hidden." She took a step closer. "You'll never find it."

"No, he might not, but I have." Eldridge's voice echoed out of the shadows and he appeared beside Eli, raising the swinging talisman into the air.

Scarlet's eyes widened. "You will give that to me," she ordered, reaching out her hand.

"I most certainly will not. If you wish to take it from me, by all means, do what you will."

The High Priestess remained where she stood contemplating what to do next. She knew the warlock's powers far surpassed her own.

Eldridge's left eyebrow arched. "Well?"

Scarlet had to attempt something otherwise she and her coven would be at the mercy of the warlock. She pointed her finger at the jewel and said, "Dispareo."

The talisman vanished from Eldridge's hand and Scarlet disappeared before their eyes.

FORTY SIX

Paige had an important decision to make. With Eli gone, she had to determine whether they should do as Matthias had suggested – go out to the cabin and ambush the coven – or wait to see if Eli and Eldridge Crane returned with the talisman. The Alpha's words rang in her ears, *'You're waiting for the warlock to step in and take control and he might not return. What do you plan to do then?'* He made a valid point. The longer she waited the more their lives were in danger. And she had no idea what Scarlet Balfour had planned for them.

After discussing her thoughts with Archer, Abbey, and Clarissa, Paige had made a choice. "Everyone… everyone, please, I have something I want to say."

The hall fell silent.

"Thank you. As much as I would like to wait for Eli and Eldridge to return, I think Matthias is right." Her eyes darted to him then back to her audience. "If we sit here and wait we're in danger of being taken by surprise, ourselves. So, I've made the decision to fight. We do have the manpower now and I'm confident that if we can attack the coven while they are unprepared we will create an opportunity to forestall the battle." She paced then turned around. "I do have one stipulation – that we capture the witches, not kill them."

The cacophony of voices of concern exploded inside the hall.

Paige raised her hands in an attempt to quiet everyone down. "Please… please hear me out."

Matthias stalked up to her. "You know they wouldn't hesitate to kill all of us. Why be so generous with their lives? Your decision is bound to come back and bite Moon Grove in the butt." He folded his arms and glowered at her.

"I think we can learn something from them if we contain them somewhere they can't use their magic. Perhaps we can persuade some of them to help us defeat Remus."

"You're out of your mind!" Matthias strutted back to his pack, waving them out of the pew. "Come on, we're outta here."

"Matthias, wait." Paige rushed over to him.

The Alpha swung around. "For what? To be attacked here where we have no means of escape?" His angry gaze moved to his men. "Let's go."

"You gave Eli your word you would help us," Paige reminded.

He stopped in his tracks, turned around and walked back down the nave to her. "That was before you decided to put our lives in danger. The witches need to be eliminated. Do you think they'll give up that easily?"

Others in the group were of the same opinion.

"I'm sorry, Paige, but I have to agree," Rosemarie said.

"If we show leniency we'll appear weak. And that will be our downfall."

"Matthias is right, sis. We have to stand strong. If we lock them away somewhere they're bound to find a way out and when they do we'll all be dead. They won't show us any mercy," Brent told his sister.

Paige ran her frowning gaze around the assembly. "All right. We'll take a vote." She looked along the nave at Matthias. "Are you staying or leaving?"

"We'll vote." He and his pack returned to their seats.

Paige swallowed hard. She had a fair idea she would lose this poll. "Let's have a show of hands for those in favor of eliminating the coven."

Everyone in the church hall raised their hands.

At that moment, the church doors imploded sending wood, leaves and other debris flying into the hall.

Eli rushed over to where Scarlet had been standing then looked at Eldridge over his shoulder. "What just happened? Why didn't you tell me what you planned to do?" He turned around and walked back to the warlock. "Now we have no idea where the talisman is. Is that the real reason you came to Moon Grove – to weaken our defenses?"

"I came to help you. This minor setback will not prevent me from doing that."

"Then if you had the ability to stop the coven without the talisman why are we here?"

"I had something else I needed to collect. Something of great significance to our cause."

"Yeah? Like what?"

The warlock gave him a shrewd grin. "This." He held up the book Remus had stolen from them when he'd abducted Archer.

"How…"

"The shadow realm is a perverse replica of the world outside its boundaries." He ran his gaze around their ominous surroundings, aware that they were being watched. "Let us not waste any more time here, we have work to do." Eldridge raised his hand and a crackling, circular electrical vortex appeared in the hazy atmosphere ahead of them. "Come along." He grabbed Eli by the arm, pulled him closer, and leaped into the black void.

When the doors burst open, Ruby and Clarissa sprang to their feet, raised their hands and chanted an incantation to prevent the witches from entering the church. Would it hold? Not for long. "Paige, you need to get everyone out of here," Clarissa called to her.

Paige shook her head. "I'm not leaving without you."

Ruby continued to chant while Clarissa tried to talk some sense into Paige.

"You must. It's the only way to save Moon Grove," the old woman told her.

"There has to be another way." Paige frowned into Clarissa's eyes. "I can't leave you here to fight the coven alone."

"Paige, you must prepare yourselves for the battle. You must!"

A single tear slipped down Paige's right cheek. "But

what about you?" Her gaze moved to the witch standing next to Clarissa. "And Ruby?"

"We'll be all right. I give you my word. Now go." She spun around and thrust her hand toward one of the side doors. It blew outward off its hinges, the gusty wind picking it up and hurtling it towards the trees. "Go!"

Everyone raced across the chancel and out the open doorway into the storm.

Matthias rushed up to Paige. "We need to get somewhere safe."

Paige nodded. "I know a place."

Abbey grabbed Rosemarie by the arm and tugged her into the trees. "Stay here," she said, then turned and raced back to Paige. "Where are we going?"

"To the council's mansion. It's empty. We can work on our next plan of attack there."

Abbey nodded then rushed back to collect Rosemarie. "Come on. We're going to the mansion."

Ruby and Clarissa continued to chant their incantation. It would prevent Scarlet and her witches from leaving the area. At least for now.

Lightning crackled across the sky, the clouds growing even darker than before, thunder rumbling beneath the car as Paige, Rosemarie, Abbey, Brent, Linda and Archer sped out of town toward Remus's manor. The others would follow, either in their vehicles or the wolves would shift and travel there on foot through the woods, while the vampires traveled through the air.

When they arrived at the manor, Paige swung the Jeep around back and pulled up at the garage. "Let's get out of the storm."

Linda whipped the garage door open and the group followed her into the house.

Once inside, Paige headed to the double front doors to let the others in. Matthias and his pack arrived first. They had chosen to travel by car. Daniel and his pack wouldn't be far behind. Max, Blake and Christopher dropped out of the sky onto the front balcony and entered the building. "Have the other vampires arrived yet?" Max asked.

"No, not yet," Paige told him.

Max frowned and stepped back out onto the landing. "They should've been right behind us."

Daniel and his pack arrived in two cars, skidded to a stop near the front stairs, scrambled from the vehicles and raced up the double staircases into the mansion. "That storm is fierce. It almost knocked us off the road."

"I'm glad you're ok," Paige said. "Head into the library. First door on the right." She pointed along the hallway. "We'll make a plan to get rid of the coven once and for all."

A smug grin crossed Matthias's rugged features. "So you've decided they're too dangerous to keep around?"

Paige gave him a disgruntled frown. She didn't like being told 'I told you so' no matter in what form. "Yes, Matthias, you were right. Happy now?"

"I wasn't trying to be right. I'm trying to help you keep everyone alive." He glowered at her then turned on his heel, marched down the hall and into the library.

Paige's eyes followed him and she let out a frustrated huff, then turned to face the open front doors.

Max was still on the porch.

Paige stepped outside and stood beside him. "Still no sign of them?"

Archer's brother turned to look at her. "No, and I'm worried. They were the last to leave. Maybe the coven got their hands on them."

"Maybe the storm has something to do with it. Give them another few minutes." She decided to wait with him.

A bright flash of light tore open the gloomy fabric of the storm, and Eldridge and Eli stepped out of the glowing portal onto the front lawn.

Paige's eyes widened when she saw the pair and she raced down the stairs, ran across the lawn, and threw her arms around Eli. "I'm so glad you're back. How did you know we were here?"

"We didn't. Eldridge came here to look for Remus… he has a copy of the book."

"But how?"

"The shadow realm. I'll explain later." Eli glanced up at the sky just as it opened up and heavy rain bucketed down on them. "Let's get inside."

When Eli entered the house his eyes searched for his grandmother. "Where's Clary?"

Paige gave him a sorrowful look. "She and Ruby stayed behind to keep the coven from killing us."

Eli frowned into her eyes. "She what?"

"She promised me they'd be safe. I believe her."

"She's an old woman, Paige…"

"No, Eli, she's an accomplished witch that has been able to hold off Scarlet and her witches so far. Her abilities are phenomenal."

At that moment, Paige's cell went off in her pocket. She snatched up the phone and frowned at the screen. "Hello?"

"Paige, it's Ruby. We're at Clary's. We're safe."

Paige gave a relieved sigh. "Thank goodness. Well, stay put. It's the safest place for you both right now."

"We will. Call us when you need us."

"Ok." She ended the call and pushed her phone back into her jacket pocket, Eli's curious gaze remaining on her. "Ruby. She said they're safe at Clary's."

"Thank God." Eli glanced over his shoulder at Archer's brother standing on the front balcony. "What's up with Max?"

"The four vampires that came to town haven't arrived. He thinks the coven may have them."

"That's a possibility. How long since you left the church."

Paige glanced at her watch. It had stopped. "Uh, fifteen, twenty minutes, maybe."

He turned toward the front doors. "Max?"

Max swung around. "Yeah?"

"You could be right about the coven removing the vampires from the fight."

"Yeah." He stepped into the mansion and closed the twin doors. "Doesn't help us much, does it?"

"Fear not," Eldridge told them. "I can handle a few witches."

FORTY SEVEN

Paige paced the entry hall, her eyes moving to her watch, then along the hallway to the library door. She bit her bottom lip. Could she be correct in her assumption? She marched down the hall to the library and peered inside, her eyes roaming the group for Eli. When she spotted him she walked over to him. "Eli, can I talk to you outside for a moment?"

Eli stopped the conversation he'd been having with Archer and his brother. "Sure. What is it?"

Paige crossed the library and stepped out into the hallway, Eli behind her. "I think the coven has stopped time."

Eli gave her a dubious frown. "What makes you think that?"

She raised her wrist. "My watch has stopped."

His gaze moved to the watch then back to her. "Maybe the battery died."

"What about yours?" She motioned to his wrist with her head.

Eli checked. "Oh. Mine's stopped too."

"I wonder what that means." A look of concern crossed her face.

"I don't know. Perhaps Eldridge will. Let's go talk to him."

The pair walked back along the hall and into the library.

"Eldridge, can we talk to you for a moment?"

The warlock turned around. "Of course. Is something wrong?"

"Let's go out into the hallway."

"Very well." Eldridge motioned for Paige to go ahead of him then followed Eli out.

The pair walked through the curtained archway into the entry hall.

"Is there a problem?" Eldridge gave them a curious stare.

"Paige... *we* think the coven has stopped time." Eli folded his arms.

The warlock's left eyebrow arched. "Oh? What makes you think that?"

"Our watches have stopped," Paige told him.

Eldridge hurried to the double front doors, whipped them open and stepped out onto the balcony. The storm had subsided and everything lay still. "I believe you are correct."

"What does that mean?" Paige asked, her voice shaky.

"It means they are on their way here and are not far away. We need to prepare."

The witches flew across the dark sky in a V formation similar to that of ducks migrating for the winter. When they reached the mansion, they lowered themselves onto the front lawn and stood facing the entry to the triple story, gothic building. Scarlet raised her hands in the air and chanted an incantation. The wind whipped around them blowing up leaves and other debris in a spiral toward the house. She continued to chant.

Eldridge stepped out onto the balcony. "Be silent woman. You have no dominion here, Scarlet Balfour. Leave while you still can."

The High Priestess's laughter echoed around him. "We do not answer to you, Eldridge Crane." She thrust out her hands and hurled a flaming ball of fire at him.

Eldridge raised his left hand and called out, "Saeclum."

The ball of flames dissolved in mid-air before it reached him, droplets of fire raining down onto the damp lawn, hissing as they connected with the moisture.

The cloaked witches fanned out and chanted along with Scarlet.

Thick fog encapsulated the mansion making it difficult to see beyond the front steps.

Eldridge stepped back into the house, closed and locked the doors. "Let's move into position. Is everyone ready?"

All in the entry hall nodded.

"Scarlet and her witches cannot set foot inside the mansion, but they can break windows and send spells and other dangers into the house. You will all need to keep your wits about you otherwise you may be attacked in such a way." He moved to the window on the stair landing and gazed outside.

At that moment, the double front doors burst open, the gusty wind driving the fog into the entry hall.

"Move. Quickly!" Eldridge ordered.

Everyone scattered to different areas within the mansion, all but Matthias and his pack.

"Why should we run scared? Why don't we fight?"

Eldridge turned around to face the Alpha. "Because I will deal with the coven. I'm doing what I can to avoid bloodshed and loss of life."

Matthias frowned into Eldridge's eyes. "Or you're planning something."

"Why would I? I came here to help."

The Alpha's stern gaze remained on the warlock. He hadn't trusted him from the moment he'd set foot in Moon Grove and still didn't. "Why did you allow that witch to hide the talisman when you knew it would help us win this fight?"

"I do not have time to debate my intentions with you. Go to your positions and allow me to take care of this."

Matthias's gut told him something wasn't right about the warlock. He had his own agenda. He turned on his heel, his men in tow, and stalked along the hallway. He needed to talk to Eli.

Scarlet sent her witches to stand at different areas around the mansion. They would form the points of the pentacle and emanate black magic energy into the house. It would be easier than the High Priestess had anticipated. Everyone inside would be imprisoned in a vortex of darkness and she would expedite them into the shadow realm to be lost forever.

Each witch raised their hands into the air and chanted in unison, "I call on the dark lord to imbue me with his power to propel this house and all inhabitants into the realm of shadow. As it is below let it be on earth."

Thunder rumbled across the charcoal sky and stark flashes of forked white lightning prodded a singed circle into the ground around the mansion.

Eldridge flung open the double front doors and thrust his body into the blustering wind, chanting an incantation to ward off the spell the coven attempted to place on the building and those inside.

Clary and Ruby appeared on the balcony and stood on either side of the warlock, repeating the same words alongside him, the power of three as strong as the thirteen.

The thunder resembled war drums booming across the sky, the sound growing louder and louder until the three on the front landing couldn't hear each other. The thick fog rolled in, blue streaks of bright lightning crackled across the balustrade close to them, chunks of concrete breaking away and falling into the garden bed below.

Eldridge turned to the women beside him and shouted. "Let's get inside. It is too dangerous out here."

The trio raced into the entry hall and slammed the doors shut.

Eli, Paige and Archer rushed through the curtained archway. "What's happening?" Eli yelled over the cacophony of loud thunder and crashing lightning, pulling his grandmother into his arms and giving her a tight hug.

"Scarlet and her coven are trying to send us and the house to the shadow realm," Eldridge told him. "We need to continue the spell."

Clary tugged free from her grandson and stood with Ruby and Eldridge and they continued to chant the countering incantation.

The walls vibrated and the building shook beneath their feet.

Daniel, Matthias and both of their packs appeared in the entry hall. "What's going on?" Daniel shouted.

Eli rushed across to the group. "The witches are attempting to send us to the shadow realm. Eldridge, my grandmother and Ruby are doing what they can to prevent that."

"Will it work?" Matthias asked.

"All we can do is pray it does."

The house continued to shake, panes of window glass shattered and imploded around them.

Abbey, Brent and Rosemarie flew down the stairs to the others. "What the hell's going on?" Abbey shouted. "That sound is driving me insane. It's making my wolf want to emerge." She pressed her hands to her ears.

Rosemarie rushed over to Paige. "How are we going to stop them?"

Paige wrapped her arms around the woman. "That's what Eldridge, Clary, and Ruby are trying to do right now."

"What are the witches doing?"

A grim expression crossed Paige's face. "They're attempting to send the house and us into the shadow realm."

"What?!" Rosemarie pulled free from Paige's embrace. She rushed over to the trio of witches, joined hands with Clary and began chanting with them.

Paige's and Eli's eyes widened. Rosemarie was a witch.

FORTY EIGHT

Matthias stalked across the entry hall. "I can't stay in here any longer. We need to end this." He whipped the front doors open, then he and his guys shifted into wolf form and disappeared into the foggy storm. Daniel and his pack did the same. Paige raced across to the doorway and peered outside, unable to see anyone through the dense haze. She hoped they'd be all right. She pushed against one of the doors in an attempt to close out the gale force wind, but it flew out of her hands and crashed against the wall.

Eli rushed up behind her, both of them together pushing one door then the other closed. "I hope Matthias and Daniel and their packs will be ok."

"Me too." Paige's gaze returned to Eldridge, Clary, Ruby, and Rosemarie. She couldn't believe the receptionist had hidden the fact she was a witch and she wondered why.

A bolt of lightning cracked against the turret spire outside. The thunder grew even louder.

Abbey continued to press the palms of her hands against her ears. "I can't stand this anymore. Open the door and let me out."

Eli raced over, opened one of the double black front doors and Abbey dissolved into the hazy wall of fog, howling as she shifted.

Brent was about to do the same when Paige grabbed his arm. "Don't. Please."

He gave her a perplexed frown. "Paige, I can't let mom go out there alone."

"She's not alone. Matthias, Daniel and both their packs are out there. I need you to stay here."

"Why?"

Tears stung the backs of her eyes and she blinked them away. "Because if anything happens to mom you're all I have left."

"Don't you think that's selfish? She needs me." He tugged free and hurtled himself through the open doorway, shifting before he disappeared into the mist.

Within minutes, everything stopped.

The wind.

The rain.

The thunder.

The lightning.

The stillness set Paige's nerves on edge and she shivered. Had the wolf packs knocked some of the witches out of the fight? She hoped so.

Archer rushed up to her and Eli. "I'm going out there."

A tear slipped down Paige's cheek. "Please don't. We can't see what's happening out there. Who knows who'll survive? I can't lose you too."

The editor gently gripped her arms and pulled her close for a moment. "I have to do something. I didn't do what I did, drink your blood, to stand here and let others fight."

Max and his friends came up beside him. "We're coming with you."

Archer eased Paige out of his embrace. "We'll be ok. I promise."

"You can't make that kind of promise, Archer."

He gave her an uncertain smile and marched over to the front doors. Before stepping out behind his brother, he turned to look at her and said, "Wish us luck."

Paige nodded. She couldn't speak for the painful lump lodged in her throat.

Eli closed the door, crossed the entry hall to Paige and pulled her into his arms. "He'll be ok."

More tears spilled down her face. "I hope you're right."

Cooper came flying down the staircase. "The roof has fallen into the attic. Must've been that crack of lightning." His eyes roamed the entry hall and through the curtained archway. "Where's everyone?"

Eli stepped up to his newbie wolf. "They've gone out to fight."

"Then let's go." Cooper strutted over to the front doors.

"Wait." Eli crossed the entry hall to his deputy. "Some of us need to remain here."

"Why?" Cooper gave his Alpha a confused frown. "We need to help the others." He threw open one of the double doors. "Coming?"

Eli's gaze moved to Paige.

She shook her head, asking him silently not to go, and another tear slipped down her cheek.

"No. And neither are you."

Cooper bounced on the balls of his feet. He wanted to go out and fight alongside Matthias, Daniel, Archer and the others. "Don't make me disobey you, Eli. I can't stay here and do nothing." The massacre of their pack out on the front lawn by Gregor Petrov prodded his thoughts, something that constantly haunted his dreams. "This is where Bobby and the others died. We can't let that happen again."

Paige walked across the entry hall to the pair, giving a heavy sigh. She knew he was right. "Then we'll go together."

Clary glanced over her shoulder at the three standing in the open doorway. "Eli, no."

"I'm sorry, Gran, I have to." With that said, the trio shifted into wolf form and dissolved into the fog.

The silence seemed deafening as Eli, Paige, and Cooper padded through the haze, their Lycan ears pricked to pick up any sounds around them. Where were the witches? And what about Matthias, Daniel, Archer and the others?

The three werewolves continued forward with caution.

Matthias knocked down one of the witches, his sharp wolf incisors tearing the flesh from her throat. She gave a bloody, gurgled gasp and her body evaporated into the earth beneath him. *One down*, he thought as he made his way through the mist in search of the next witch in the coven.

Daniel hurtled his huge wolf frame at one of the witches. She tumbled to the ground, raising her hand in an attempt to attack him with a spell. His long snout clamped around her wrist, biting through flesh, sinew, and bone. The witch gave a shrill scream, agonizing pain radiated up her arm, her eyes wide as he inched closer. She dug her heels into the lawn, pushing herself backwards on her bottom. Daniel loomed over her and, with one sharp thrust, his muzzle took off her head.

Archer and Max had become separated from Blake and Christopher but pushed through the fog in search of the coven.

"I don't hear anything," Max said. "No heartbeats. Nothing."

"Perhaps Scarlet placed a protection spell on them to make it difficult to find them in this miasmic pea soup." Archer continued to move forward, Max beside him. His vampire hearing picked up a sound close by and he swung around as a wolf lunged out of the mist.

Max darted in front of his brother and sprang onto the wolf, the pair tumbling across the lawn and disappearing into the fog. Hissing, Max jumped to his feet, eyes darting in all directions. The wolf flew toward him, swiping out with one of its massive clawed paws. Max leaned backwards, the wolf's claws missing him by inches. It would mean a death sentence if he got scratched or bitten by the creature.

He hurled himself onto the wolf, sinking his fangs into its massive neck, before it could attack again, its huge body slumping to the ground. Why would one of the wolves attack them when they were working together to win this fight against the coven?

Eli, Paige, and Cooper appeared through the haze, Eli shifting back to human form. "What happened?"

Max climbed to his feet. "That wolf tried to attack Archer." He peeled off his knee-length leather jacket and passed it to the sheriff.

"Thanks." He shrugged into it and buttoned the front. "Is it dead?"

"Yeah, and faster than I would've expected. Must be the enhanced abilities caused by the serum."

The wolf morphed back to human form.

"Matthias!" Eli frowned at the naked body lying on the ground in front of him.

"Why would he attempt to kill my brother?" Max asked, his gaze roaming the surrounding gray vapor in search of others that might attack them.

"I don't know," Eli replied, shaking his head. "I knew he didn't like vampires, but this…"

"Let's not waste time hypothesizing," Archer said. "We need to keep moving."

Blake and Christopher came upon one of the witches, Blake grabbing her from behind and wrapping his arms around her to keep her hands by her side. Christopher's fangs snapped into place and he plunged them into her throat, drinking deeply, but pulled back as heat traveled the length of his tall frame, his body bursting into flames, and disintegrating into a pile of ash. Stunned, Blake jolted backwards, his eyes wide. The witch had garlic running through her veins. He twisted her neck and tossed her body onto the grass, then headed further into the fog in search of Archer, Max, and the others.

FORTY NINE

Eldridge, Clary, Ruby, and Rosemarie stopped chanting the incantation. Something felt different about their current circumstances. The potency of the black magic wielded by the coven seemed weaker. They released hands and stepped out onto the balcony, the fog slowly dissipating. "I believe the threat has been thwarted," the warlock said, a thin smile crossing his handsome face.

"How can you be sure of that?" Rosemarie asked.

"There has been a shift in the atmosphere." He glanced at each of the women's wrists. "Ruby, is your watch working?"

The young woman raised her hand to her face and checked the time. "Yes, it is."

"Then the battle is over." Eldridge descended the stairs and crossed the lawn to Eli.

As the haze around them cleared, the group surveyed the living and dead around them.

Paige shifted back to human form and raced across the lawn to her mother and brother, not caring that they were all naked, and threw her arms around them. "I'm so glad you're ok."

Bodies lay strewn across the grass.

Daniel had lost four of his pack.

Matthias's pack had lost six.

The witches had been a force to reckon with despite their numbers.

Blake came around the corner of the mansion and Max rushed up to him. "Where's Chris?"

His friend shook his head, a grim expression on his face.

"No."

"The witch's blood had been laced with garlic."

Ruby, Clary, and Rosemarie came down the front steps with black robes they'd found in the hall closet and handed them around to those who needed them.

Eli's eyes roamed the scene. "Where's Scarlet?"

"I do not sense her presence," Eldridge told him. "I think she has absconded with the remaining witches of her coven."

"That means they could try to finish what they started," Eli said, turning and frowning into the warlock's eyes.

"Indeed, that could be true, but I do not believe they will."

"Why?"

"She needs thirteen in order for the dark magic they each possess to be potent enough to do any real damage. Strength in numbers, as they say." He wandered the lawn and stopped in several places before returning to the others. "Scarlet lost six of her coven."

"How do you know that?" Eli asked.

"Their essence still lingers in the earth. Scarlet will need to find others as powerful to take their place. I think they would have left Moon Grove by now. The High Priestess would not risk losing any more of her witches."

"Good. But we still have Remus to deal with."

"Yes, we do. And we will."

Linda appeared on the front landing. She had chosen not to fight.

Eli's gaze moved to the top of the staircase. Linda would have to wait. The thought crossed his mind that she might still be involved with Remus and the council. He hoped not because if that were true next time he wouldn't be as lenient. Right now, he had more important matters to focus on, but he would keep a close eye on her.

When the group reached Moon Grove, everything appeared to be back to normal. People were on the streets, the sun beamed in the cloudy blue sky, and nothing seemed out of place. Because Scarlet had stopped time and suspended the human residents in a coma-like sleep, the township had no idea of what had taken place.

Eli swung the Jeep into the church parking lot and turned off the engine. They needed to debrief before stepping back into their lives within the town, even if it was only for each of their own sanity. Once again, they had lost good people that couldn't be replaced. He stepped out of the four wheel drive, opened the rear passenger door on his side, then rounded the hood, and opened the passenger doors for Paige and the other ladies. Paige and her mother were still wearing the black robes Rosemarie had given them. "Come on, let's get inside and change." Eli glanced down at himself. He had on the jacket Archer's brother had offered him.

Eldridge climbed out of the second vehicle and walked up to Eli. "We will need to devise a careful plan to get to Remus as soon as possible."

Eli nodded. "Yes, and I have an advantage."

The warlock's left eyebrow arched. "Oh? And what is that?"

"I have someone on the inside."

Eldridge pondered that information for a moment before speaking. "And you are sure he or she can be trusted?"

Eli had to give the question some consideration. *Am I sure?*

"You seem uncertain, Sheriff Blackwood."

"No, well, maybe. He has been helpful so far. But…"

"You cannot say for sure that he is trustworthy?"

Eli shook his head. "No, I can't."

"In that case, we need to consider dissolving the council in its entirety," Eldridge offered. "If you cannot be sure of this vampire's intentions, and believe he may be a threat in the future, then he needs to be dispatched alongside Remus and the other members."

Eli thought about that. Could he do what the warlock suggested? Could he become what he had believed Alistair to be, a double agent? "Maybe we should give him the benefit of the doubt for now. He has offered to help get rid of Remus and I believe he'll stick to his word because he wants to become the council's new leader."

"Have you considered the possibility that he is telling you what you want to hear, so you will help him usurp Remus and then rule the town in the same manner?"

Eli needed to give what the warlock had said some serious thought. "Look, let's get inside and debrief first. I'll let you know what I decide later."

"Of course." Eldridge gave a nod, clasped his hands behind his back, and headed to the front doors of the church.

After cleaning up and changing into clothes that had been stored in the office, Eli, Paige, Brent, and Abbey entered the hall. Daniel and his remaining pack members had gone back to the Inn to change and had just arrived, Matthias's men didn't return. Eli knew he would have to go out to the cabin and speak to them at some point. They had lost their Alpha and other members of their pack and would need to organize their funeral.

Eli didn't want to encroach on Matthias's pack, but they would need a new Alpha to lead them, and if he could talk them into joining him it would be beneficial for all.

Daniel stepped out of the pew and approached Eli. "Can we talk for a minute?"

"Sure." Eli walked over to a column near the office door. "What do you need?"

"I want to relinquish my Alpha status and become part of your pack. We need someone like you to lead us, Eli. We've lost good men and I doubt there are other wolves out there willing to join me."

Eli gripped the Alpha's shoulder in a gesture of comradery. "You'd be a welcome addition to our pack, Daniel, but are you sure this is what you want?"

"I've talked it over with my guys and they're ok with whatever I decide. So, yes, it *is* what I want."

"Then, once we've finished our fight with Remus and the council, I'll organize a place for you to stay." He gave Daniel a warm smile and squeezed his shoulder. "Thank you. I'm happy to have you onboard."

"We're grateful." Daniel turned on his heel and went back and took his seat with his men.

Paige came over to Eli. "What did he want?"

"He asked to join our pack."

"He did?" Paige's eyes widened. "That's wonderful. We need good men like him and his guys."

"Yeah, we do."

Paige returned to her seat beside Rosemarie, Cooper, Abbey, Brent, Linda, Archer, Max, and Blake.

"Listen up, everyone. Although we've lost good people today the fight isn't over. We have to find Remus and rid Moon Grove of his hold over our town, once and for all. But, before we move into the next phase of our battle, I want each of you to tell me how you're feeling. We need to talk about what happened at the mansion for the good of our well-being."

Before anyone could begin, the church doors crashed open and Alistair and the other members of the council stalked inside.

Daniel and his men flew out of their seats and blocked the nave. Archer, Max, and Blake stood with them. Brent and Cooper raced across the chancel and stepped up beside the vampires.

"Alistair? Why have you come here?" Eli pushed through the group and walked up the nave to him.

"I am here as a gesture of good faith, as I have already discussed with you. You wanted Remus dead... he is dead." Alistair reached into a leather bag and tugged their leader's severed head out of it. "The fight is over, Eli. We can now move forward and bring in a new governing body that will work with the residents of Moon Grove for the betterment of all."

FIFTY

The council's twist in their plan to take down Remus had been a complete and utter surprise to Eli... to everyone. He hadn't expected Alistair to orchestrate murdering their leader. He'd always believed the vampire didn't have the courage. It seemed he had underestimated Alistair once again. What did that mean for their town? Could Eldridge be correct in his assumption that the council member – now the council principal as he preferred to be addressed – would hide the truth about his intentions for Moon Grove? Only time would tell. And he would be watching the new governing body closely.

Eli lay on his back staring up at the ceiling, Paige asleep beside him, the threat to their town gone... for now. He thought about his new deputies. He'd had a feeling they suspected something. Could he be right? He would have to keep an eye on them as well. Who knew what would happen to them if he didn't? And what they could find out.

Paige stirred and let out a soft sigh. Eli wondered what she was dreaming about. It felt good not to be on his guard for the first time in a long while. But how long would that last before another danger threatened their town?

He turned over, wrapped his arm around Paige and spooned her. He liked to feel her body close to his. After a while, his eyes closed and he drifted off to sleep.

Eli wandered the shadowed main street of Moon Grove, his gut wound tight. Something seemed wrong about his home town. Where had everyone gone? Why were the shops and businesses closed? He continued along the sidewalk, heading to the Tribune office. Would Archer still be there?

As he crossed the road, someone called out his name from behind him. Eli swung around. He recognized that voice. His eyes widened when he spotted the mayor coming toward him. "How are you here?"

Ross Redmond gave him a peculiar smile. "I'm not. You are."

Eli frowned at his cryptic reply. "What does that mean?"

The mayor raised his hand and motioned along the street. "Take a look around you, Sheriff. Where do you think you are?"

Eli's gaze roamed the business hub of the town before returning to the mayor. "Moon Grove. Where else?"

Redmond let out a fiendish chuckle. "*Wrong.*"

"Then tell me where I am." Eli frowned into the man's glowing eyes. *Why are his eyes glowing?*

"Come on, Sheriff, you're a smarter wolf than that." The mayor turned on his heel, crossed the street, and disappeared into the mayoral chamber building.

Eli followed, his tight gut now churning. "Wait. Ross." He entered the lobby. Redmond wasn't there. Where had he disappeared to so quickly? "Ross, where are you?"

The lobby and hallway were in complete darkness.

Eli's Lycan vision expanded so he could see more clearly. "Redmond?" He continued along the deserted hallway to the mayor's office. When he reached the door he found it ajar. Pushing it open, he stepped into reception and ran his gaze around the room. Ross's office door stood open. Eli wandered over to it and peered inside.

Ross Redmond was at his desk. "Come in, come in. Close the door behind you. We wouldn't want anyone to hear our conversation, would we?" He gave another devilish chuckle and motioned to the chair opposite him. "Take a seat."

Eli eased his tall frame across the office with caution but remained standing. "Tell me why you brought me here."

"The book, Eli, the book. Now do you want to sit?"

"Where did you get it?" Eli moved around the chair and sat down."

Redmond raised his right hand, index finger pointed upward. "Ah, that's a good question."

"Are you going to give me an answer?" His perplexed gaze remained on the mayor.

"All in good time, Sheriff." He clasped his hands on the desk blotter in front of him. "I believe Remus is dead."

Eli's frown deepened. "How do you know that?"

"News like that has a way of getting around the grapevine quickly."

"I want to know how you got the book."

"What do you know about Eldridge Crane?" the mayor asked, changing the topic of conversation.

"Why? Do you know something I should know?"

"I asked you first."

"We're not children, Ross, tell me what you know."

"You have to figure it out for yourself."

"If that's the case then why are you here?"

Redmond pointed his index finger at the sheriff. "But I'm not. You are. Remember?"

"You're not making any sense."

"Just give it time, Eli. The pieces will soon fit together. Have you figured out where you are yet?"

Eli gave his question some thought. The sudden look of awareness crossing his handsome face. He jerked out of his chair, his heart hammering in his chest. "The shadow realm."

"Bingo!" Ross vanished before his eyes.

Eli jerked awake and sprang up in bed, his eyes roaming the shadows in the room, his heart thumping against his ribs. *What the hell had that been? Why did I dream about Ross Redmond?* He knew the answers would come, eventually. They always did, and often, not in a good way.

Paige sat up. "Hey, are you ok?"

Eli pulled her into his arms and lay down again. "Yeah, I think so."

"Did you have a bad dream?" She brushed his face with gentle fingers.

"More like a nightmare. I was in the shadow realm with the mayor."

She frowned into his honey colored eyes. "Ross Redmond? Do you think it means something?"

"I'm sure of it."

Paige leaned in and kissed his lips.

He eased her away from him and sat up. "I want to apologize for not telling you I knew the location of the council. I…"

Paige shushed him, placing her index finger against his lips. "I was hurt at first, but I do understand why you did what you did. You had no idea who the mole was and there hadn't been enough time to talk about it after we found out it had been Linda."

"I'm sorry, Paige. I know I can trust you heart and soul."

"Yes, you can."

"From now on there will be no secrets between us."

Paige smiled. "I'm glad to hear it." She eased him back onto the bed, straddled him, and planted a firm kiss on his lips.

FIFTY ONE

T he next morning, Eli went into the station earlier than usual. He wanted to be there when Taylor and Rick arrived. Cooper came in and headed to his boss's office. "Hey, Eli, great morning, isn't it?"

"Yeah, but winter is fast approaching. I saw snow in the fields on my way into town."

"Yeah, I noticed that too. Christmas is right around the corner."

"I know. I've been hinting for Paige to give me gift ideas. I already have one in mind, though."

"Oh, yeah? What's that?"

Eli stood up and came around his desk, heading to the kitchen to make coffee. He realized how much Rosy did around the office now that she wasn't here. "I'll keep it to myself for the time being. Want some coffee?"

"Sure. Any donuts to go with that?" Cooper followed Eli down the short corridor.

"Yep. Picked them up myself."

"Cool." Cooper always had an appetite and figured it had to be the Lycan gene that made him hungry.

The station door opened. Both Eli and Cooper could

hear it from where they were.

The deputy walked back along the corridor and peered into reception, then turned around and went back to the kitchen. "Just Taylor and Rick."

"Good. I want to have a conversation with them." Eli picked up his mug of coffee and took it with him. Stepping into the station house he said, "You two follow me."

He waited by the door until both deputies entered his office then closed it and motioned for the pair to take a seat. He sat down behind his desk, setting his mug of steaming black coffee on the blotter. "I want to discuss something with you."

Rick and Taylor gave each other a sideward glance before returning their gaze to their boss. "What is it?" Taylor asked.

"News on the grapevine travels fast around here. I've been told you've been asking questions about the town and its residents. That true?"

Rick's Adam's apple bobbed above the collar of his shirt and he glanced at Taylor again. "Uh, is that a problem?"

"I don't know. Why don't you tell me?" Eli leaned forward, resting his clasped hands on his desk.

"How are we supposed to get to know the town if we don't ask questions?" Taylor offered in their defense.

"It depends on the kind of questions you're asking." Eli's gaze moved from one deputy to the other. "You've mentioned something about a creature?"

Taylor popped up from her chair. "We saw something last week that we can't explain. And why is the church locked?" she blurted.

Rick gave a heavy sigh. "Now we're in trouble," he

said under his breath.

Eli stood up. "Sit." Taylor remained on her feet. "I asked you to sit down." His serious gaze remained on her. She backed into her chair. "Do you want to tell me what you think you saw?" He perched himself on the corner of his desk and folded his arms.

Taylor looked at Rick, then at Eli. "At first, I thought it might have been a dog, but after thinking about it I realized it had been too big. Then I thought maybe it had been a wolf…"

"There are no wolves in this area," Eli told her.

"Yeah, that's what Rick said." She shrugged.

"And the reason the church is closed is because it's out of town. We've had vandals in Moon Grove before and they did some serious damage up there. That's why it's locked now."

"That makes sense, and something I already thought of." Taylor felt stupid for allowing her imagination to run wild. She needed to get her act together… she was a cop, after all.

"If you have questions in future I'd like you to bring them to me. Ok?" Eli rounded his desk and sat down again.

"Sure," Rick said.

Taylor nodded without speaking.

"Ok, you can go now."

The pair stood up and walked across the office.

"I mean what I said. If you have questions come to me."

"We will." Rick opened the door and waited for Taylor to step out first then followed her and closed it behind them.

Eli watched them return to their desks through his office window. Had he averted their curiosity for now? He hoped so.

Cooper knocked and entered. "What was that all about?"

Eli sipped his coffee. "They've been asking unusual questions around town. And they both encountered a wolf a few nights ago."

"What?!"

"Yeah. We're going to have to keep an eye on them. For their own safety."

"What do you want me to do?" Cooper may not have been happy to have the newbies at the station but he didn't want to see anything happen to them.

"Take Taylor out on rounds with you again. I know we had a problem while I was abducted but, now things are kind of back to normal, you'll be able to keep an eye on her movements."

"Sure. Whatever you need me to do."

"I'll take Rick with me. When I'm not here I'll confine him to desk duty. That should solve the problem for the time being." He frowned at Cooper. "You haven't said anything to them, have you?"

His deputy looked sheepish, his cheeks flushing.

"Cooper?"

"I... may have inadvertently said they should get out of Moon Grove while they could."

Eli lurched out of his chair. "Why would you do that?"

"Because I didn't want them here. I wanted Bobby, Rebecca, Paul, and Ryan back. I know what you're thinking and I'm sorry. It won't happen again."

"You've put doubt in their minds, Coop. That seed will

continue to grow no matter what I tell them."

Cooper raised defensive hands. "I'm sorry, Eli… I am."

"Well, you'll have to make sure you keep a tight leash on Taylor while you're on patrol. Some of the residents aren't happy about her digging around."

"Will do." He opened the door. "I *am* sorry, Eli. From now on I'll keep my big mouth shut."

"Just make sure neither of them continues to dig into what makes this town tick."

Cooper nodded and stepped outside.

Eli sighed as he sat down. Now he would have to keep an eye on Cooper as well.

FIFTY TWO

Paige sat across the lunch room table contemplating whether or not to broach the subject of Rosemarie being a witch with her. She didn't want to upset the woman who had become a friend. But she did want her to know that she didn't have to hide who she was anymore. She sipped her coffee and took a bite of one of the cookies the receptionist had brought in this morning. What could she say to start the conversation off without it being awkward?

Rosemarie's gaze met hers. "Is there something you want to say to me?"

Paige dropped the rest of her cookie onto her plate and cleared her throat. "Yes, Rosy, there is."

"Oh, ok, what is it?" She frowned, set her coffee mug down, and clasped her hands on the table top.

"Well... I – I wanted to talk to you about what happened at the mansion." She took a sip of her coffee and cleared her throat again.

"I'm not sure I understand what you mean." Rosemarie gave her a perplexed stare.

"I'm referring to what you did, Rosy."

"Oh?" Her cheeks flushed.

"Why didn't you tell Eli you were a witch? It's nothing to be ashamed of."

Rosemarie's expression darkened. "I'm not ashamed. I just prefer not to announce it to the world."

"I understand."

"Do you, Paige. Do you really? I've wanted to have as normal life as I could. I didn't want people expecting me to create spells for ridiculous reasons like winning the lottery or making someone fall in love with them. I take my gift very seriously."

"I do understand, Rosy. It's difficult being someone different. *I know.* Sometimes, it changes everything."

Rosemarie gave Paige a wry smile. "You're right. And I'm sorry for being... you know."

Paige reached across the table and gave the woman's hand a gentle squeeze. "It's ok. Eli and I would never take your abilities lightly. And I know he would never ask you to do anything you didn't want to do."

The receptionist nodded. "Yes, I know."

Eli crossed the sidewalk to Ruby. She had just finished loading her suitcase into the trunk of her car outside the Moon Grove Inn, and he had spotted her as he was traveling back to the station. He'd figured she hadn't wanted to say goodbye because they were always difficult. "You're leaving?"

"Yes. There's nothing left for me to do here now that Remus is dead. And, besides, I'm sure Paige will be happy to know I've gone." She stepped closer to Eli, wrapping her arms around him. "It's been good seeing you again."

Eli eased Ruby away from him. "Yes, it has. Have a safe trip back."

"I will." She smiled and rounded the car. "If you need me you know where to find me now." She climbed in, buckled her seatbelt, and pulled away from the curb.

Eli watched the car head along the main street toward the highway, then crossed the road and entered the Tribune office. "How are things? Max and Blake get away ok?"

Archer came around his desk. "Yeah, they did. So what now?"

"Now we wait for the next threat to our town. There will always be one."

The editor nodded. "Can I buy you a coffee?"

"Sure, why not." He checked his watch. "I have some time. The Inn?"

"Yeah. Let's go."

Once the pair was seated at a corner table, away from prying ears, Archer told Eli he'd been looking into Eldridge Crane. He told him he knew he'd heard the warlock's name before in his travels and decided to do some research. Carmichael had emailed a file the governing body had on him and it wasn't good.

"What are you telling me?" Eli asked.

"Eldridge Crane is not who he professes to be."

A look of awareness crossed the sheriff's face. "He has a copy of the book."

"Yes, and that not only concerns me it concerns Carmichael as well. Nothing good can come from him possessing that book."

Another thought crossed Eli's mind. "Alistair has the

original, along with the artifacts. Why didn't he give them back if he plans to make changes to the way the council has been doing things?"

"Good question." Archer leaned back on his chair and folded his arms. "Want to go out there and ask him?"

"Yeah, I do, but right now I'm more concerned about Eldridge."

"I wonder if the book he brought out of the shadow realm is exactly the same as the one here."

Eli's frowning gaze met Archer's. "What are you thinking?"

"That, perhaps, it possesses a darker magic... because of where it has come from. What if Eldridge came to Moon Grove to take over leadership of the town?"

Eli's gut tightened. What if that were true?

"And what about Scarlet and her coven? I know she lost witches, but nothing happened to her. Maybe Eldridge had something to do with that because they had been an item once."

"They had?"

"It appears so, from what I've read in his file. Perhaps he's the reason she got away."

The pieces started to fit together. Eldridge had come to Moon Grove to rid it of the competition so he could take possession of their town. That meant Alistair and the other members of the newly formed governing body were in danger.

Eli stood up. "I've had another thought. What if Eldridge needs both books to complete his mission?"

Archer rose from his seat. "That would mean..."

"Yeah. Let's go."

Eli sent a text message to Daniel, Cooper, Abbey and

Brent asking them to meet him at the mansion. They had to stop Eldridge before he killed the vampires and used the books to do something that couldn't be undone.

When they reached the mansion, Eli got out of the Jeep and marched over to Abbey. "Where's Eldridge?"

She gave him an agitated frown. "How should I know?"

Eli stood with hands on hips. "Isn't he staying with you?"

"He left this morning."

"And you didn't think to tell me?"

"Why would I? The war has been won. He's free to leave any time he wants." She folded her arms.

"He has…"

Archer rushed up to the pair. "We need to get inside. The doors are wide open. Something's happened here."

Eli raced across the lawn and climbed the stairs to the front landing, everyone else behind him. He had chosen to leave Paige and Rosemarie out of it this time. He stopped at the threshold and ran his gaze around the entry hall before stepping into the mansion. No sign of an altercation so far. His gut did a flip under his buckled belt. Alistair never slept, it seemed, so if he was all right he should be somewhere in the house. "Alistair?" Eli called, the sound of his voice echoing around the silence. He stepped inside. "Alistair, are you here?" No answer. He glanced over his shoulder at Archer and the others. "Let's spread out in pairs and take a look around. And be careful."

Abbey and Brent stopped beside him. "What's going

on, Eli?" Abbey asked.

"Eldridge came here to get his hands on the book and artifacts. While we were in the shadow realm he found another copy. I believe he needs both books to do whatever he has planned for Moon Grove."

Abbey's eyes widened. "That can't be right. He has an impeccable reputation in supernatural circles."

"The hierarchy Archer works for has a file on Eldridge and it isn't good."

"That doesn't make any sense. He has rid other towns of serious threats. Why would he do what you think he's done now?"

"I don't know. I only know I will not allow him to take over our town without a fight. Are you going to help me or…"

Abbey nodded. "Of course." She didn't want to believe she had been deceived by the warlock. She and Brent took the stairs to the upper level of the mansion.

"Eli?" Archer came up to the curtained archway. "In here."

The pair walked along the hall to the library. Ashen remains were scattered around the room.

"Looks like he got what he came for," Archer said.

Eli sighed. "Yeah, it does."

"Where would he have gone?"

"I don't…" A thought popped into Eli's head. "The cabin out at Peak's Ridge trail."

"Then let's get out there and stop him." Archer headed for the door.

"Wait."

The editor turned around. "For what?"

Eli crossed the library to him. "You and I should go out

there and check first. No point in everyone going if he isn't there."

"Ok. Let's do that."

When the pair reached the entry hall, the others were waiting on the front balcony.

"Find anything?" Daniel asked.

"Yeah, the remains of the council are in the library." Eli stepped outside. Archer followed and closed the doors.

Abbey came up to Eli. "Then Eldridge has the book."

"Yes, both of them. And we have no idea what he's planned for our town." Eli strutted past Paige's mother and down the front steps. The group followed. "I'll let you all know if we locate Eldridge. In the meantime, be safe out there."

Everyone dispersed, leaving Eli and Archer alone on the front lawn.

"Ok, let's head out to the cabin." Eli climbed into the Jeep, Archer alongside him.

FIFTY THREE

Eli pulled the Patrol Jeep onto the shoulder and turned off the engine. "We need to get up to the cabin without being seen." He pulled the keys from the ignition and stepped out of the vehicle, closing the door with a quiet click.

Archer did the same. "Why don't I go in first? Like I did when we were searching for Gregor. I can suss out if Eldridge is there and he won't know."

"Are you sure you want to do it alone?"

"I'll be in and out in a few seconds."

Eli sighed. "Ok, be careful."

The editor gave him a shrewd grin. "Always. That's how I've managed to stay alive this long." He disappeared through the trees in a blur and was back in an instant. "He's here. What do you want to do?"

"He's too powerful for us alone."

At that moment, Eldridge's voice echoed through the tall pines around them. "Eli Blackwood, I want to talk to you. Alone."

Eli frowned at Archer. "I thought you said he wouldn't know."

The editor shrugged. "Like you said, he's powerful."

The sheriff contemplated what he should do. If he went in alone he may not come out. But if he didn't, all hell would break loose in his town. He'd had enough of maniacs that wanted to rule Moon Grove. "I'm going in."

Archer grabbed his arm. "No, Eli, it's a trap."

"Probably, but I don't have a choice. Don't follow me." He shrugged out of the editor's grasp and headed through the legion of trees. When he came upon the cabin, the warlock was on the front porch. "What do you want, Eldridge?"

"To talk. That is all." He motioned for the sheriff to climb the steps onto the veranda. "Won't you indulge me?"

"I can hear you from here. What is it you want to say?"

"I dispatched the council so that Moon Grove would be free of its tyrannical reign. You can never trust a vampire craving control. You should know that."

"The only vampire I trust is Archer. The others in the town stay to themselves and adhere to the rules."

"Do they? Are you sure?"

"Yes. Now, what do you want?" He would not show fear, even though his anxious gut churned.

"I want you to know that I have no intention of taking control of your town. I came here to help and I have done my part."

"Have you? Then why did you take the books and artifacts?"

"They serve a higher purpose. One I do not care to discuss at this time."

"The governing body Archer works for has a large dossier on you, Eldridge, and none of it good."

"What they have has been fabricated. They want me to appear to be a mercenary, which I am not."

"Why would they?" Eli folded his arms. "What purpose would it serve?"

"Because I have been doing what they should be and they do not care for it. It makes them appear antediluvian, which they are."

"How can I believe anything you say?"

"Believe this. I am leaving Moon Grove and I shall not return. The town is yours to do with what you will, Eli Blackwood. As I said, the books and artifacts are for a much more important undertaking than the leadership of your town."

"All right. But you need to leave soon otherwise the supernatural residents may come out here on a witch hunt."

"Do not concern yourself with my well-being. I will be gone before the end of the day."

Eli turned around and headed back through the trees to Archer.

"What did he want?" the editor asked.

"He told me he's leaving Moon Grove. That the books are for another purpose."

"You believe him?"

"Yes, I do."

"I hope you're right about that. What about the file on him?"

"He said it's been fabricated to make him look bad because he's been doing the work the hierarchy should have been doing. How long have you been working for the governing body?"

"Longer than you've been alive. But that doesn't mean I know everything about it."

"You might want to be careful about the information you share with Carmichael from now on."

"I will."

The pair climbed into the Jeep.

"While we're out here, I want to go see Matthias's guys," Eli told Archer. "I need to check on them."

"They may not be very receptive after everything that's happened." Archer clipped in his seatbelt.

"I know, but as an Alpha I'm obligated to make sure they're all right." He started the engine.

"Fair enough."

Eli did a U-turn and headed out to Matthias's cabin. When they arrived, he turned off the engine and looked at Archer. "You wait here. I won't be long."

"Are you sure you want to face them alone. They'd be pretty angry about losing their Alpha in a fight that wasn't theirs to begin with."

"I realize that but I think I'll be fine. There are certain Lycan laws that can't be broken, and killing another pack's Alpha is one of them."

"Ok. But if you're not back in fifteen minutes I'm coming in."

Eli gave the editor a thin smile. "Sure. Ok." He closed the door and headed into the trees.

A voice echoed out from behind the trunk of a tall pine. "What are you doing here, Sheriff?"

"You lost good men, including your Alpha, and I came to make sure you're all right."

"Don't concern yourself with us, Sheriff Blackwood. We'll make our own way." Heath came around the tree trunk. Samuel close behind him.

"Look, I wanted to say how sorry I am for what happened."

"Yeah, you should be. It wasn't our fight." Heath folded his arms across his checked shirt.

"Matthias offered his assistance and I'm grateful for that. None of us knew who would survive and who wouldn't. He decided to fight and that was his choice."

"So it's his fault he got himself and our other pack members killed, is that what you're saying?" Samuel's frown deepened and his wolf eyes glowed.

"Not at all. His bravery is something we will be forever grateful for." He wouldn't tell them that their Alpha had made an attempt on Archer's life.

"Why are you really here?" Heath asked. "To ask us to join you?"

Eli wanted to be honest with them. "I thought of it, yes, then I realized you needed to make that decision for yourselves. If you're ok with being lone wolves it's up to you, I wouldn't try to change your mind."

"Good, because we don't want to join you," Samuel told him.

Eli raised defensive hands. "Ok. Fine. Do you need anything?"

"Not from you."

"All right. If you do you know where to find me." Eli turned on his heel and headed back along the path to his car. He had done what he could. If the pair changed their minds sometime in the future he'd be happy to have them as part of his pack.

Archer waited for him to get into the Jeep. "How'd it go?"

"They're grieving right now and don't want my help. That could change later on though."

"Or it may not. They're a couple of angry wolves that might need to be monitored."

"I know. And we will." Eli started the engine and headed back to Moon Grove.

FIFTY FOUR

Eldridge Crane left as he'd said he would. Eli had gone out at the end of the day to make sure and there had been no sign of the warlock. He wondered what Eldridge planned to do with the books and artifacts he had taken with him. No point in hypothesizing. As he traveled back into Moon Grove he spotted the old movie house on the opposite side of the main road, and thought it would be a great place to have a date night. He and Paige could sit in the back row like teenagers and make out while the movie played on in the foreground. A smile crossed his handsome face. Yes, he'd tee it up with Ted Blaxland in the morning for that evening, and arrange dinner beforehand at the Jade Dragon. It would be nice to get back to some kind of normal for a while. He knew the peace in the town wouldn't last for long, it never did, but while it did he would make the most of it with Paige.

They had never discovered what had happened to the four hybrid vampires Archer had organized to come to their town to help. The coven had to have cast a spell on them and, possibly, sent them into the shadow realm, or worse, killed them. Something else they would never have an answer to.

The dream he'd had about their dead mayor, Ross Redmond, crossed his mind. Maybe he *had* been in the shadow realm again. He realized the dream, or whatever it was, had been about the fact that Eldridge wanted the books and artifacts. Strange, though, that Ross hadn't actually given him the information he'd asked for. He remembered what the mayor had said, 'You have to figure it out for yourself.'

He drove along the road, pulled into the driveway behind Paige's car and turned off the engine. It seemed Eldridge hadn't been the harbinger of death they had believed him to be. Would they see him again? Who knew? But he hoped not. Eli slid the key from the ignition and climbed out of the Jeep.

Paige opened the door as he stepped onto the front porch. "Hey, you're home early."

"Yeah, I thought, after everything we've been through, I could play hooky for once and spend a quiet evening at home with you. Cooper can manage without me."

She smiled, wrapped her arms around his neck and planted a firm kiss on his lips. "That sounds like a wonderful idea."

Eli entered the house and closed the door behind him. "Maybe we could make a night of it." He brought his hand around from behind his back, displaying a bottle of Merlot."

Paige took the wine from his hand. "Sounds like a plan."

"Hey, I've been thinking… want to go to the movies

tomorrow night? I'll organize everything. You just need to be dressed and ready to go by seven."

Paige gave him a curious frown. "A movie night?"

"Yeah, they're playing an oldie but a goodie."

"Oh, which one?" She uncorked the wine, poured two glasses and handed one to him.

"An Affair to Remember."

"Cary Grant and Deborah Kerr. Love it. It's a date. But I do have to warn you, that movie always makes me cry." She gave him a wry smile and sipped her Merlot.

"That's ok. You can have my shoulder to cry on." He breathed in the aromas from the kitchen. "Something smells good. What's for dinner?"

"Mini chicken pot pies… and for dessert… apple pie and ice cream."

Eli set his glass down on the bureau, reached for her and pulled her into his arms. "I kinda hoped you'd be dessert." He pressed his lips to hers in a passionate kiss.

Paige eased herself out of his embrace. "There's always room for more than one dessert." She gave him a cheeky smile.

"That is true."

A knock echoed into the entry hall interrupting their seductive banter. Eli gazed over his shoulder at the door. "I wonder who that could be."

"Only one way to find out." Paige followed him to the door.

"Clary. Come on in." Eli stepped aside allowing his grandmother to enter the house. "Is everything all right?"

"Everything's fine, dear. I just came over to borrow a cup of sugar. I'm making brownies."

"Of course you can," Paige said, taking the cup from the older woman's hand and heading into the kitchen.

Clarissa leaned to her right and glanced through the doorway at Paige before returning her gaze to her grandson. "The cards told me someone is coming to Moon Grove."

Eli frowned into his grandmother's eyes. "Do you know who? And are they a threat?"

She shook her head. "No, I don't know who yet. But, yes, they are a threat. I didn't want to worry Paige with it, I would've preferred not to have had to tell you, either. You've been through so much already."

"It's ok. We need to be…"

Paige came back into the entry hall with the cup of brown sugar. "Everything ok?"

Clarissa took the cup from her hand. "Everything's fine, hon." She turned toward the open front door. "Thanks for the sugar. I'll bring some brownies over tomorrow."

"That would be lovely, Clary, thank you." Paige saw the old woman out and closed the door. "Want to tell me what that was about?" She knew the sugar had been a ploy to get her out of the room.

"I'm not sure. Clary said the cards told her someone's coming to Moon Grove but she didn't know who."

"Then let's go over and talk to her. Perhaps she can do a reading while we're there and tell us who it is. Or, at least, tell us what kind of threat it will be."

Eli pulled her into his arms. "Let's not. Let's just stay here and enjoy the night together."

The next morning, Archer pulled his car into the curb outside the Tribune office and turned off the engine. He sat for a moment admiring the newness of it and the features it offered. It had taken a while for the insurance company to organize it, but, at last, he could drive around in comfort instead of in the clunky Tribune van.

Paige spotted him as she stepped out of her sedan and crossed the street. She whistled and ran her gaze over the sleek, obsidian black convertible with burgundy seats and plush interior. "Nice wheels."

The editor smiled up at her. "Thanks. I think I'll enjoy driving this around."

"Who wouldn't? It's gorgeous."

"Hop in and we'll go for a spin." His grin widened.

Paige sighed. "I wish I could but I've got an early appointment," she said, glancing at her watch, "that'll be arriving any minute. Raincheck?"

"Absolutely. Anytime you're free." He climbed out of the car. "Hope your day goes well."

"Yours too. See you later." She crossed the road.

"Yeah, see you." When Archer stepped into the office Eli was waiting for him. "Hey, something up?"

"Clary came over last night and told me there's a new threat coming to Moon Grove. She read it in the cards."

"Did she say what kind of threat?"

"I spoke to her this morning and she still isn't sure. She said she'll keep trying until she can tell me more."

"Damn! Can't this town ever get a break?" Archer walked down to his desk, shrugged out of his jacket and dropped it onto his chair.

"I wish. In the meantime, I have something I want to

tell you, but you have to promise to keep it to yourself for now."

"Of course. What is it?"

Later that day, Paige drove out to her old family home. She sat in the car for a long time, her feelings conflicted, before opening the door and stepping out onto the dirt road. She sighed as she rounded the hood. Her eyes roamed the dilapidated, double-story, rotting gray structure. This house had been where her father had died. She wished she could remember him but she had been only a little girl at the time.

Paige wondered what had brought her out here today. The last time she had been here was when she and Eli had been shot at by men sent by his father. The house needed to be demolished. It held too many bad memories for her, her mother, and brother. She made the decision to call and organize it as soon as she arrived back at her office. The past needed to be let go. She headed to the driver's door and before climbing in took one last look at her childhood home. Checking her watch, she realized she needed to get a move on. Eli had planned their date night and she didn't want to be late.

FIFTY FIVE

After dinner, Eli took Paige's hand in his and they strolled along the main street to the movie house. He had arranged for the theater to be theirs for the evening and when they entered, Ted stood behind the refreshments counter, his face beaming. "Good evening, and welcome to Gem Movie Theater." He handed the pair a bucket of popcorn and two Cokes, then walked over to the double doors and opened one for them. "Enjoy your movie."

Paige ran her gaze around the dimly lit interior and whispered. "Where is everyone?"

Eli shrugged. "I guess it's too cold for them." He sidled into the back row and moved to the center seats. Paige followed and sat down beside him.

"It feels weird being here alone," she said. "Don't you think?"

"Not really. Gives us more privacy." He gave her a cheeky wink.

She play slapped him and giggled. "Oh, you."

Eli popped their drink cups into the arms of the chairs

and sat the tub of popcorn on the seat beside him. "There's something I want to say."

Paige's eyebrows rose. "Oh, what's that?"

He took her hand in his. "From the very first day I met you I felt something. I know now it's because we were destined to be together. As strange as that is." He gave her one of those heart-stopping smiles. "I couldn't see myself without you in my life. I know we went through a bit of a rough patch, but we came through it knowing how much we mean to each other. I love you, Paige O'Connell... I'm *in love* with you." He reached into the pocket of his jacket and tugged out a small, black, ring box and flipped it open. "Would you do me the honor of becoming my wife, Paige? It would make me the happiest man in the world."

Tears welled in her eyes as she looked into his beautiful, sincere, honey colored gaze. "I couldn't see myself without you in my life, either, Eli. I am so in love with you." She touched his handsome face with gentle fingertips. "Yes, I want to be your wife."

His smile widened as he plucked the diamond ring from the satin lining and slipped it onto her finger. "I am so happy right now." He leaned in and pressed his lips to hers in a long, slow kiss.

The theater lights dimmed to darkness and the screen flashed a milky aura around the movie house, the musical introduction adding to the special moment between them.

The month leading up to Christmas had been relatively quiet. Life flowed along without any major drama and the town seemed at peace as the residents geared up for the winter pageant, once again. The holidays were the best time of year and everyone looked forward to the cheer it brought to their town.

Clary's cards hadn't revealed anything more regarding the impending threat but Eli figured they would in time, when the danger became more imminent. Until then, they would continue on with their lives, making plans for the future, and working together to keep Moon Grove safe.

Paige had had her childhood home razed, the land standing eerily empty now. She had no plans for developing it. In fact, she had signed the deed back over to her mother, not wanting any part of the place now. Abbey donated the land to the town for redevelopment and left it up to the new mayor to decide what should be done with the extensive block. Like Paige, she wanted nothing more to do with it, the memories of that tragic night too painful.

Winter had settled into Moon Grove, the chilly snowy days keeping many residents indoors.

Eli patrolled the streets alone, choosing to keep the new deputies on desk duties over the winter months. He knew if there were any wolves out there that they would wander into town in search of food and he couldn't have Taylor and Rick stumbling across one on their rounds. Yes, he had allowed them to ride together again because Cooper had gone to the city for further training and would be gone for six months.

Rosemarie had requested to stay with Paige and Eli had agreed. Even though he missed her at the station, he knew she would remain an asset to Paige's practice. Would he replace her? He didn't think so. He had enough on his hands with his deputies.

Matthias's guys had remained aloof and Eli wondered if they'd be all right on their own. Nothing he could do about that. They had made the choice to remain lone wolves and he had to respect their decision. He hoped, sometime in the future, they might change their minds and come join his pack. The more wolves he had the better protection they could offer the town.

As he traveled home, he thought about the plans he and Paige were making for their wedding in the New Year. In six months they would be Mr. and Mrs. Blackwood. A smile spread across his face. He liked the sound of that. He thought about kids and wondered how soon Paige would want to try. Something they would need to talk about. He hoped it would be soon, because he had always envisioned himself being a dad. He knew there were certain implications to them having children, but he wanted a family of his own and he knew Paige did too.

When he pulled into the drive, his grandmother was just leaving. She gave him a wave and blew him a kiss, then continued down the path and across the street.

Eli came up onto the front porch. "Why did Clary run off so fast?"

"I guess she has things to do. Quick, get inside, it's freezing out here." Paige ushered him into the warmth of the entry hall, the fire in the living room fireplace crackling behind them, and closed the door.

Eli shrugged out of his police issue anorak and hung it on the coat rack before taking Paige's hand and heading into the warm space. "How was your day?"

"Good. What about you?"

"The town is quiet. Not many people on the streets. I guess the snow is keeping them inside."

"I guess. Want some coffee?" She turned and headed to the kitchen.

"Yeah, that'd be great." Eli followed.

"Why don't you sit and I'll bring it over to the table?" Paige walked across to the counter, poured two mugs of coffee and set them down in front of him, then brought the plate of brownies over Clarissa had dropped off.

Eli picked up his mug and took a cautious sip before reaching for a brownie. "I love these." He took a large bite.

"I know. Your mom's recipe."

"Yes." He ran his gaze over her face for a moment. "Is something wrong?"

"I guess that depends on how you look at things."

Eli frowned. "What do you mean?"

She stood up, came around the table to him, and sat on his lap. "I have something I want to tell you, but…"

"Sweetheart, you know you can tell me anything."

"That's what Clary said."

Eli dropped the rest of his brownie onto the plate. "Ok, what's going on?"

She cleared her throat. "You know all those plans we've been making for our wedding?"

"Of course."

"We may have to change them."

Eli scooted her off his lap and stood up. "Why? Are you having second thoughts?"

She stepped close to him, reached up and planted a gentle kiss on his lips. "Never, Mr. Blackwood, you're stuck with me."

"Then what?" His frown deepened.

"You might want to sit down."

He shook his head. "No thanks. Tell me."

"Ok." Paige waited for a moment. "Eli…" She sighed. "Eli, we're having a baby."

It took a moment for the information to register with him. "Wait, what?"

She smiled and nodded. "We're going to have a baby."

Eli lifted her into the air and swung her around, laughing. "We're having a baby. You know, I'd been thinking about that on the way home and thought we needed to talk about it. But now we don't have to." He set her down, pulled her face close and kissed her lips. "A baby."

"I'm so glad you're happy about it. I wasn't sure how you'd take the news with everything that's happened in Moon Grove recently."

"This is the best news. How far along are we?" He held her close and stroked her silky hair.

"About eight weeks."

"This is the best Christmas present ever."

"Isn't it? We're not only going to be Mr. and Mrs. but we're also going to be mom and dad."

"He raised her face up to him. "Is Clary the only one who knows?"

"Yes. And I'm sorry it wasn't you first. It's… I wanted to ask her what she thought you might think and she told me your reaction would be this."

"Of course it would be. I love you, Paige, and want us to have children together. As many as you want."

"Well I'm glad to hear it, because I want a house full." She smiled up at him, then pulled him close and kissed him again.

It would be a wonderful Christmas and New Year, at

least for a while. No one could predict what would come to Moon Grove the following year, but if Clary's cards were correct they would face another new threat to their town. In the meantime, they would enjoy making plans for their upcoming wedding and the birth of their baby boy or girl in July. Danger would continue to be a part of their lives and, just as they had always done, they would meet it head on when it arrived.

Did you love this book?

Tell other readers by posting a review
Visit the author's Amazon page
https://amzn.to/30VSxXl

READ AN EXCERPT FROM
BOOK FOUR
WOLF BONDS

ONE

Paige's shrill scream woke Eli with a jolt. He threw back the covers, flew from the bed, his sleepy gaze searching their room for an assailant, before he realized she'd been having another nightmare. He came around her side of the bed, sat down, and pulled her into his arms. "Are you all right, sweetheart?" he said, frowning into her welling eyes.

She pressed her fist to her mouth, shaking her head, her body trembling, the tears spilling now.

Eli flicked on the bedside lamp, plucked a tissue from the box sitting in front of it, and wiped Paige's tears. "You've been having these dreams since you told me you were pregnant. Maybe it has something to do with the Lycan gene."

Paige didn't want to be analyzed. She needed to be held and comforted. "I don't care what's causing them. I just want them to stop. I can't imagine what my anxiety is doing to the baby." Another tear slipped down her cheek.

Eli brushed it away with his thumb. "Why don't we get away from Moon Grove for a while? Go on vacation somewhere tropical? Lay on a beach in the warm sunshine?"

"I wish I could, Eli, but I don't have anyone to take over my patients while I'm away. My appointment schedule is choc-o-block." She let out a heavy sigh.

Eli pulled her into his arms again and stroked her hair. "Do you have any idea why you're having these dreams? Apart from the obvious, that is."

"I have no idea."

"Maybe talking about it will help." He slid his index finger under her chin and raised her face up to meet his gaze. "I'm here for you, you know that."

"I know. The strange thing is, once I'm awake I can't seem to remember much about it. I only know it's the same dream every time. And it terrifies me."

"You could always make an appointment with the shrink in Bellehurst. Perhaps he can help."

She shrugged. "I don't know. Maybe you're right, maybe it's hormones or something."

"Paige, if you need to see someone then go see them."

"I don't. I'll be ok."

He kissed her forehead. "Want some warm milk and honey? Maybe that'll help you sleep better." Eli headed for the bedroom door.

"Thank you. You're right, it might." She gave him a smile and watched him walk along the hallway and into the living room. *Why am I dreaming about Stephanie? It's been almost a year since she ended our friendship. And why is the dream so frightening? I wish I could remember it.*

www.ingramcontent.com/pod-product-compliance
Lightning Source LLC
Chambersburg PA
CBHW022134170626
46807CB00005B/1935